Praise for Deryn Lake's other
John Rawlings Mysteries

One of the best mystery series to hand at present is the John Rawlings
historical crime line . . . ten out of ten'
DR JONATHAN GASH

'John Rawlings and the Blind Beak are developing into my favourite
historical mystery heroes – tenacious in their search for villains, daring as
they outwit them, yet always ready to pause for a moment of delightful
domestic life. I'm eager for the next!'
LINDSEY DAVIES

'evocative Georgian mystery . . . if you love a good whodunnit
you won't be disappointed'
Evening Argus, Brighton

'an absorbing murder tale set in Georgian London . . . splendidly evokes the
atmosphere of the capital with all its elegance and intrigue. Wonderfully
descriptive, it deserves to be a success'
The Kent and Sussex Courier

'A wealth of marvellous characters parade across the pages, their dialogue is
lively and John Rawlings is proving to be a real charmer.'
Eastbourne Herald

'An effervescent tale. . . the author organises her large cast
and colourful background with skill and gusto through
a racily readable drama.'
FELICIA LAMB in the *Mail on Sunday's*
Night & Day Magazine

Also by Deryn Lake

Death at The Beggar's Opera
Death at the Devil's Tavern
Death on the Romney Marsh
Death in the Peerless Pool
Death at Apothecaries' Hall
Death in the West Wind
Death at St. James's Palace
Death in the Valley of the Shadows
Death in the Setting Sun
Death and the Cornish Fiddler

About the author

Deryn Lake is the pseudonym of a well-known historical novelist who joined
the popular ranks of historical detective writers with her gripping
John Rawlings Mysteries.

Deryn Lake lives near the famous battleground of 1066.

Death in the
Dark Walk

Deryn Lake

Back-In-Print Books Ltd

Published by Back-In-Print Books Ltd 2002
ISBN 1 903552 37 0
Previously published in Great Britain by
Hodder and Stoughton 1994 under ISBN 0 340 60702 5

A CIP catalogue record is available from the British Library.

Cover illustration by Tim Barber based on an old print.

Printed and bound on demand in Great Britain by
Lightning Source.

Back-In-Print Books Ltd
PO Box 47057
London SW18 1YW
020 8637 0975

For Henry James
my bright new star
and
Dicky Douglas-Boyd
star of old aquaintance

Acknowledgments

My grateful thanks are due to Beryl Cross, poet and friend, who helped me during my original search for John Rawlings, and to Mark Dunton, archivist at the Public Record Office, Kew, who also went on the trail with me. Thanks, too, to Major Charles O'Leary of The Worshipful Society of Apothecaries of London, for looking through the Society's records and giving me some further details about John. And to Lyndi Clements Telepneff for filling in the background of Jonathan Tyers, Proprietor of Vaux Hall Pleasure Gardens, from her expert knowledge. Two more people deserve my gratitude: Ros Bacon, for typing the manuscript so beautifully, and Maureen Lyle, who read, approved and enthusiastically encouraged. Thank you all.

This is a Back-In-Print Book.

- This title was out of print for some time but Back-In-Print Books has brought it back in to print because of demand from Deryn Lake fans.
- This re-print was produced on demand using up-to-date digital printing technology.
- Paper and print quality are higher than most conventionally printed paperback novels.
- Digital printing may cost somewhat more but ensures that book titles need not go out of print as long as there are readers who want them.

What other titles are available from **BiP**?

Check out our web site at www.backinprint.co.uk for other titles released by Back-In-Print Books Ltd and news about forthcoming titles.

Do you want any other titles?

If you know of a title which is out of print and you think there might be a reasonable demand please contact us.

Back-In-Print Books Ltd
PO Box 47057
London
SW18 1YW
020 8637 0975

e-mail: info@backinprint.co.uk

Chapter One

It being such a delicate night, all stars and moon and silk soft breeze, John Rawlings, well satisfied with the day's events and having kissed his father goodnight, stepped forth from number two Nassau Street, so named in honour of the marriage of the Princess Royal to the Prince of Orange-Nassau, and hailed a chair to take him to the river.

Gone eight o'clock as it was, the fashionable world had just set out on its nocturnal perambulations and as the swaying sedan made its way through Leicester Fields, past the house of ill repute hidden discreetly amongst the trees, John peered through the small window at the elegant parade which strolled the London streets. Ladies in hooped skirts, some as wide as fifteen feet, minced along beside gentlemen in flared coats, dazzling waistcoats and breeches with silver buckles at the knee. Bows were exchanged and tricorne hats raised as couples, passing one another with difficulty, made their way to the balls, assemblies and gaming houses that provided the beau monde with its nightly entertainment.

John, dazzled by the splendour of it all, stared through his quizzing glass, a patent affectation for someone who only that morning had still been a mere apprentice lad, and called and waved at two beautiful whores who preened through the crowd like a pair of decadent doves.

Unhindered by the antics of its occupant, the sedan continued its journey across Castle Street, down Hemmings Row, then into St Martin's Lane, past St Martin's in the Fields and on to the Strand. Here a maze of alleyways led down to the Thames but as these were the haunt of footpads and cut-throats, the chairmen turned instead into the square of Hungerford market and set their passenger down at his destination, the top of Hungerford Stairs which descended to the very edge of the water.

A faun-like creature emerged from their conveyance, gleaming a grin at them as he searched in his pocket to settle the fare. Of average height and supple build, for all that their passenger gave the impression of possessing a certain wiry strength and this feeling was endorsed by the construction of his face. High-cheekboned, strong-jawed, it was capped by a white wig which barely concealed the thick bush of cinnamon curls beneath, cut short though they might be. A pair of dark quizzical eyebrows which moved expressively when he spoke danced above eyes the colour of fresh-picked delphiniums, eyes which in certain lights could deepen to a tint resembling wild lilac.

Shaded by curving lids and a sweep of thick black lash, still the animation in them, the curiosity, the love of living in all its aspects, could hardly be hidden. Yet belying this awareness of every nuance of life, the man's face was composed, tranquil almost, a fact that in the past he had many times used to his advantage. Only his mouth, with its crooked disconcerting smile beneath his long straight nose, endorsed the fact that here stood an imp of intelligence, a wild hare of a being, ready to move off at the slightest whisper of the word adventure.

Already there ahead of John, leaning nonchalantly against the wall, waited a vast windmill of a fellow with a thick thatch of flaxen hair covered by a wig a size too small for his head. On seeing his friend alighting he hurried forward and shook him warmly by the hand.

'Well, is it done?'

'Aye, it is. Seven long years successfully over. This morning my Master freed me from my indentures and you are presently crushing the fingers of John Rawlings, Apothecary. And what of yourself?'

'Just the same. Greet Samuel Swann, future Goldsmith of the City of London. My apprenticeship ended last week and my Master there and then gave me leave to apply to the Guild for Freedom.' With those words Samuel threw his hat in the air, failed to catch it, and watched in dismay as it floated down over the wall and landed in the river.

'Then it's time for celebration,' John answered joyfully, slapping him on the back. 'Wine, women, I'm ready for it all.' And he, too, removed his hat, though more cautiously keeping fast hold of it, and, pushing his wig to one side, tugged a lock of the springing hair which grew beneath.

Several boatmen were moored by the stairs and, engaging the services of a likely fellow who had ingratiated himself by rescuing the sodden headgear, the two young men stepped aboard his bobbing craft and gave orders to proceed down river to Vaux Hall Gardens. Thus settled, they sat down back-to-back, leaning upon one another companionably, taking sips from a flask of brandy which Samuel had secreted in the pocket of his best satin coat. In this state of high contentment they watched the banks of the great waterway lit clearly by the beams of the moon, and thought of nothing but the delightful evening that lay ahead of them.

Having left behind the houses of the city as they passed Millbank Terrace, the landscape became rural, the trees and market gardens of Tothill Fields giving way to rolling meadowland. As they caught sight of the lights of the Pleasure Gardens distantly reflected in the water, the faint sound of music suddenly became audible. But the gentle mood created by this romantic mirage was rudely shattered by the scene on arrival at Vaux Hall Stairs. For here was moored a positive flotilla of craft, all of varying sizes, including a confusion of wherries and one private barge, very grand and superior, with a crew of liveried oarsmen who looked down their noses at the watermen. People attempting to land were bawling and swearing at one another, quarrels were breaking out, and despite the presence of the Vaux Hall beadles, there to keep order, a parcel of ugly fellows were running into the water to pull people violently ashore. Thankful that Samuel Swann's size prevented any angry approaches, John and his companion managed to negotiate their way onto dry land.

At the top of the stone staircase lay a walkway, visible from the river, leading directly to rather an unimposing entrance. This consisted of an austere brick wall joined to a windowed three-storeyed house, the doorway of which contained half doors, like those of a stable, which swung to and fro.

Attached to these somewhat unattractive buildings and completing the complex was the Proprietor's private residence. Yet here all semblance of reality ceased, for having paid their shilling and gone down the dark passageway that lay beyond the swing doors, the friends found themselves in the full blaze of the Gardens, lit with its thousand lamps. This was the greatest moment for any visitor to Vaux Hall and the couple simply stood there, thunderstruck, and gazed about them.

Before them lay the Grand Walk, planted on each side with elms, extending about nine hundred feet, the entire length of the Pleasure Gardens, to the pleasant meadows of Kennington beyond. At the far end of this walk stood a huge gilded statue of Aurora, glittering in the light of the sparkling lanterns, while running parallel to it was another incredible boulevard, even more exotic – if that were possible. This last, known as the South Walk, was spanned by soaring triumphal arches and allowed a distant glimpse of a large painting of the ruins of Palmyra. Connecting these two major promenades was the Grand Cross Walk, which ran from one side of the Pleasure Gardens to the other and also contained a representation of ancient Gothic decay. Thinking that only a romantic and complex mind could have planned such a fantasy, John sauntered into the Grand Walk as if he had been perambulating there all his life.

To his right, the Grand Cross Walk terminated in a long shadowy avenue known sometimes as Druid's Walk but more frequently as Lovers' or The Dark Walk. Here a verdant canopy towered overhead in which nightingales, blackbirds and thrushes built their nests and sang, while sweethearts sported in its shady seclusion, hidden from prying eyes by the leafy dimness.

Turning his head to look left, John saw that the Grand Cross Walk crossed the Grand Walk at right angles and then ended in the Wildernesses and the Rural Downs. In this part of the Gardens the theme was natural and springy turf covered the ground, interspersed at intervals by firs, cypresses and cedars to break the flatness. Narrowing his eyes, John tried to catch a glimpse of the leaden statue of Milton, seated and listening to music, but was unable to do so. Smiling to himself, he recalled that in this area of Vaux Hall were the famous Musical Bushes where a band lay concealed, playing fairy tunes and frightening the maidens – and also coming off the worst of it when gentlemen chose to relieve themselves, unaware of the hidden musicians.

'Shall we go straight to supper?' asked Samuel, breaking in on his friend's thoughts.

'Certainly,' answered John, and increased his pace towards The Grove, a quadrangle of about five acres lying between the Grand Cross Walk and the entrance. Here could be found the raised bandstand, an elaborate dining pavilion known as the Turkish Tent standing immediately behind it. Also situated in this area, beyond the trees and standing on either side of The Grove, were the supper boxes and booths, placed in long rows or arranged in a semi-circular sweep. The more exotic of these emulated temples and follies, but even the other, simpler, booths were decorated with paintings, some executed by Mr Hogarth himself, representing sports and pastimes or scenes from popular comedies. Swaggering nonchalantly, John and Samuel passed the magnificent Rotunda, in which the orchestra performed on wet evenings, together with the Picture Room which led into it, on their way to dine.

There seemed to be lights everywhere, adorning the arches, the pillars, even the garlands of flowers looped between them. This brilliant illumination, combined with the fine clothes of the people who promenaded or sat down to eat, created an unforgettable impression. Overawed by such splendour but desperately trying to look as if they belonged in these elegant surroundings, the two young men took their seats in an unoccupied booth.

'Waiter,' called John.

'Yes, Sir?' responded a knobbly-kneed fellow with a supercilious expression.

'A jug of punch, if you please.'

'The celebrated Vaux Hall punch? The Arrack?' the man asked, obviously picking them out as newcomers despite John's fancy clothes. 'It's very strong, you know.'

'Then we'll have two,' the Apothecary replied grandly, and winked at his friend as the man went off.

'I feel as if I've flown to Paradise,' said Samuel ingenuously.

'The place is certainly full of angels,' John agreed, and gazed round at all the many beauties who strolled on the arms of exquisites or sat with gallant gentlemen in their boxes. 'My God, look at that incomparable creature!' he added in an undertone.

'Where?'

'Sitting in the booth next to ours. Take a peep but be discreet. I know what you're like.'

Sliding to the end of the bench seat, the Goldsmith peered round the corner and saw a veritable feast for the eye. For there, right next door to them, sat one of the finest, freshest Beauties it had ever been his privilege to look upon. Strawberry hair piled up beneath a cascade of fresh flowers enhanced a complexion of snow and country roses, while the girl's small pert nose was placed most prettily above her full, rather pouting lips. Even from that distance, the flirtatious play of the Beauty's black lashes round eyes so extraordinarily light a blue they resembled forget-me-nots, was clearly visible. Without thinking, Samuel let out an appreciative whistle before returning to his place, mouth agape.

'What a lovely girl. And with a gentleman of means, I see! Did you notice the quality of his clothes?'

'Very stylish. I wonder who the lucky rogue is.'

'Shall we saunter past and get a better look at them?'

'By all means.'

The friends stood up to go but their plan was brought to an abrupt halt by the appearance of the waiter bearing the punch and the menu. Sitting down again, John and Samuel stared at the selection of meats, consisting mainly of thinly sliced ham, chicken or beef, then turned their attention to the savouries and sweets. On offer in this last category were a tart at one shilling, a custard or a cheesecake, fourpence, a heart cake, twopence, and a Shrewsbury cake for the same amount. They settled for chicken followed by custard, but with this order transacted looked up to find that the girl had risen from her place and was making her way down the Grand Walk on the arm of the gallant. Every red-blooded male she passed bowed and raised his hat to the Beauty, though she ignored them, putting her chin high in the air, whilst in coquettish contrast she openly kissed her lover on the lips from time to time.

'Ah ha,' said John, smiling his uneven smile. 'So she's either a Duchess or a whore.'

'What makes you say that?'

'It's obvious. She lacks too much prudery to come from the middle classes. I'll wager that girl is either from the highest or lowest walk of life.'

Samuel gazed at him in astonishment. 'You've become very observant.'

John grinned but did not answer, and with that they fell to eating the meal that was set before them.

The repast consumed, the two strolled forth to hear the inimitable Miss Burchell rendering an aria, standing in front of the raised orchestra box, music in hand. Then, having blown her flourishing kisses and been rewarded with a flattering if somewhat grave bow of her head, they hastened towards the north side of the Gardens in response to the ringing of a bell. This denoted that the hour of nine o'clock had arrived and the famous Cascade was about to be lit. With much excitement, the friends jostled amongst the crowd who had already foregathered to witness the spectacle.

The lamps were suddenly extinguished so that all stood in darkness and then, as if by magic, an enormous curtain was drawn to one side disclosing a landscape scene illuminated by concealed lights. A fine grotto became visible, surrounded by the statues of Neptune, a mermaid, a dolphin and various other sea creatures, all placed in, as the woman in front of John remarked, 'very agreeable attitudes'. Behind the statues fell showers of crystal water which plunged into a spacious basin, full of swimming fish, then spouted heavenwards once more through the mouth of a grinning dogfish. Despite the *oohs* and *aahs* and thunderous applause, John found himself rather in agreement with *The Connoisseur* who had described the sight, somewhat scathingly, as the 'tin cascade'. And, as was his habit when slightly bored, the Apothecary found his attention turning to the crowd, thinking that people were always more interesting than mechanical effects.

It seemed that the *beau monde* had gathered in force at Vaux Hall this night, for amongst the throng John recognised the Duke of Richmond, notorious young man about town and the idol of his contemporaries. Lost in admiration, John saw that the nobleman was wearing a blue coat of quite stunning splendour and wondered if the day would ever come when he would be able to afford such a fabulous garment. Standing beside the Duke was his brother-in-law, Henry Fox, older than Richmond by far, and one of the most celebrated politicians of the day. He was also wearing blue, though a far more sober cut.

Next to them, part of the melée and yet somehow alone, there hovered an extravagant being, a female of both mystery and fascination, whom John had glimpsed earlier sitting in a booth with a rouleau of rakehells, part of a small group all bent forward eagerly as the dice box rattled. Though there were no gaming tables at Vaux Hall, what people did in their private booths was their own affair, but that a member of her sex had been seen gambling in public would have been intriguing enough, without the fact that this one was also masked. John studied the extraordinary creature closely, wishing he knew her identity.

She was quite tall for a woman, in fact not a great deal shorter than he, yet supple for all that, a delicate racehorse of a female. Her facial bones, too, looked as if they might well be good, what John could see of them behind the concealing scarlet mask. Yet the full mouth with its lovely tilt of amusement was superb, its owner's sense of fun impossible to hide. Staring at her, wondering what colour her hair might be, for that, too, was concealed, swept aloft into a wire turban set with glittering brooches, John longed to know more about this elegant denizen of the town.

And he was obviously not the only one, for the Masked Lady was catching the attention of a tall man of foreign appearance, dressed from head to toe in a black cloak, only a hint of blue at the throat revealing the colour he wore beneath. John's eyes wandered on and took in the fact that two old harpies, dressed in identical blue gowns in a horrid pastiche of young female twins, were also jealously regarding the exotic being who lingered so close to them. Wondering why everyone in the Pleasure Gardens seemed to be wearing the same colour, and feeling hopelessly out of fashion in his new mulberry satin, John continued to observe.

An apprentice lad, too small to see over the heads of the crowd, had crept forward and was crouching in front of the circle of onlookers in order to get a better view. He looked so tiny, a rascally little fellow in a coat of such fine stuff, inevitably a dazzling shade of blue, that John immediately wondered if he had stolen the garment, for how else could a poor 'prentice manage to be so smartly clad. The Apothecary watched him with amusement, seeing the boy's youthful profile turned in wonder towards the shining waterfall and its fanciful aquatic attendants. Then he forgot all about the apprentice as he saw who stood behind him: the Beauty, her escort gone and now quite alone, had joined the throng.

The scene took on the frozen quality of a painting; the crowd intent upon the Cascade, their faces glowing in its reflected light, the loveliness of the girl dominating all. Then the moment passed. The lights dimmed on the spectacle and the great curtain fell. The throng, with nothing to look at, began to move away, and John turned to find that Samuel was no longer standing beside him. Gazing in all directions, the Apothecary saw that most people were milling towards the bandstand where the concert and supper were about to resume, though others who had already eaten or wished to take the air were starting to promenade down the two great avenues. With no idea where Samuel could have gone to, John eventually decided to traverse the Gardens in search of him.

It was a quivering night of argent moonshine and purplish shadows, the breeze bustling in the leaves, the smells and sounds of the black satin Thames drifting on its breath. The sky was dark as a cloak, yet spangled with a million sequinned stars, while the big indolent moon bathed in milk, throwing a shower of white about itself. There was a stirring everywhere, a nervousness abroad, as though a splinter of lightning might at any moment crack across the heavens and transform the evening's gaudy beauty into something fierce and uncertain.

Feeling slightly uneasy, the Apothecary strode on and, having reached the point where the Grand Walk and the Grand Cross Walk met, John turned into the crossing avenue and walked determinedly along, staring all about him, particularly when he reached the South Walk, at which point he stopped beneath one of the vast archways and peered up and down its length. Still there was no sign of that familiar windmill figure, and John had no option but to go on towards The Dark Walk, whose inky depths lay before him. It was then, just as he stood hesitating, not knowing whether to turn left or right, that he heard the sound of a scream, a momentary anguished cry which ended abruptly, as if a hand had been clapped over the mouth of the woman calling out.

John waited uncertainly, poised like an animal ready to race, wondering whether he had merely heard sweethearts at play or whether that choking cry denoted something far more sinister. Then came another noise, a dull thud as though something had fallen to the earth. It was enough to spur him into action and John hurtled into that dark cavernous avenue, turning left, the direction from which the sound had come.

He had entered a pit where the tall trees blotted out the moonshine and there was nothing but the high hedge on one side and dense woodland on the other. Hardly able to see, John rushed on, regardless of the fact that his hat had fallen off, that his fine stockings were tearing, his one purpose to find the woman who had cried out in despair. And it was then that he glimpsed a figure rushing out of the trees and speeding away as he approached. Just for a second he saw an oval of a face turn in his direction, saw a dim flash of blue as the creature hastened off. Then, charging into the clump of trees from which the figure had run, John Rawlings tripped over the other occupant of The Dark Walk and found himself lying prostrate beside the Beauty.

She lay sprawled upon the grass like a shattered doll, her strawberry hair streaming out about her, the flowers that had so recently bedecked its curls trampled and broken where they had fallen. In a second the Apothecary was on his feet, stooping to lift the inert form, then delicately turning it over. The glorious eyes stared into his sightlessly, but still he felt for her heart, kneeling and leaning low to the lips to catch any sign of breath. Then a shaft of moonlight came slanting through the trees and John saw that the roses in her cheeks had turned to snowdrops, that there was a blueness about her mouth, and round her neck, twisted like an obscene serpent, was the thing that had choked the life out of her.

Very gently, almost with reverence, John laid the Beauty back on the ground and straightened out her clothing, which had become torn and disarrayed as she had helplessly fought her attacker. One of her legs was bare, he noticed, the other covered with a black stocking held up by a garter. Her stays and small clothes seemed undisturbed, suggesting that this was no common rape, that sexual molestation had not been the reason for this killing. Leaning over the body once more, John stared hard at the thing drawn tightly round the girl's neck and recognised it for what it was. This most lovely of creatures had been brutally strangled with her own dark stocking.

'Is she dead?' asked a tremulous voice, making the Apothecary leap in fright.

A wide-eyed girl, clinging to her sweetheart's arm as if it were an anchor, was approaching him through the trees.

'I fear so,' John answered, standing up and brushing his knees.

The girl went paler than the moon, staring at the body in horror.

'What's that around her neck?'

'A stocking. She's been strangled.'

'Oh God's faith!' 'she exclaimed, clapping a hand over her mouth, while her lover, a burly boy if ever there was one, turned his eyes up in his head and fell to the earth without a sound.

''Zounds!' said John irritably, dragging the young man into a sitting position and thrusting his head between his knees. 'What next I ask?'

'Oh Giles, Giles!' cried the girl, dropping to the ground beside her sweetheart and grabbing his hand. 'Speak to me!'

'He'll speak to you quicker if we can cool his head. Go and soak your handkerchief in one of the cascades,' John ordered, then realising how high-handed he must sound gave her a smile. She stared at him, sighing a little, then sped off, returning some minutes later with a dripping scarf which she wove round her lover's head like a turban. John saw the colour come back into the young man's cheeks.

'I think it might be best if the two of you go for help,' said the Apothecary firmly as Giles's eyes swivelled once more in the direction of the dead girl. 'Try to find one of the beadles and ask him to tell Mr Tyers, the Proprietor, that there's been a fatality in The Dark Walk and that a constable must be sent for. Can you manage that?'

'Certainly,' answered the boy, standing up, clutching at the threads of his dignity.

'Good. Now there's no time to waste. I'll stay with the body until someone comes.' Realising that he was giving orders to people only a year or so younger than he was, John added contritely, 'Do you think that's the most sensible plan?'

'Indeed I do,' answered the girl, dimpling at him despite the ghastly circumstances. 'Should we tell the beadles to raise a hue and cry?'

John shook his head. 'Whoever did this is well away by now. I think it might be wiser to say nothing until the authorities have been informed.'

'Then let's make haste,' Giles put in, with a huge attempt at being decisive.

'Indeed,' John replied solemnly.

The couple needed no further bidding, hastening off through the trees as quickly as they could, and just at that moment the shaft of moonlight grew more intense, enabling John to take a clear look at the scene.

It seemed to him from the way she had fallen that the girl must have been sitting down and that her attacker had sprung on her from behind. There was no doubt that she had put up a brave fight for her life, for her fingernails were torn and bleeding where she had clawed and scratched her assailant, while her sleeves were ripped from the wild thrashing of her arms. But obviously the struggle had proved too much and her loveliness had passed from the world face-down in the grass, with no-one to save her. Sadly, John Rawlings dropped a kiss on the cooling forehead, paying his last respects to one who, in life, must certainly have been one of the most beautiful women of her day. It was then that he noticed something held in one of the battered white hands. Bending low, he carefully removed it and held it up to the moon: a piece of blue brocade material.

'Torn from her murderer's coat!' John exclaimed softly, and with deft fingers wrapped it in his handkerchief for safe-keeping.

Any hopes he had cherished of keeping the news of the death in The Dark Walk secret, were most rudely dashed. Within a few minutes a crowd had gathered, gaping and pushing avidly, and it was only the appearance of the entire troop of beadles employed to preserve order in the Pleasure Gardens, together with Samuel Swann, looming large and somehow giving the impression of possessing a giant's proportions, that kept sightseers from coming irreverently close.

'I can't believe it,' Sam kept repeating as he was allowed through the cordon to join his friend. 'Barely an hour ago we were ogling her.'

'And wondering whether she be whore or Duchess. Well, it doesn't matter much now, does it?'

'Only in the eyes of God, I suppose.'

'I suppose,' John echoed softly.

It was at that moment that a beadle approached with a cloth, probably from one of the tables the Apothecary couldn't help thinking as he placed it over the body, closing the girl's eyes as he did so. He had not wanted to touch her again, feeling that everything should be left for the constable to observe as accurately as when he had first found her. But the sight of that beautiful blind gaze was too much for him and he drew down her lids.

'Your Master trained you well,' Samuel remarked quietly.

'What do you mean?'

'You've no fear of the dead.'

John shook his head, his blank face not revealing his seething emotions. 'He taught me that they can do no harm. He said only the living are capable of that.'

The friends stared at one another sombrely and then a distant sound broke into their consciousness. Judging by the reaction of the crowd, the constable was approaching, and John thankfully stepped aside as two men came into his line of vision, one quite small and black-haired, the other very lively and loud.

Without saying a word, the dark one knelt by the body, drew back the cloth and made a quick and expert examination. There was something about the way he set about the task that made the Apothecary think that here was no ordinary constable, chosen reluctantly by rote to fulfil the office for a year. It seemed to John Rawlings that Mr Tyers, the Proprietor of Vaux Hall, had, perhaps in order to protect the reputation of his Pleasure Gardens, sent a rider to Bow Street; that he was now watching one of Mr Henry Fielding's expert Thief Takers, 'all men of known and approved fidelity and intrepidity', latterly nicknamed the Beak Runners – so called after Henry's half-brother John, who had succeeded him as Metropolitan Magistrate.

The man stood up and shook his head at his companion who promptly turned to look John squarely in the face, his bright eyes suddenly hard as flint.

'Was it you, Sir, who found the body of the murdered woman?'

'Yes.'

'And can you tell me who you are?'

'I'm John Rawlings, apothecary, of number two Nassau Street.'

'I see. And how did you come to discover her?'

'I was looking for my friend here. We became separated after the lighting of the Cascade. I had just reached The Dark Walk when I heard a scream. I waited a moment lest it was simply a lovers' tiff, then heard the sound of a thud. It was that which made me decide to investigate.'

'And what did you find exactly?'

'Nothing at first, it really was damnably dark. And then I glimpsed someone who ran away as I approached.'

'Did you behold the person clearly enough to know them again?'

'No, it was too black. I could only make out a pair of breeches and a flash of blue coat.'

John reached into his pocket to fetch out the piece of torn brocade but was cut short by the dark fellow who asked abruptly, 'Why did you not go in pursuit, Sir?'

'Because I fell over the dead girl, landed lying in the grass beside her, in fact. I am a trained apothecary and as dedicated to saving life as a physician, therefore my instinct was to help her for I did not know whether she might merely be stunned.'

Mr Fielding's men exchanged a glance but said nothing. 'By the time I discovered she was dead,' John went on, 'I knew it would be hopeless to search. Her killer would have rejoined the crowd. It would have been like looking for a needle in a haystack.'

'Ah!' said the dark man, and gave him a long hard stare which left John in no doubt that his story was not altogether believed.

'The young couple there can vouch for me,' he added, just a shade too quickly. And pointed at the hovering pair whom he had sent to get assistance.

'We most certainly saw him,' the girl put in at once.

'Kneeling by the body?'

'Just getting up.'

'Ah,' said the Beak Runner again, and the Apothecary was filled with dread, realising that he was under suspicion of murder.

'I had nothing to do with her death,' he protested vehemently, dropping his lids, aware that his eyes would reveal how nervous he felt even though his features remained composed. 'I did not even know the girl.'

'As you have probably guessed, Sir,' answered the lively one, 'we are not constables but attached to the Public Office at Bow Street. We must, therefore, request you to come with us to tell your tale to Mr Fielding personally. It is his expressed wish to question important witnesses himself.'

Putting his hand in his pocket to check that the piece of material still lay safely within his handkerchief, John decided that he would indeed have more chance of proving his innocence with the great John Fielding, London's Principal Justice of the Peace, a man whose wit and intelligence were a thing of legend.

'I should be delighted to meet him,' he answered calmly, though his mobile eyebrows inadvertently drew into a frown.

'Then we will go now, if you please, Sir. And you two young people as well,' replied the Beak Runner, bowing politely to the couple, who looked aghast.

John drew Samuel to one side. 'I'm suspected, I know it. For God's sake go to my home and tell my father what's afoot.'

His friend rolled his eyes. The road to the city was fraught with hazard to those who left the Pleasure Gardens late, and he had no means of transport other than to go by water, which would take too long.

'I'll do my best,' he said through gritted teeth.

'Then we'll be on our way, lady and gentlemen,' the dark man announced, sounding very courteous but very firm.

Looking round, John saw that the crowd had dispersed, that only a few stragglers remained at Vaux Hall, a blight having fallen on the entire evening. He also saw, as the ragged group set off towards the main entrance, that two soberly dressed men carrying what looked like a stretcher were making their way down The Dark Walk.

'It's all right,' the lively Beak Runner called to them, 'we've seen all there is to see. Take her away.'

Bowing his head as a mark of respect, the Apothecary, in a terrible parody of his arrival at the Pleasure Gardens, passed through the swing doors, this time escorted by Mr Fielding's Brave Fellows, on his way to the Public Office at Bow Street. While down at the water's edge, the Beauty also departed Vaux Hall, her earthly shell loaded on to a wherry to make its last tragic journey to the city mortuary, leaving behind for ever the scene of what only a few short hours before had been her final triumph.

Chapter Two

Samuel's dilemma as to how to get to London in the small hours of the morning, yet remain unrobbed and alive, was solved by two gentlemen who were just leaving Vaux Hall by the Kennington entrance, clambering into a coach accompanied by three young ladies, their direction Back Lane and the city.

'Room for one more,' called one of them jovially. 'Jump in, young Sir.'

'Gladly,' answered Samuel, scrambling aboard and cramming his large frame between two of the girls.

The man who had offered assistance held out his hand. 'Frobisher, the Honourable Frederick. And these are the Misses Carter, Miss Bealieu and Lord Bramcote.'

'Damme,' said his Lordship, 'rum do tonight, what? Who'd have thought poor Lizzie would have gone like that.'

'Lizzie?' repeated Samuel in astonishment. 'Did you then know the victim, Sir?'

'Me, and half of London. She was, that is until two months or so ago, when she left mysteriously, the favourite of the Leicester Fields brothel.' His Lordship cleared his throat and added, 'Forgive frank talk, ladies. Forgot myself.'

'Not a Duchess then!' Samuel exclaimed, and everyone laughed.

'A Duchess in her way,' put in the Honourable Frederick, suddenly solemn. 'The usual story, I'm afraid. An innocent country girl looking for work in London and snatched up by a procuress. Then taking to the life, alas.'

'You're certain it was her?'

'Positive. I saw her face before your friend covered it up.'

'I wonder if they know this at Bow Street.'

'They're sure to find out soon enough.'

'But where has she been recently?' said Samuel, almost to himself.

Lord Bramcote frowned. 'That's the damnable odd part. Nobody knows. I think a fancy fellow must have set her up, couldn't bear to share her, what?'

'George, please!' remonstrated one of the Misses Carter.

'Sony, Sal. 'Zounds, but it's a wicked world, ain't it?'

'So wicked I fear we may be robbed tonight,' she answered, shivering.

'If a highwayman comes I'll blow his head off,' Milord stated cheerfully, and produced a loaded pistol from an inner pocket.

Sam sat mute, thinking that this evening, which had started with so much promise, was turning into one of the most nightmarish of his entire life. In fact he was never more glad of anything than when the coach reached the outskirts of London, clattered over Westminster Bridge, opened to the public four years earlier, and set him down at the top of The Hay Market. Hurrying down Coventry Street, from which place he could glimpse the brothel in Leicester Fields where the dead girl had worked, Samuel ran the rest of the way to Nassau Street, startling the Night Watch as he panted up to the front door of number two.

When the street had been created in the 1730s, a uniform group of elegant residences had been erected, each four storeys high and three windows wide, their interiors furnished in handsome style. As Samuel Swann was shown into the hall by the night porter, he remembered with fondness the house next door where he had lived as a boy, nostalgically wishing he were still there. His father had long since moved away to the unspoilt rural retreat of Islington, while Samuel lodged with his former Master in West Cheap, as yet not settled in a home of his own. Yet looking round him now as the porter went to waken Sir Gabriel Kent's valet to see if John's father might himself, in his turn, be awakened, Samuel experienced a great surge of longing, a yearning for boyhood, for the past. And when Sir Gabriel appeared at the top of the stairs, clad in a night rail and turban, the younger man hurried forward to greet him just as he had when he was a child.

'How very glad I am to see you, Sir,' he exclaimed and, without thinking, raised Sir Gabriel's hand to his lips.

The man who was to all intents and purposes John Rawlings's father, for he had raised the child since it had been three years old, smiled and nodded, and Samuel stepped back to look at him properly.

At seventy years of age, Sir Gabriel stood a magnificent figure. Always dressed in black and white – black and silver for balls and other festive occasions – during daylight hours he made it his custom to wear a full-bottomed wig with long curls which flowed down over his shoulders. His eyes were extraordinary, sometimes fierce as an eagle's, at others gentle as a deer's, and an unforgettable shade of amber-flecked gold. But beyond his unique way of dressing and arresting features lay a powerful charm that drew even the smallest child to Gabriel's side. He possessed the kind of magic that won many friends and, therefore, also attracted certain enemies.

'My dear Samuel,' he said now, 'what brings you at this late hour? Has aught befallen John?'

'In a way, yes. Oh he's perfectly safe,' the young man added hastily as he saw a frown cross the planes and hollows of Sir Gabriel's face. 'But there's been an extraordinary event.'

'Shall we discuss it in the salon? Come, you look fraught,' and without waiting for a reply, John's father strode, straight and tall and not in the least bowed down by the weight of years, into a room that led off to the left of the entrance hall. Samuel followed and sat down on the padded sofa with relief, glad that despite the unusual hour Sir Gabriel had poured two glasses of port and placed one in his visitor's hand.

'Tell me everything,' he said, fixing his guest with a compelling gaze.

Almost as if he were speaking to his own father, Samuel let the story come out, only omitting the fact that he and John had been making sheep's eyes at the murdered girl.

'And you say she was a whore in Leicester Fields?'

'Yes, Sir.'

'Then she may well have had many enemies. Men grow indiscreet in the arms of a beautiful woman. A murmured secret that might jeopardise a marriage, a business matter, even the state, could prove fatal. The one in whom too much information has been entrusted is always in danger of being silenced for ever.'

'I wonder what happened to the man she was with,' Samuel answered thoughtfully. 'A fine young dandy if ever I saw one. Monied, too. Halfway through the evening he seemed to vanish off the face of the earth.'

'Perhaps they quarrelled and he abandoned her? Who knows? But enough of him. You say that John is at the Public Office now? That he is under suspicion of the crime?'

'Ostensibly he was taken there to tell what he saw. Those who came to investigate said that Mr Fielding likes to question witnesses himself. But John fears that they do not believe his account of what took place.'

'I do not consider he will come to any harm,' Sir Gabriel answered after a moment's thought. 'John Fielding is known to deal fairly with those who play straight with him.'

Samuel yawned. 'May I beg a bed for a few hours, Sir?'

Sir Gabriel rose to his feet, and despite his sudden and immense fatigue, Samuel could not help but remark how lithely he moved for a man of his age.

'My dear young friend, pray forgive my thoughtlessness. Watkin shall show you upstairs at once.'

'And what of you, Sir?'

'I shall await John's return. I have slept quite long enough.'

But in this John Rawlings's adopted father was dissembling, for it was far from his intention to sit idle. As soon as Samuel had safely disappeared, the older man's valet helped him into black breeches, a fine white shirt, and a stark coat relieved only by its white velvet buttons. Then, as the first pink smudges of dawn appeared in the London sky, a dark coach with milk white horses set forth from Nassau Street and down towards Leicester Fields. There, it turned left into Bear Street, picked its way through a narrow alleyway, only just wide enough to allow the conveyance to pass through, then crossed St Martin's Lane on its journey towards Covent Garden and the Public Office at Bow Street, situated in the home of Mr John Fielding, Principal Justice of the Peace, in whose hands alone lay the responsibility for policing the lawless metropolis of London.

* * *

Hastening from Vaux Hall, the carriage bearing John Rawlings and his two companions, whose names had been revealed during the ride as Lucy Pink and Giles Collings, turned into the Great Piazza of Covent Garden, on its way to the Public Office at Bow Street, cutting a slow path through the crowd as it went. Even at this dawning hour the vast square was already thronged with traders selling their wares from baskets set on the cobbles before them, the air filled with their cries. 'Cabbages O! Turnips', 'Fine strawberries', competed with 'Buy my sweet roses', and 'Cherries O! Ripe Cherries O!' in boisterous cacophony, the whole uproar punctuated with the noisy barking of alleyway curs and dismal wails of neglected street children.

John, surveying the tatterdemalion pageant with a jaded eye, thought about death and wondered if any member of this motley mob might face his end before nightfall. Shivering at this sudden stark awareness of mortality, the Apothecary attempted to summon up the last of his flagging wits as the carriage turned out of Russell Street into Bow Street, and drew to a halt before the third residence on the left-hand side.

The Public Office, which he was now contemplating with dread, was situated on the ground floor of a four-storey house, the upper areas of the same still, surprisingly yet by custom, serving as the private residence of the Metropolitan Magistrate, Mr John Fielding. This practice had started some years earlier when, in 1738, Sir Thomas de Veil, Colonel of the Westminster Militia and Justice of the Peace for four counties beside, had moved to a new home in Bow Street. Despite his terrible reputation with women, Sir Thomas had been highly respected as a legal man, no mean feat in view of four marriages, twenty-five children, and lusty extra-marital liaisons. Indeed, it was a known fact that the magistrate had used a private examination room in his house for the interrogation of pretty female witnesses, a room from which a lady would always emerge with a smile on her face.

Yet other, more serious, legal matters had also been conducted at de Veil's dwelling place and in this way the Public Office had been born. Since Sir Thomas's death it had become the custom for the Principal Justice of the Peace to live at the Bow Street residence. Now, looking at its tall thin shape as he got out of the carriage, John's dark brows drew down once more at the prospect of what lay ahead of him.

The hallway of the famous house was much like any other, a beautiful curving staircase leading upwards, while four doors and a passageway marked the entrance to the other rooms. An ornate mirror hung on the right-hand wall and, despite his feelings of dread, John was amused to see that all three of them, Lucy and Giles reacting just as he did, stopped to stare into it, hastily attempting to smarten their dishevelled appearance. He looked wrecked, the Apothecary thought; his wig askew, eyes circled and heavy, his crooked mouth compressed into a harsh line, the mobile brows straight and frowning.

'God's life!' he exclaimed, and pulled his headgear straight over his springing curls.

'This way if you please, Sir,' said the dark Beak Runner and, much to his dismay, John found himself shown into a small room on his own, spying out of the corner of his eye that Lucy and Giles were also being separated one from the other.

'Mr Fielding won't keep you long,' the man added. Then the door closed and John Rawlings was alone for the first time since he had taken that fateful stroll down the Grand Walk. Pacing restlessly, the Apothecary began to examine the objects about him, rapidly coming to the conclusion that he had been put into Sir Thomas de Veil's famous interrogation room. In any other circumstances a grin would have lit his impish features, but tonight even his ready humour was wearing thin.

A long and comfortable sofa ran the length of one wall, a chair and table, together with a coffer, the only other furnishing. Opening the lid of the chest a spark of amusement momentarily returned and John chuckled to himself as he noticed several different items of female clothing and what appeared to be a collection of fans.

'Well, well!' he said, and smiled his crooked smile.

The sofa was even better to sit on than it looked and as he sunk deep into its long padded cushion, the Apothecary suddenly realised he was weary to the bone. With a yawn that started in his boots, he closed his eyes and instantly fell asleep, but whether for an hour or merely a few minutes he never afterwards knew, for he was abruptly awoken again by a persistent noise. From somewhere in the silence of the house was coming the distant sound of tapping and as it drew nearer, John identified the source as a cane rapping on floorboards. He froze as the sound progressed steadily towards the room in which he waited, then snatching at his rebellious wig, fallen forward while he slept, John turned to face the door.

It opened slowly, dramatically, as if the person beyond were making an entrance in a play, and the Apothecary felt his heart quicken in fear as he stared into the gloom. A man waited silently in the shadows beyond, a vast figure, well over six feet in height, whose broad shoulders and powerful build filled the entrance in which he stood. John saw a long white wig which fell to the shoulders, a thin nose with flared nostrils, a black bandage where there should have been eyes. In awe and terror he watched as the Blind Beak, Mr John Fielding, the most powerful and respected man in London, tapped his way into the room, felt for the chair opposite the sofa and sat down on it.

'Mr Rawlings?' asked the Beak in a voice which sent a shiver down John's spine, and turned his sightless gaze in the Apothecary's direction. Even though he could not be seen, the younger man rose to his feet in respect.

'You are addressing him, Sir,' he answered, and to his ears his tones sounded as pitiful and fluting as the squeaks of a mouse.

'Then kindly retake your seat.'

John obeyed, closely surveying the face turned towards his, its trenchant profile lit by the early morning light which was by now streaming through the window.

'I believe it was you who actually discovered the body,' the Magistrate began without preliminary. 'Pray describe the scene for me exactly as you saw it. Take your time.'

It was a relief to talk at last to a man known for his fairness, for his acute mind and grasp of situations. Almost with alacrity, John began to recount the story of his solitary walk, of the muffled cry, the glimpse of the figure in blue running away. Yet throughout this discourse the Blind Beak said not a word, the black bandage turned intently in John's direction, the man not moving in the slightest degree.

'Tell me of the body,' he said at last. 'Every detail if you will.'

'I fell over it to be honest, Sir. Landed face-down on the grass beside it. Then I rose and lifted the dead girl, turning her upwards. Perhaps your Brave Fellows have told you, Mr Fielding, that I am an apothecary. That is why I did not give chase to her murderer but stayed with the victim to see if I could restore her to life.'

'But you could not?'

John gave an involuntary shiver. 'No. She was gone. Choked to death with one of her own stockings.'

The Magistrate nodded. 'So what did you do next?'

'I put her back on the ground and straightened out her clothing, which had become disarrayed during the struggle. Yet this was no common rape, Sir. I could not help but notice that the girl's small clothes were undisturbed.'

The Blind Beak pursed his lips but made no comment, instead asking, 'Was the body still warm to the touch?'

'Yes, Sir. I believe, taking into account the time elapsed between her scream and finding the victim, that the girl had been dead only about ten minutes.'

The bandaged gaze drew slightly closer to John's own. 'Was there anyone else near you? Did anybody else witness your stumbling over the corpse?'

'No, Sir, I was quite alone, though a young couple who are presently here in the Public Office, arrived shortly afterwards.'

If Mr Fielding had been a sighted man he would have been staring the Apothecary straight in the eye. 'You are probably aware, Mr Rawlings, that because of this fact you yourself are under suspicion. You see, it is a known trick for a killer disturbed in the act to pretend that he was the first upon the scene of the crime. It has been done many, many times.'

'That's as may be,' John retorted angrily. 'But the fact is I did not even know the dead girl. What possible motive could I have had for doing away with her?'

The Blind Beak looked grim. 'It would seem that some do not need a motive to take life. That thwarted lust, a craving for excitement, can be reason enough in themselves. I am damning the whole of mankind when I tell you that gratuitous crime is commonplace.'

'That might well be true,' the Apothecary answered with indignation, yet for all that feeling the vile lurch of fear in the pit of his stomach. 'But I can assure you upon my oath, Mr Fielding, that I did not kill the poor wretch.'

The Magistrate's sightless gaze moved away and after a long silence he said, 'I know that.'

'You know!' repeated John, both astonished and relieved. 'Then I thank God for it. But how could you tell?'

'When I lost my sight at the age of nineteen, Mr Rawlings, certain compensations were granted me. The rational delights of reflection, contemplation and conversation were one. Another was more practical; a keen improvement in my hearing made me aware of almost all that goes on around me. I heard you shudder when you described the victim, and though such an act may have been put on to deceive a sighted man it would have been pointless to impress one who is blind.'

John could not reply, only grateful that the pall of suspicion had been removed from him. Then remembering the fragment of torn material he turned to face the blind man once more.

'There's something else, Sir, something of which I did not tell the Beak Runners because I wanted to show it to you personally. The girl had a small piece of blue brocade clutched in her hand, pulled from her murderer's coat.' John reached in his pocket and took the thing from its resting place of safe-keeping within his handkerchief. 'Here it is. Look for yourself.'

Having said those words he could have died of shame. Yet if the Blind Beak's feelings were wounded he revealed none of it. Instead, he took the torn brocade and delicately turned it over and over in his fingers.

'So you believe that this was ripped off during the struggle?'

'It must have been, Sir. What other explanation could there be for its presence? It did not come from her own clothing.'

In the silence that followed, John peered into Fielding's face, trying to hazard a guess as to what the Beak might be thinking, Eventually, the Magistrate spoke again. 'The Duke of Midhurst wore blue last night.'

The Apothecary stared at the blind man uncomprehendingly. 'The Duke of Midhurst?'

'The young rip who accompanied the dead girl. He was found asleep in his barge, drunk as a wheelbarrow, or apparently so. His story is that he quarrelled with his light of love and, leaving her to her own devices, returned to their box, then eventually staggered down to the river and went aboard.'

John frowned. 'Mr Fielding, Sir, there were many at Vaux Hall wearing blue last night, so many, in fact, that I began to suspect there must be a rage for the colour.'

'Did you know any of them?'

'Some, by sight.'

'Then tell me who they were, Mr Rawlings.'

John flashed a series of pictures into his mind's eye and came up with that of the crowd, jostling and laughing as the Cascade was lit in its pretty grotto.

'Well, there was the Duke of Richmond and his brother-in-law, Henry Fox.

The younger man was stunningly arrayed and the elder not greatly outshone. They were both in blue. Then next to them stood the Masked Lady...

'Who?'

'A fascinating woman, dressed in scarlet and gold with a red domino, a most mysterious creature. Strangely, there was a tall man in a black cloak who was staring at her almost as hard as I was. He had a blue garment beneath his mantle. Then there were two middle-aged ladies and their servant. They were got up very finely, though rather ridiculously.'

'In what way?'

'Their gowns matched, as if they were twins. I got the impression they were trying to look younger than they were.'

Mr Fielding's expression did not change. 'And the maid?'

'She was simply clad, in grey. But of course there *was* the apprentice.'

'Who was he?'

'A young lad, far too grandly dressed for his station. I put him down for a thief.'

The Blind Beak said, 'Ah!' but made no further comment and lapsed into another of his long silences. Finally, he asked, 'What do you look like, Mr Rawlings? Are you regarded as a handsome man?'

'I don't know, Sir,' John answered modestly.

The bandaged eyes drew frighteningly close. 'Don't mince with me, Mr Rawlings. Describe yourself. Every detail.'

'Well, I'm of medium height and build, not conspicuous in either of those things. My father maintains that I move with elegance, though not in a dandified way you understand. My hair is curly, auburn in colour, more red than brown, and my eyes are blue, quite a dark shade.' John paused. 'I find this a little embarrassing, Sir.'

Mr Fielding made an impatient noise. 'Really, Mr Rawlings, when one is dealing with a case of wilful murder, the solving of the crime must override all other considerations.'

'But I don't quite see...'

'There is a reason for everything I do. Continue, if you please.'

'Well, I'm good at hiding what I think. Sir Gabriel maintains I have a gambler's face, rather composed of feature. Oh, and when I smile I do so crookedly.'

The Blind Beak made a slight sound in response to this and John stared at him suspiciously. But Mr Fielding's features remained impassive. 'So other than for your strange grin would you say there was anything that sets you apart from the crowd?'

'No, Sir.'

The Magistrate put the tips of his fingers together. 'Tell me about your memory. Does it work pictorially?'

'Yes, I see scenes as if they were paintings in which I can recall every detail. It is the same with the written word. I can summon it back and read it once more.'

'That must have been very useful to you in your studies.'

'It was.'

The sightless eyes turned fully in John's direction and yet again there was a protracted silence. The Apothecary caught himself thinking that if this were a trick to throw witnesses off balance it certainly worked most effectively.

Mr Fielding cleared his throat. 'You have unusual powers of recollection, I believe, Mr Rawlings,' he said at last.

'It has been my gift since childhood, Sir.'

'Then in that case I would like you to undertake a commission for me.'

The hare in John Rawlings quivered, getting the scent of something rare, and at that moment he looked anything but one of the crowd, burnished and graceful, yet strong as wire. 'And what is that, Sir?' he asked.

'To find the owner of the garment from which that piece of material was torn.'

The gambler's face vanished and John's features lit up before he drooped his lids to hide the expression in his eyes, forgetting momentarily that Mr Fielding could not see his reaction.

'You want me to act as one of your Runners, Sir?' he asked, astonished yet thrilled.

'I do.'

'But why not choose one especially trained for such a task?'

'Because they did not see what you saw. They did not glimpse that elusive figure taking to its heels and fleeing from the scene of the murder. Nor, Mr Rawlings, do they have such a formidable memory as you claim to possess.'

John looked up, dark-eyed, glinting with the thoughts that teemed through his mind.

'How would I start? How should I go about such a quest?'

'The Duke of Midhurst is here in the Public Office and has already been questioned. He tells me that the dead girl was called Elizabeth Harper and until a few months ago worked in the brothel in Leicester Fields. You must begin by going there to discover all you can about her: where she came from, who her friends and enemies were, where she went between leaving the brothel and being put under the Duke's protection.'

John's smile appeared briefly. 'And you believe I am capable of this?'

'Why not, Mr Rawlings? You are a trained apothecary, which fact declares you to be of no mean intelligence.'

'But would people confide in me, do you think?'

'That remains to be seen. I shall give you a letter of authorisation which will convince those like Mr Tyers of Vaux Hall that he must co-operate with you. It is his proud boast, incidentally, that he knows more about his visitors than they do themselves. Should that be true, it would prove very useful.'

The smile reappeared and remained. 'I'll do it,' said John.

The Magistrate's face stayed expressionless beneath its full white wig and the Apothecary found himself wondering how old the Blind Beak actually was. Despite the large build and heavily jowled chin, despite his aura of power and authority, the younger man guessed shrewdly that John Fielding was probably still in the early part of his thirties, probably little more than ten years older than John Rawlings himself.

'Do you ever play chess?' Fielding asked by way of answer.

'I do indeed, Sir.'

'Then, Mr Rawlings, you are about to embark upon the finest game of your life. By your skill and ingenuity you will track down the evil being who choked the life from poor Elizabeth Harper and bring him to the justice he deserves. Before you leave here a letter of authorisation and five guineas for expenses will be yours. You have, Sir, entered the service of the Public Office, albeit unofficially.'

With those words the Blind Beak got to his feet, thrust the piece of material back into John's hand, then made for the door, his stick tapping in front of him.

'When shall I report back to you?' asked John, nervous again.

'When you have something of genuine interest to tell me. Good day, Mr Rawlings.'

And with that the Metropolitan Magistrate was gone.

Chapter Three

He had fallen into a restless sleep almost as soon as he had closed his eyes, dreaming of murder and violence, of voices raised in quarrel, of seeing a man hurrying down the Grand Walk, of hearing a girl cry out. Then the sound of wheels had awoken him abruptly and Samuel had sat bolt upright, briefly unable to get his bearings, before realising that he was in one of Sir Gabriel Kent's guest rooms and that the noise which had disturbed him was that of his host leaving the house. With a sigh, Samuel wondered if it was time to get up, but the faint light reflected on the bedroom ceiling told him that the day had not yet broken, so he lay back on his pillows thinking about the dream and whether it had any substance in reality.

Though it would certainly not sound well if he were questioned, Samuel had to admit that he had followed the fated Beauty deliberately, longing to have a closer look at her, walking just a few paces behind her down the Grand Walk, trying to pluck up the courage to introduce himself. He had attached himself to the throng leaving the Cascade, with that intention, if truth were to be told, but had lost his chance when she had been joined by a man in a black cloak, a man who had taken her by the arm and shouted at her in anger. Then a crowd of people had got in the way, and by the time Samuel had been able to get another look both the man and the girl had gone. The only thing he had seen was the elegant creature who had escorted the Beauty to Vaux Hall striding out of The Dark Walk and turning towards the river.

The thought of John, incarcerated in the Public Office, and a sudden feeling that he ought to go and help him, ought to seek out Mr Fielding and tell him what he had eye-witnessed, had Samuel leaping out of bed and crossing to the window to draw back the curtains. But then, seeing the gardens below, small but elegant and presently filled with an abundance of spring flowers, a wave of nostalgia engulfed him once more and, with a sigh, he sat down on the window seat and remembered.

He and the man who was to become his closest friend had originally been introduced as children, when Samuel Swann senior had moved into the town house next door to that of Sir Gabriel Kent. Nassau Street had been in existence only a few years then, in 1737, and was considered a good address for those of the professional class. Thus, the fathers became friendly and the sons followed suit, while Mistress Marjorie Swann, clapping her eyes on the motherless child who clung to her own boy's hand so pitifully, had taken pity on the poor soul, all great eyes and curling hair as the imp of humanity had been. But Marjorie had died of a fever two winters later and the children had been thrown together even more, both of them brought up by a father and servants, and no other young people around for company.

In 1741, when the boys had been ten years old, John and Samuel had been sent together to the Reverend Mr Johnson's boarding school for twenty pupils, situated in a house on the edge of Kensington village. The Principal had promised the two widowed fathers that as well as learning arithmetic and geometry, plus trigonometry plane and spherical, as applied to navigation and astronomy, to say nothing of book-keeping after the Italian method, his scholars would dine with the Master, be kept clean, and have bedchambers, beds and bedding as fine as any gentleman could desire for his son. He also assured the enquiring parents that his charges would be instructed in Latin so well they could converse in it, and would in addition read the best authors in the English language. Furthermore, they would be taught to read and write grammatically and spell most true.

Mr Johnson's academy had kept John and Samuel within its learned walls for six years, when a final examination had proved to the Principal's satisfaction that they were now qualified to go out into the world and the time for them to take indentures had come – for apprenticeship was still the best method of entry into the companies which governed the economy, and indeed the only way of obtaining the freedom of the city of London.

In that year of 1747, when John and Samuel were both sixteen, apprentice lads and lasses came from all walks of life, for girls that did not go into service young could also expect to endure the rigours of being sent into a strange household at an early age. Indeed, the daughter of one of Sir Gabriel's servants had been apprenticed to a milliner in the sum of twelve guineas some months previously. But where orphans and paupers could look forward to little else other than an apprenticeship to an obscure workman, the sons of gentlemen and merchants had their future guaranteed, knowing that they would become men of substance and prominent citizens when their indentures finally came to an end. Thus, his formal education over, John Rawlings had been apprenticed to Richard Purefoy, Apothecary, of Evans Row, for the sum of £200 and Samuel Swann to Edward Hall, Goldsmith, of West Cheap, for £50 less. The premiums had been high but one Master had been a member of one of the Twelve Great Livery Companies, the other the Worshipful Society of Apothecaries, and could, within limits, charge what they wished.

'And now it's over,' Samuel thought. 'And we can apply to be made free.'

And with that he remembered the celebrations of the night before and their violent and terrible end.

'John!' he exclaimed out loud. Furious with himself for lapsing into a daydream, Samuel hurled on his clothes and hurried from the house, still doing up his cravat.

* * *

One of the most enviable qualities of Sir Gabriel Kent, in the estimation of his adopted son at least, was his ability to remain silent when the situation so demanded. Indeed John was never more grateful for this attribute than during the short journey back to Nassau Street from the Public Office. Having seen his son emerge onto the step of the house in Bow Street, Sir Gabriel had merely held open the carriage door and beckoned him inside, then called to the coachman to take them home. After that he had simply remarked that it promised to be a fine day and had said nothing further. At home, he had behaved similarly. Wishing his son good morning and saying that he would speak to him over dinner, John's father had disappeared in the direction of his study leaving the Apothecary no option but to go to bed and sleep off the effects of such a devastating night.

Awoken by bright sunlight at three, John, having but one hour left in which to prepare, hastily took a bath in the tin tub brought to his bedroom for the purpose, shaved, then dressed carefully in dark satin breeches, fine white stockings, a pink coat and floral-patterned waistcoat, thinking to himself that it had been some years since he had worn such elegant clothes at mealtimes.

Dinner was served in the first floor dining room from which there was a fine view of the grounds of Leicester House and the gracious building itself. It was at present occupied by the Prince of Wales, George II's grandson, who preferred it to the royal residences, some said because it got him away from his domineering mother Augusta, widow of the King's son Frederick. Looking out of the window, John thought how pleasant it was to be at home again after his seven years of study, during which he had lived in his Master's house, only allowed to go out on Sundays and generally kept in order. Then he remembered Mr Fielding's commission and glittered his disturbing smile at his father.

Sir Gabriel looked up from the delicate sherry which he was sipping before the meal commenced. 'Do you wish to tell me everything now or shall we wait until the port?'

'That might be a better time, I believe.'

His father understood and nodded, for once the meal had been served the servants would be dismissed and they would be alone to talk frankly. Thus, John chattered of trivialities as he devoured every cover set before him, relishing the fine cooking of home. Sir Gabriel, on the other hand, ate like a connoisseur rather than a gourmand, his fork flying amongst the tastier fishes and meats, his silver knife delicately peeling the skin from the fruit with which he ended his repast.

'I've missed you, you know,' said John, his features alight with affection.

'But you've seen me. We have been in constant touch.'

'It is not the same as living under your roof.'

Sir Gabriel leant forward, the curls of his long wig brushing against the white damask tablecloth. 'And do you not think I have missed you? That this house has not seemed full of ghosts without your presence?' He looked up over John's shoulder at the full-length portrait of Phyllida, Lady Kent, painted by Thomas Gainsborough before the artist had returned to live in his native Suffolk.

'Tell me, Father,' said Gabriel's adopted son, reading his father's thoughts and carefully changing the subject, 'what do you know of Mr John Fielding?'

The tawny eyes looked thoughtful. 'A remarkable person, part of a remarkable family. Why, his half-brother Henry, now alas a very sick man, must be one of the most talented people alive. Not only did he write my favourite novel, *Tom Jones,* to say nothing of the most bitingly satirical plays in the English language, he also began the policing of this lawless capital.'

'I thought Sir Thomas de Veil did that.'

'Sir Thomas was Principal Magistrate but he did not have a force of Brave Fellows. It was Henry Fielding who first trained the Thief Takers, and let no one forget it.'

'And what of John?'

'The Blind Beak? An exceptional human being. To do all that he has done to impose law and order in so short a time since his brother's retirement, and without the use of his eyes, is almost beyond belief.'

John looked up and saw that they were alone, that the port, both white and red, had been set before Sir Gabriel and the servants were bowing their way out of the room.

'Father, I must speak to you now that we are private together,' he said urgently. 'How much do you know of what occurred last night?'

'I am aware of most that happened at Vaux Hall. Samuel made his way here and told me the whole story.' Sir Gabriel drank deeply as if to arm himself for what lay ahead, and John did likewise.

'What he didn't tell you, because he did not know of it, was that I found something of importance on the dead girl. She had a piece of blue brocade clutched in her hand, obviously pulled from her murderer's clothing.'

Sir Gabriel said nothing, his face alight with interest.

'I told Mr Fielding of it and he has enlisted my help in finding the owner of that torn garment and bringing him to justice.'

'God's wounds!' exclaimed Sir Gabriel, whistling slightly beneath his breath, an action which John found most endearing. 'What an honour! To be picked for such a task by a member of so great a family. What did you say?'

'I agreed.'

'Quite rightly.'

'Yet there was doubt in my mind when I did so. With my indentures formally ended it occurred to me that I should be starting out on my career, that I might be set back by such an adventure.'

Sir Gabriel smiled a worldly smile. 'My boy, you are but twenty-three years old. Many, many years lie ahead in which you may compound your great and many pills and brews and, indeed, experiment for the good of mankind. But now fate has called you out and I am gratified to hear that my son has risen to such a challenge.'

As he spoke words of lineage and parenthood, the old man was filled with bitter-sweet memories, remembering the first glimpse of John and his mother, and acknowledging reluctantly that the young man was only his adopted son after all and not related by ties of blood.

He had seen them initially from the window of his coach, the mother and child begging in the streets, dirty, dishevelled and desperate for food. He had noted them in a vague abstracted way, the dewdrop of a girl, fresh as a brook, the boy all eyes, all innocent despair. The fact that his carriage had knocked them flying, thrown them down into the filth of the gutters, had torn his heart from his body. Shouting to his coachman to stop, he had lifted them himself, carried them, bruised and bleeding, into the safety of his conveyance. At that moment, even though he had not been aware of it, had begun the grand passion of his life. Sir Gabriel Kent, widower of the parish of St Anne's, Soho, victim of an arranged, loveless and childless marriage, had felt the first stirring of an emotion unfamiliar to him.

He had taken the beggar woman and her son to his newly-built home in Nassau Street, his intention to feed them, let them recover from their cuts and bruises, then send them on their way. But he had reckoned without the sweetness they had brought into his elegant soulless mansion, without the trust of the three-year-old who had thrust his small dirty hand into that of Sir Gabriel almost immediately. He had also reckoned without the delicate beauty of the child's mother, revealed in all its splendour as the grime of the London streets was washed away from her.

He had started by employing her as a servant, for she was no more than a simple country girl from the village of Twickenham, her accent rural, her social status low. Her name, so she told him, was Phyllida Fleet, but the boy she referred to as John Rawlings.

'But he is your child?' Sir Gabriel had asked her.

'Yes he is, Sir,' she had answered truthfully.

And later, when she had become more than a servant, when her master and she had entered the world of indescribable joy which only lovers know, she had told him everything. How the boy's father had come from the great Rawlings family of Twickenham, the local landed gentry; how she had worked in the kitchens; how the son of the house had fallen in love with her.

'Though I do not believe he intended to betray me, Sir. When he knew I was pregnant he went to London to find somewhere to lodge so that we might be together. Yet he never came back. I waited for the postchaise to return but he was not on it. Nor any of those following.'

'What happened then?'

'John was born in shame, alas. Still, as soon as I was able I came to town to look for his father.'

'But you did not find him?'

'No. John Rawlings, for I named his son after him, had vanished off the face of the earth.'

Being the man he was, Sir Gabriel Kent had educated Phyllida Fleet as if she were his own daughter. She had learned to read and write, to draw and embroider, to play the harpsichord, an accomplishment at which she excelled. Then, when she felt ready to accept a higher station in life, he had married her. For two years they had shared what both could only think of as heaven on earth. And then she had gone, giving birth to the child he had always wanted, taking her infant daughter with her to the grave. Even now, with so many years passed by, Gabriel Kent sighed as he looked again at Mr Gainsborough's masterpiece, which hung on the far wall beyond John's shoulder, the boy and the portrait the only tangible memories left of Phyllida Fleet.

'Don't be sad,' said his adopted son, following the direction of Sir Gabriel's gaze.

'I'm not. In fact I was thinking how proud your mother would be now that your apprenticeship is over and her son a qualified apothecary.'

John tugged a wayward curl. 'She might not be quite so proud that I am currently involved in the hunt for a murderer.'

'On the contrary,' his father answered, 'having once lived in the streets of London she knew the dangers of city life. I think she would be delighted that you have become Elizabeth Harper's champion.'

'Yet how shall I start?' John queried anxiously, repeating the question he had asked of John Fielding. 'Where amongst all the people in town do I find the wretch who killed her?'

'You must begin at the beginning,' Sir Gabriel replied sensibly. 'You must go to the house in Leicester Fields and discover all you can about the dead girl. Somewhere amongst the people who knew her is your man, you can be certain of it.'

The youthful Apothecary's cheeks flushed. 'That's what Mr Fielding advised. But you know the strict rules of apprenticeship, Father. I've never been inside a place of that sort. I would find it most embarrassing.'

Sir Gabriel fingered his chin, his lids lowered to conceal the expression in his eyes. 'Indeed, indeed. Of course, you could announce yourself as the Blind Beak's agent but that might well do more harm than good. I think you should perhaps take Samuel and play the part of two young men about town.'

'I suppose so,' John answered doubtfully.

'Yes, that would be the best plan,' his father continued briskly. 'Now, my boy, let us drink to your future and to success in *everything* you undertake.'

John looked at him suspiciously but Sir Gabriel's face was as straight as if he were playing cards.

'To the future,' the Apothecary echoed, and drained his glass.

Chapter Four

From a distance, the house in Leicester Fields, discreetly hidden from the gaze of the great Leicester House by a clump of sheltering trees, appeared almost respectable. So much so, that the disparate emotions of relief and disappointment could be seen clearly warring in the faces of John Rawlings and Samuel Swann as they walked down the path approaching it.

The two companions had joined forces again earlier that evening, Samuel having arrived at Bow Street only to find that John had already left and being obliged to retrace his steps.

'But I didn't waste my visit,' the Apothecary's friend had informed him. 'I asked to see Mr Fielding and he granted me an interview in which I told him all I could remember.'

'Which was?'

'That I observed the victim quarrelling with a man in a black cloak.'

'Was he foreign looking?'

'Yes.'

'Then I saw him too, earlier on. He was at the lighting of the Cascade. I particularly noticed him because he was staring fixedly at that amazing woman wearing a mask.'

Samuel had looked important. 'I saw something else as well.'

'And what was that?'

'The chap she was in the box with, that elegant dandy. He was rushing out of The Dark Walk as if the devil himself were on his trail. He headed for the river at great haste.'

'Really? How very interesting. By the way, I've discovered who he is.'

'Oh?'

'The Duke of Midhurst no less. The dead girl aimed high, it would seem. Anyway, he was at Bow Street when I got there. Apparently he told the Blind Beak that he argued with his lady love and went to his barge where, for consolation presumably, he drank himself into oblivion.'

'Then as I saw him running away from there he must have fallen out with her in The Dark Walk.'

'Yes,' John had answered thoughtfully, stroking his chin. 'It would seem that the victim did a great deal of quarrelling that night.'

'Obviously. I suppose you don't know the identity of the man in the black cloak as well, do you?'

'I'm afraid not.' John had given his friend a quizzical smile. 'Mr Fielding has asked me to act as his eyes, Sam.'

'What do you mean?'

'The dead girl had a piece of blue material clutched in her fingers. The Beak wants me to find the owner of the garment from which it was torn.'

'Does he indeed! Are you going to do so?'

'Yes. I admit I was undecided momentarily, but the thought of such an adventure was too good to pass by.'

Samuel had stood up, banging a hand as big as a melon into the palm of the other. 'Then I will assist you, as much as my Master will permit, that is.'

'But you're free of him.'

'I intend to stay on as a journeyman until I can set up on my own.'

John had given his friend an uncertain smile. 'Then if you mean what you say, I've a commission for you this very night.'

'I'm at your command,' Samuel had answered eagerly.

'I sincerely hope so. Both Mr Fielding and Sir Gabriel feel I should go to the brothel and make enquiries about Elizabeth. I want you to come with me.'

Samuel's expression had undergone a rapid transformation. 'But I've never set foot in such a place, you know that. City regulations prohibit apprentices from doing so.'

'Of course I was not apprenticed in the City,' John had answered smoothly. 'Then you...?'

'No, of course not. I would have told you if I had. Now, my father thinks we should masquerade as men of the world, so I suggest we pose as bloods.'

'Bloods!' Samuel had exclaimed, sitting down heavily on one of Sir Gabriel's elegant spade foot chairs which winced beneath his sudden considerable weight. For a keen young blood was something to emulate indeed, being a member of male society much favoured by the ladies, amongst whom he was known to be mighty with the sword, gallant in a ballroom, at ease in gaming hells, and incomparable behind the closed doors of a boudoir.

'We'd never get away with such a charade,' he added dolefully.

'Courage,' John had answered cheerfully. 'My father can find some clothes for you and I shall wear my new embroidered coat.'

Samuel had gulped. 'But...'

His friend had stared at him in sudden earnest. 'Samuel, I need you. Please say you will accompany me. The truth is, despite my great show at Vaux Hall last night, I know hardly anything about women.'

His friend had sighed heavily. 'No more do I. As I once told you, my experience amounts to no more than a few romps with my Master's servant, Mollie. Naturally, he caught us at it and put her out of doors, while I got a beating for breaking my pledge of no liaisons.'

John had nodded gloomily. 'My story is much the same, as you know. Like you, I had to swear solemnly not to fornicate, marry or run away. So when my Master discovered me in bed with sulky Sukie, his kitchen maid, he gave me a swipe that nearly flew me out the window. He said the only reason he kept me on was because he respected my father.

'Did he betray you to Sir Gabriel?'

'No, not he. He's a good man, is Master Purefoy.'

'So what are we going to do?' Samuel had asked.

'Still pretend to be bloods. Perhaps the guise will rub off on us.'

'It might on you,' Samuel had answered sombrely. 'My mother always said that you were so charming an imp you could get away with murder.'

'An unfortunate phrase,' John had replied crisply, and had gone to see about finding the clothes they should wear.

A discreetly dressed maid answered their knock on the brothel door, dropping a polite curtsey as she ushered the friends into a hall of classic design. But here any similarity between an ordinary house and that in Leicester Fields ended. Samuel's eyes bulged at the sight of the many young women, all scantily dressed, who draped themselves on sofas or leant on the pillars in the hall in the manner of statues *vivantes*.

'God's teeth!' exclaimed John, and his mobile eyebrows danced a jig at the very sight.

An older woman swept down the stairs in answer to the maid's ringing of a handbell, a woman who, even as she approached, seemed somehow vaguely familiar. John set his memory to work but came up with nothing, and then it was too late to concentrate for she was upon them, reddened lips simpering, eyes darting, shrewd as a counting clerk's.

'I do not believe I have had the pleasure,' she said, dropping a curtsey. 'Allow me to introduce myself. I am Madame de Blond.'

As her accent was extremely suspect, John doubted any French origins but none the less made her a bow, so elaborate that it left Samuel gaping, and said, 'Recommended here by my cousin, Ma'am. He spoke of your establishment in glowing terms. Thought I ought to pay a visit as my friend and I are newly arrived in town.'

'Ah, just so,' she replied. 'Pray consider yourselves at home. Would you gentlemen care for some refreshment while you make your choice? We have a very fine punch.'

'A large jug,' said John, waving a careless arm, and with that sat down upon a sofa to hide the fact that his legs were shaking.

He noticed from his vantage point that other gentlemen of fashion were seated at small tables in an open-doored room leading off the hall which seemed to serve as some kind of coffee house. Waiters hovered discreetly, arms draped with white napery, and pipe smoke filled the air. In fact all would have appeared normal had it not been for the fact that the girls wandered amongst the tables, overtly displaying their wares.

'My word!' said Samuel beneath his breath.

John turned to Madame de Blond. 'When it comes to choice I have a particular request to make, if you'd be so obliging, Ma'am.'

'Oh yes?' she answered, all smiles.

'My cousin spoke highly of one of your young ladies, Elizabeth Harper. I'd like mightily to make her acquaintance.'

A shadow crossed the woman's face but she recovered herself quickly. 'Elizabeth does not work here any more. I believe she was taken under the protection of a gentleman of substance. But I have another girl very like her, one Diana Linacre. I believe she is free at the moment. Shall I fetch her for you?'

'Has Diana been here long?' asked Samuel, speaking for the first time.

Madame de Blond stared at him in some surprise. 'A twelve-month. Why?'

He looked cunning. 'Because then you'll have trained her well, Ma'am, if you understand me.'

'The old dog!' thought John in admiration.

Light dawned on the Madame's face. 'Ah, you would like to share her. Is that it?'

The friends stared at one another in consternation, not quite sure what to answer. 'Yes,' said Samuel as 'No,' chorused John.

Madame de Blond smiled archly, the make-up on her face cracking lightly as she did so. 'Well, gentlemen, I'll leave you to make your minds up in private. Your punch will be served in the coffee house.'

With those words she was gone as some new customers came through the front door.

'What do we do?' asked Samuel frantically.

'I'll speak to Diana alone. She's bound to have known Elizabeth if she's been here that long. It was clever of you to ask.'

'Thank you. What happens to me in the meantime?'

'Pick someone else and try to find out all you can. I'm sure you'll manage.' And John could not help but laugh at the expression on his friend's face, fear and delight mixed so obviously in equal quantities.

Yet, tease Samuel as he might, no-one could have been more nervous than he when Diana Linacre, a comely young woman of about nineteen years of age, approached the table at which they sat.

'I hear you wanted me, Sir,' she said, displaying a set of small white seed pearl teeth.

John summoned up his courage. 'I really asked for Lizzie Harper, her reputation being so highly spoken of. But the Madame told me she had gone and that you were as fine in every way.'

'That is true, Sir.'

'None the less I would like to quiz you about her if I may.'

'Certainly,' Diana replied, then added firmly, 'but we would be far more comfortable talking in my apartment.' This said she put her hand under John's arm, eased him to his feet, and led him towards the curving staircase. Turning to look over his shoulder, he saw that a very beautiful black girl, obviously a runaway servant, had approached their table and taken his vacated seat.

'Good luck, old friend,' the Apothecary muttered silently, and continued up the stairs.

Diana's room, from the bed to the curtains, was furnished throughout in red, one wall completely taken up by a mirror.

'Now, Sir,' she said, unbuttoning her shift, 'what can I do to please you? Is it Lizzie's tricks you're after?'

'No!' answered John urgently and, as she gaped at him, amazed himself with his own ability to deceive by saying, 'Damme, my cousin will never forgive me if I don't find out more about the girl. He's quite head-over-heels in love with her.'

Diana stared at him narrow-eyed. 'Your cousin?'

'Yes, let me explain. We're a country family, from Twickenham you know. My cousin, when he was last in town, came here and met Elizabeth Harper. Most taken with her, he was. I believe he's thinking of putting her under his protection.'

'A bit late for that,' answered Diana, sitting down on the bed and indicating the place beside her. 'Someone's got in ahead of him. She left here several months ago with a wealthy rake who set her up in lodgings.'

'Was it the Duke of Midhurst?' asked John, making his first mistake.

The girl stared at him in surprise. 'Why do you say that? No, he was no Duke, unless he was a French one.'

'She went off with a Frenchman?' the Apothecary exclaimed, trying to hide his astonishment.

'Yes. Louis de something. He was very dandified, very rich, and she thought he could give her a better life.'

'Where did he lodge her?'

'In Vigo Lane, behind Burlington House. In a very nice set of rooms. I went there once,' Diana added just a little wistfully.

Suddenly sorry for her, John put his arm round the girl's shoulders.

'What happened to Elizabeth? Have you seen her since?'

'No, she turned too grand for the likes of me. Didn't want to be reminded of her past, I imagine. I haven't clapped eyes on her from that day to this.'

Those words confirmed more clearly than anything else that news of the murder had not yet reached the brothel and John silently congratulated himself on acting so promptly. John Fielding had been quite right in suggesting that the enquiry should begin there. It was obvious that at present suspicions had not been aroused.

'So, as far as you know, she still dwells in Vigo Lane?'

'I believe so, yes.'

'May I know the number in case my kinsman should wish to call?'

Diana looked mischievous. 'I wouldn't advise that. The Frenchman is very jealous. He would probably challenge him to a duel.'

'My cousin is a grown man and can take care of himself,' the Apothecary answered smoothly.

'Then it's number twenty-four, tell him.'

'Elizabeth went a long way for a simple country girl,' John commented wryly.

'Many of us begin like that,' Diana answered bitterly, then added, 'How did you know where she came from?'

'Because my cousin told me,' he replied swiftly. 'So am I to presume that you also did not start life in London?'

'I came to the city from Winchester and went into service. But the footman took advantage of me and I was put out of the house. One of the two Madames found me and brought me here. It was better than life as a street drab after all.'

'One of the *two* Madames?' the Apothecary repeated, something beginning to take shape in the back of his mind.

'Yes, there are two Madames de Blond – sisters, not twins, though they look as if they are. One of them runs this house, the other is out and about procuring any innocent she can get her hands on. They're a hateful pair, truly, though they feed and protect us well enough. By the way, they both set about the Frenchman when he took Lizzie away. Called him all the vile names under the sun and punched him with their fists. He sent one of them flying.'

'Really?' said John, amused.

'Yes. But just a minute, Sir,' Diana went on, suddenly earnest, 'I have to ask you something. Do you want me or don't you? We've spent so long talking I am no longer sure what you came for.'

'As I said, I really wished to help my cousin out of his dilemma.'

'Very well,' the girl answered resignedly, buttoning up her clothes, 'but don't tell Madame de Blond that nothing happened between us, will you?'

'Of course not. I'll pay her just as if it did.'

'It's not because you don't like me, is it?'

'Indeed no. You're a very desirable girl.'

Diana's fingers hesitated over the last button. 'Well then...?'

John lowered one lid till the black lashes swept his cheek, while the other blue eye regarded Diana Linacre in a brilliant stare. 'Well then,' he said, and gave her a slow and extremely disconcerting smile.

It was while he was seated in the coffee house drinking a restorative brandy and waiting for Samuel Swann to come down the stairs and join him that Madame de Blond suddenly flitted across John's line of vision, only to be followed a moment or two later by what appeared to be her double, neither of them dressed in identical blue today but certainly recognisable.

John cast his memory back to the scene at the Cascade and envisaged them, staring up at the waterfall, rubbing shoulders with Henry Fox, who had appeared to know them.

'I'll wager he did too!' thought John. But what new avenues did this discovery open? Had they gone to Vaux Hall in pursuit of Elizabeth, perhaps hoping to lure her back? Could her death be an awful warning to any girl from the brothel who might think of going astray in future?

With his mind mulling over all these ideas, John Rawlings ordered another brandy and decided that the very next day he must visit number twenty-four Vigo Lane and see what clues, if any, the silent home of a dead girl might yet yield up.

Chapter Five

After some discussion with Sir Gabriel over a hasty but hearty breakfast, it had been mutually decided that the role of young blood, much as John had enjoyed it, should be put aside in favour of some less conspicuous guise. Therefore, with a great deal of reluctance, the Apothecary found himself once again putting on the sober attire of an apprentice. City regulations insisted that those under indenture must wear only garments provided by their Master and that hair should be 'cut in a decent and comely manner', though the latter rule was frequently violated, John having been one of the worst offenders in this matter. Yet dark respectable clothing had been a necessity of life.

'I had hoped to put this sort of garb behind me now,' the Apothecary grumbled as he buttoned himself into a long serviceable coat.

'I would imagine that Mr Fielding's men adopt many strange disguises,' Sir Gabriel had answered him calmly.

Nothing could have mollified his son more effectively and John had left the house in Nassau Street with the serious look of one whose purpose in life it is to track down criminals.

Vigo Lane, which ran behind the magnificent gardens of the great mansion, Burlington House, was easy to reach on foot from Nassau Street, and today John chose the route that led him through Compton Street and the Huguenot quarter. Here so much French could be heard, so many French people passed, that it was almost possible to believe oneself in France, while leading off Compton Street was Greek Street, where a Greek colony had settled in the seventeenth century. But John turned away from this fascinating quarter and, instead, made his way down Knaves Acre, Brewer Street and Glass-House Street, into Vigo Lane.

Number twenty-four was easy enough to find. A tall terraced house built within the last forty years and not unlike the dwellings in Nassau Street in appearance, it had a fanlight and simple segmental hood above its front door and three steps leading up to the entrance. Moving with hare-like speed, John ascended them and seized the knocker, only to find that the door moved beneath his touch. Giving it a cautious push, the Apothecary saw to his astonishment that the catch had been left open. Hardly able to believe his good fortune, Mr Fielding's man stepped into the entrance hall.

An elegant angled staircase rose almost directly before him, to its left an internal access obviously leading to a suite of rooms. It occurred to John at once that the two upper floors mirrored this one and that the whole house consisted of three sets of apartments, though whether the place had been built in this manner or converted at some later time he could not be certain. Going to the door, John tapped on it lightly but there was no reply, no sound from within. Feeling somewhat apprehensive, the Apothecary cautiously turned and made his way upstairs.

He had guessed correctly. The first floor was laid out in exactly the same way as its lower counterpart, but once again a knock at the entry drew no audible response. Preparing, if there was no other alternative, to pick the locks, John decided to try his luck on the top storey, climbing the graceful stairway as silently as he could. Much to his astonishment, as he rounded the bend he saw that the inner door leading to the second floor apartment also stood slightly ajar. Carefully and quietly, John crossed over and peered inside.

The suite consisted of three rooms: a parlour – into which John was now gazing – together with a dining room, which he could glimpse through yet another open door, a third room leading off it which the Apothecary took to be a bed chamber. Knocking politely, John called out, 'Is there anyone at home?' He was greeted only by an overwhelming silence. Feeling daunted and decidedly nervous, he took a few steps inside.

The parlour was brightly though cheaply furnished in a mixture of styles without a cohesive theme. Looking around at the French tables and chairs, obviously obtained from immigrant craftsmen, and the old-fashioned Dutch walnut couch, which had plainly seen far better days, John guessed that whoever owned this lodging had been forced to buy mostly second-hand goods. Calling out as he went, John proceeded into the dining room.

Here, someone had made a gallant effort to produce the Oriental look. The mania for Oriental furnishings and ornamentation had come to England with William and Mary, and now John found himself gazing at a black reproduction cabinet with lace-work panels, embellished candle stands and an ornate bedragoned fire screen. Crowning all this self-conscious Chinoiserie was a vivid Chinese wallpaper flaunting birds of every hue, complete with a rainbowed peacock glinting starry eyes. The total effect was garish and slightly repellent and smacked of a country girl let loose in London with a purse of money to spend, though obviously not a very large one. Looking round him, John Rawlings became convinced that he was standing in the rooms of the murder victim.

The bedroom confirmed his suspicions. A large and old-fashioned bed, hung with scarlet and gold damask, had a mirror cunningly arranged to reveal its occupants. But it was the clothes in the marquetry press, most attractively decorated with a floral design and the finest piece of furniture in the apartments, that revealed all. Hanging in the cupboard were a selection of vivid gowns, their elegance and style declaring that they belonged to a slim and beautiful young woman. While in the drawers beneath were the petticoats and hoops, the small clothes, handkerchiefs and gloves, of a creature of fashion. The final proof lay in her perfume, for from all the garments wafted the faint but delicious smell of otto of roses and sandal, a scent that John remembered vividly lingering on the corpse, trained as he was to recognise such properties.

'Poor Elizabeth,' he said aloud, and knew that he had found what he was looking for.

The very drawers into which he was presently staring seemed as good a place as any to start searching for papers, and John went to the task with his usual elegant haste. Tipping the contents on to the bed, he riffled methodically, replacing the contents where he had found them after he had examined each item. However, other than a bottle of medicine which John put in his pocket to examine later, little of interest was revealed. Furthermore, there was something none too pleasant about the task, smacking as it did of violating a dead girl's possessions. There was something else too, an eeriness in the fact that Elizabeth's clothes and belongings were still in place, just as if she were due back at any moment. Indeed, so strong was this feeling that John caught himself listening to the silence, almost as though he expected it to be broken by the sound of the murdered woman returning home.

Then he froze, his blood turning to ice, for there *was* a noise. Faintly but distinctly came the tap of a light footfall as someone climbed the stairs towards the second floor. Thoughts raced through John's mind: a ridiculous notion that Lizzie's shade was revisiting its old haunts dismissed by the idea that he had been wrong all along, that this apartment belonged to another female entirely who would come storming through the door at any moment, demanding an explanation for his presence. Not knowing quite what to do, John concealed himself behind the dining room curtains.

He had closed the front door behind him and now his heart sank as a key was inserted into the lock and slowly turned. There was a momentary pause followed by the creak of hinges as the door swung open. Terrified, the Apothecary peered out from his hiding place and into the parlour.

It was almost a relief to discover that an old woman had come into Elizabeth Harper's apartment, an old woman loaded with various cleaning utensils, who puffed and blew with the effort of the climb and muttered to herself as she set about swiping at the various pieces of furniture with a dusty cloth. Nonplussed, John stood stock still and watched her.

'Fine business,' the woman grumbled, half-heartedly going to clean out the grate then seeing that it had not been used, 'still not come home, eh? Dirty little stop-out. God's old bones, that Frenchie won't be pleased.' And she cackled a laugh like a witch's, then narrowed her eyes. 'I wonder,' she said, and plodded through to the bedroom, walking right past John in his hiding place, presumably to see whether the bed had been slept in.

He seized his opportunity and, moving faster than he ever had in his life before, shot through the front door and down the stairs, not stopping until he was out in the street again, extremely out of breath and wondering what to do next. Then the outline of Lizzie's medicine bottle in his pocket gave him an idea. Assuming a nonchalant expression, John climbed the stairs at a leisurely gait and gave a polite knock on Elizabeth's door which still stood open as the old woman had left it.

From within he could hear the combined sounds of a clattering bucket and further grumbling, but eventually the cleaner's footsteps became audible and she appeared in the entrance.

'Yes?' she said, peering at him suspiciously.

John assumed a charming smile. 'I'm so sorry to disturb you. My name is Rawlings, John Rawlings. I am an apothecary.'

The beldame sniffed. 'Are you one of Lizzie's fancy men?'

John contrived to look slightly shocked. 'Indeed no. I have been compounding medicine for her.' He snatched the bottle from his pocket. 'And have just prepared some fresh. But, in the circumstances, I hardly knew what to do for the best.'

The old woman glared at him. 'What circumstances? What babble's this?'

John took a step backwards. 'I'd best be off. It is not fitting that I be the bearer of such tidings.'

She narrowed her eyes to slits. 'Nay, you'll come out with it, whatever it is. Speak up or I'll box your ears for you.'

He bowed his head as if in acquiescence. 'Then may I step inside?'

She opened the door a little wider and motioned him within. Sitting down carefully, John assumed a grave expression. 'Before I begin, may I know to whom I am speaking?'

'Eh?'

'I said, what is your name.'

'Oh. It's Hannah Roper. I take care of these apartments, the landlord living elsewhere, like. Now spit out your business.'

'It's about Elizabeth Harper. She met with an accident two nights ago. I shrink from giving you such grave news but that is the truth of the matter.'

'Is she dead?' Hannah said hoarsely, clearly shocked and astonished.

John nodded. 'I fear so.'

'How did such a thing happen?'

The Apothecary weighed up his answer and decided to tell the truth, knowing that sooner or later the old wretch would learn it for herself. 'She suffered a violent end at the hands of a murderer whilst visiting Vaux Hall Pleasure Gardens. I know because I happened to be there that very night. Acting as her physician, of course, I knew something of her background and it struck me that there might be several who wished her harm. Would you agree with that?'

The woman snatched a bottle of gin from her pocket and had a swig, offering John the same after wiping the neck with a greasy hand. He took a cautious mouthful as a sign of goodwill.

'Aye, there's a few who might at that,' she said, nodding agreement.

'Ah!' John answered meaningfully.

'You knew her well then? I've never seen you round here?'

'I mostly called in the evenings, merely to prescribe, of course.'

Hannah let out a wheezy laugh. 'Oh yes, of course! Well, in that case you'll know there's been quite a bit going on of late.'

John shrugged slightly. 'Well, yes and no. I didn't see her that often. Tell me.'

Hannah paused, glancing over her shoulder just as if she, too, thought Elizabeth's ghost might be walking. 'Like Lizzie being a kept plaything and these lodgings and all that's in 'em paid for by a gentleman of quality.'

'But why should that make her so disliked? It's an every day occurrence. Or was another woman in love with him?'

Hannah bellowed a laugh and drank deeply. 'I don't know about in love but there was certainly another woman. The gentleman in question is married.'

'Well, well,' said John, intensely interested. 'So who is this naughty fellow?'

'A Frenchman, one of the Huguenot immigrants living here in London. But well to do. He's Count Louis de Vignolles – or that's what Lizzie called him. But, like I said, there's been something strange happening recently.'

'What's that?'

'I reckon she'd got someone else as well as him.'

'What makes you think so?'

'She hasn't been home for over two weeks and the Count... Well, he's been here looking for her. He used to visit her when he could, but Lizzie still had plenty of spare hours on her hands, hours in which to go out searching for someone younger and richer.'

'I see,' said John – and did. For it was obvious that the wayward girl had come across the Duke of Midhurst during her idle moments when the Frenchman was, of necessity, spending time with his wife, and had thought him more worthy of her embraces.

'I reckon the Frenchie killed her,' Hannah went on. 'He was jealous as a viper. Foreign, you see.'

'What about his wife? Did she know about Elizabeth?' John asked, almost to himself.

Hannah shook her head and sucked her teeth reflectively. 'I'm not sure. She could have done. Though it's said that wives are often the last to discover such things. Anyway, Lizzie didn't confide in me. She talked more about her past than anything else.'

'Is it true she was a country girl?'

'Oh yes. Came from Midhurst in Sussex, or so she said. She travelled to London looking for work and ended up in a whorehouse.'

'A common enough event.'

'Aye. You can see the procurers hanging round the inns where the stage coaches end their journeys, luring the girls with tempting offers of employment. Little do the poor innocents know what they are letting themselves in for.'

John stood up, refusing the bottle of gin and getting a coin from his pocket. 'You've been most helpful, Hannah. You see, it is of great interest to me to know who killed poor Lizzie. Now, is there anything else you can tell me?'

She shook her head. 'No, I don't think so. Unless...'

'What?'

'Well, someone else came looking for her as well as the Count.'

'Who was that?'

'A boy, strangely enough. A lad of about fifteen or so. I took him to be an apprentice.'

John's breath quickened slightly as a picture came back of a young fellow in a fine blue coat crouching low to watch the lighting of the Cascade. 'Did this boy see Lizzie?'

'No, he came after she'd gone away. I told him she wasn't here and sent him about his business.'

'What did he look like?'

'He was quite short, I can recall that. And he had lightish hair and blue eyes. He didn't come from hereabouts because he had a country accent.'

'You are very observant,' said John, and handed over the coin.

Hannah stood up, groaning a little. 'I keep my wits about me.'

John looked at her with a professional eye. 'Do you have trouble with your knees by any chance?'

'Rheumatics make my joints very stiff. Hands too.'

The Apothecary adopted a business-like manner. 'I'll drop you in some compound and ointment when next I pass. They will at least ease the pain.'

The old woman gave him a look of servile gratitude. 'That's very kind of you, Sir. But I'm only a poor creature. What will be your charge?'

'Pay me what you can,' John answered magnanimously, delighted to receive his first commission since the end of his indentures.

'You're a good man, Master. Now, do you want to stay here and search the rooms?'

John hesitated, then said, 'No. But I'll ask you to do so in my stead. If you find any papers, regardless of what they might be, can you keep them for me until I come with your medicines?'

Hannah looked cunning. 'It would have to be in my working time.'

'I'll see that you're compensated,' John answered tersely, thinking what a grasping old bitch the creature really was and wishing he hadn't offered to treat her.

'Then I am your servant in all things, Sir,' replied Hannah and much to his consternation gave the Apothecary a somewhat alarming wink.

Chapter Six

It still being little after noon, John, recalling the Blind Beak's assertion that the proprietor of Vaux Hall claimed to know more about his clientele than they knew themselves, decided to make his way there forthwith. Going home merely to change his clothes into something more appropriate for a visit to the Pleasure Gardens and to seek his father's permission to borrow his coach and horses for the rest of the day, he set out in good spirits, feeling that certain interesting facts had already come to light and that by the end of the day, with the help of Jonathan Tyers, he might have learned some more.

In normal circumstances John would have appreciated clattering over the many arches of Westminster Bridge, then bowling along the leafy lanes of the South Bank, past that fine example of Tudor brickwork, Lambeth Palace. But today he was preoccupied, going over his conversation with Hannah, wishing he had had the sense to ask her where Comte Louis de Vignolles lived, then wondering whether the country boy who had come calling on Lizzie and the apprentice at the Cascade were one and the same person.

At this time of day, of course, the Pleasure Gardens were closed. Between nine and ten o'clock at night was the hour at which the *beau monde* made an appearance, while those less refined or who enjoyed the lighting of the Cascade tended to arrive somewhat earlier. Yet knowing what be did of Mr Tyers's character, a subject discussed quite frequently in London circles, John was fairly certain that he would find him on the premises somewhere.

Dropped at the Coach Entrance situated at the corner of Kennington Lane, the Apothecary proceeded the rest of the way on foot and, after making an enquiry at the admission gates, was shown to an office in the rooms to the left of the entrance where, sure enough, he found the Proprietor himself, seated behind a desk.

'Yes?' said Mr Tyers, not looking up from the ledger of accounts over which he was poring.

'Sir, I am here on behalf of Mr John Fielding,' John answered steadily and was rewarded not only by getting Mr Tyers's full attention but the sight of him rising to his feet as well.

It was an interesting face that John was regarding, handsome in a hawkish kind of way. The clearly defined features were dominated by a great beak of a nose above which a pair of fine, rather melancholy, eyes stared out as if they were seeing all the troubles of mankind. It seemed extraordinary to John that the creator of such a glorious fantasy as Vaux Hall should be revealed as profound rather than frenetic. Yet perhaps the very nature of such a dream world revealed a need to escape.

'How may I help you?' said Jonathan Tyers in a dark voice which, too, was tinged with a certain sadness.

'Very simply by telling me all you know about the night of the murder, Sir. Mr Fielding informs me that your knowledge of your patrons is formidable. It is my hope, therefore, that you will share some of it with me.'

Mr Tyers nodded silently, the curls of his elegant wig brushing against the hollow of his cheeks. 'I will do all that I can, naturally. Such a dreadful affair will not help the reputation of my Gardens, to say the least of it. It is in my own interest that the matter be cleared up without delay.' He sat down again, indicating the chair opposite his desk to John. 'Now, where would you like me to start?'

John took a seat, grateful beyond measure that he had changed his clothes, for the Proprietor was a man of understated elegance and enormous style. 'Well, Sir, perhaps you could begin by discussing the evening itself. Was there anything unusual about it as far as you were concerned?'

Jonathan Tyers smiled wryly. 'Yes, in that I took a night off. Normally, as you may already be aware, I sit at the counter and see the patrons in, take their money if one wishes to be blunt about it. But on that particular occasion I had gone to have supper with friends, though thankfully not far distant from the Gardens.'

'Then how did you hear about the murder?'

'I have an assistant who deputises for me when I am away or indisposed. He sent a beadle running to fetch me. I returned at once and despatched a rider to the Public Office, from whence Mr Fielding sent forth a set of Brave Fellows.' Mr Tyers smiled once more, though no humour reached the rest of his face. 'Is it not a profound indictment of our times that such men as these are always kept ready to venture to any part of the kingdom at a quarter of an hour's warning?'

John shook his head. 'I cannot entirely agree with you, Sir. I find it heartening that the Blind Beak has formed such a squad, able to fly anywhere at such short notice.'

The deep eyes fixed themselves on the Apothecary. 'And what is your connection with the Public Office, if I may ask? Are you one of the Magistrate's Runners?'

There was no question of lying to such a powerful individual. 'No, sir. Truth to tell my only association with the case is that I was the one to find the body.'

Interest quickened the hawkish features and Mr Tyers looked positively animated. 'Really? How did this come about?'

'I was one of your patrons that night. I came here with my friend Samuel Swann, celebrating the fact that our indentures had finally reached an end. I am a newly fledged apothecary and, thus, when I heard a scream emanating from The Dark Walk ran to see if I could be of assistance. But all I found was a dead girl, beyond my help or that of any mortal man.'

'Then, why...?'

'Because I glimpsed the murderer, Sir. Vaguely saw a fleeing figure.'

'And so Mr Fielding thought you could be of assistance to him?'

'That is the fact of it, yes.'

Jonathan Tyers turned to stare out of the window behind him, a window that overlooked the wonderland he had created. 'How strange to think that a murderer stalked these glorious groves,' he said softly, almost as if he were speaking to himself. 'The worm that hides in the heart of a perfect rose, no less.' He turned back to look at John. 'It has already affected my trade, you know. The Gardens had far few visitors both last night and the night before.'

'But why, for God's sake?'

'Perhaps they feel he still lurks here, mad enough to vent his spleen on any hapless woman.'

John considered the idea. 'They might be right at that. Perhaps he bears a grudge against the sex.'

'Or maybe just against whores and kept women,' Mr Tyers added quietly.

It was a thought that had not occurred to the Apothecary but it seemed to make a terrible kind of sense. 'But if there is a lunatic at large he could strike again at any moment!' he exclaimed.

'Even, perhaps, at you,' said the Proprietor, almost in a whisper.

'What do you mean?'

'That he may have had a better sighting of you than you did of him. If that is the case he might not be sure how much you actually saw.'

John shivered. 'And thus wish to silence me for ever?'

'Just so.' Mr Tyers made a sudden sympathetic face. 'You have grown pale, Sir. May I offer you a glass of claret to restore your colour?'

'You most certainly may, Sir,' John answered with feeling.

'Brace up,' the Proprietor continued, smiling and pouring two generous glasses, 'the killer may equally well have seen nothing. It seems most likely to me that he knew the girl and hated her. She had led quite an interesting life, I believe.'

'So I have been informed. Pray tell me what you know of the Comte Louis de Vignolles.'

The Proprietor sipped his claret, his long thin fingers winding round the stem of his glass.

'The dead girl's former protector?'

John nodded.

'Well, he's tall, dark and handsome in a typically Gallic manner. I believe his parents were aristocratic Huguenot immigrants, arriving in this country with plenty of good breeding but scarcely a sou between them. He solved the family's problems for them by marrying money.'

'Really?'

'Yes, the daughter of some wealthy Sussex landowner. I presume the Comtesse's father craved a title for her, albeit a foreign one. Anyway, they were wedded and bedded, and since then friend Louis hasn't looked back.'

John looked thoughtful. 'And the Comtesse? Was she aware of her husband's infidelity?'

'That is a question I cannot answer. You see, nobody knows a great deal about her. She's a veritable drab of melancholy and took to her bed some years ago, a martyr to ill health. I've heard it said that the lady likes nothing better than to spend all day lying upon a chaise suffering with the headache.'

'Are you suggesting that she seeks attention in this manner?'

'That is the consensus, yes.'

'I see. Then it is hardly surprising her husband took a mistress.'

'There was no-one in the *beau monde* who blamed him.'

'So I imagine he was extremely upset when that self-same mistress abandoned him for another?'

Mr Tyers nodded. 'Very much so.'

'Upset enough to kill, do you think?'

'Quite possibly.'

'And what of the Duke of Midhurst, the young man she was with that evening?'

The Proprietor frowned. 'It struck me as odd when I heard that he had stolen the Comte's woman. You see...' he hesitated.

'Yes?'

'I had always thought the Duke to be of the other persuasion.'

'A Miss Molly?' asked John, surprised.

'If not outrightly so, then with leanings in that direction.'

'How astonishing.'

'Indeed.'

'Mr Tyers, I saw both the Duke of Richmond and Mr Fox at Vaux Hall that night. Do you think they could have known Elizabeth Harper?'

A world-weary look appeared on the Proprietor's face. 'My dear young friend, the brothel in Leicester Fields is a favourite haunt of gentlemen of quality. I would warrant that half the men of the *beau monde* were acquainted with her, with varying degrees of intimacy, of course.'

John sighed. 'That does not make my task any easier.'

'It certainly does not.'

'I must somehow narrow the field to those who had a motive for doing away with the girl.'

'I wish you luck, Sir.' Mr Tyers refilled his visitor's glass. 'Now, is there anything further I can tell you?'

'Yes, though I doubt it would have any bearing on the case. Is it possible that by any chance you know the identity of the Masked Lady?'

The melancholy eyes suddenly brimmed with laughter. 'No, that is a question no-one can answer. All I can tell you is that she is the most notorious gambler in London. Every night she is to be found at cards or dice, involved in *deep* play, too. Yet for all that, who she is remains a mystery.'

'How extraordinary.'

'The gambling fraternity find her intriguing, you know. She is even admitted at White's.'

'I can hardly believe it!'

'It's a fact I assure you. The rumour is that she is actually the Princess Augusta. There is a vague similarity.'

'Oh nonsense!' John exclaimed. 'The Lady looks amused and amusing, whereas the Princess is as miserable as a toothpick.'

The Proprietor laughed for the first time. 'How colourfully put! Well, if you solve the enigma please let me know.'

John stood up and held out his hand. 'Thank you for your time, Sir.'

Mr Tyers rose too. 'I hope I have been of some assistance.'

'You have certainly given me a great deal to think about. By the way, one last question, do you have an apprentice lad among your regular patrons?'

'Most certainly not. The Pleasure Gardens are somewhat beyond the means of such people.'

John nodded. 'I know that from bitter experience. It was just an outside chance.' He bowed. 'I wish you good day, Sir. It has been a pleasure to make your acquaintance.'

The Proprietor's naturally sombre cast of features returned. 'Good day to you too, Sir. I shall pray you pick your way through the maze. Indeed I'll not rest easy until you do.'

'You really think he might kill again, don't you?'

'I fear it's possible,' said Mr Tyers as he showed his visitor out.

Chapter Seven

It had started to rain while he had been engaged with Jonathan Tyers, not a heavy downpour but a gentle dewing which freshened the grass and brought out the smell of blossom. All the way back, driving through the pleasant pastures and riverside stretches of the South Bank, John breathed the sweet air and felt refreshed. It was only when the coach reached Lambeth marshes, a dank unpleasant area which in Tudor times had been famed for concealing the corpses of unwanted children, that the Apothecary stopped staring out of the window with unabashed delight. Nor did he look again until the coach crossed Westminster Bridge and entered the built-up areas of the metropolis, going down White Hall to the Strand, and then through the back streets to the area known as Covent Garden, famous for its brothels and gaming houses, and also, of course, for their unlikely neighbour, the Public Office at Bow Street.

At this hour of the late spring day the city glowed with a bright clarity that would soon be tinged with rose. Every building and dwelling place looked fine and fresh, belying the fact that as soon as twilight fell the entire area would become the centre of London's night life. The whore houses and taverns, the last-named with rooms for assignation, would open their doors; the bagnios would receive their first customers, answering the call of the ladies who sat in their windows inviting the passing trade with impudent gestures and poses. Tom's coffee house, presided over by Old Etonian Tom King and in fact the most notorious gaming hell of all, would welcome its clientele of bucks, bloods, demi-rips and choice spirits of London, while the Covent Garden Playhouse would usher in its rowdy audience. Now, though, all was calm, all was quiet, almost as if Mr John Fielding and his Brave Fellows, his band of trained Beak Runners, had everything tightly under control.

The Blind Beak himself had obviously dined early and was presently sitting in his office with his clerk who was reading aloud the list of all the information taken that day, including descriptions of suspicious persons, robbers, and things stolen. Just for a moment John stood in the open doorway regarding them, and then the sightless gaze turned in his direction and the voice of the clerk died away.

'Ah, Mr Rawlings, what news?' the Magistrate asked uncannily.

Unnerved by the blind man's extraordinary powers of perception, John fell over his words as he said, 'Good evening, Sir. I've come to report on what I have discovered so far.'

'Good, good. Step inside and take a seat.' The Blind Beak motioned to the clerk who had half risen to his feet. 'Stay where you are, Jago. I would like you to take notes if you would be so kind.'

'Certainly,' the man answered, but stood politely until the visitor had taken his place on the opposite side of the Magistrate's desk, when he sat down once more, picked up his pen, dipped it in his inkwell, and stared at John Rawlings in eager anticipation.

They made an extraordinary pair, the Apothecary caught himself thinking. The Magistrate, so powerfully built and strong-featured yet so grievously afflicted, the absolute antithesis of his foxy-faced assistant whose sandy hair and bright blue eyes gave an impression of exceptional cunning and alertness.

'Begin,' said the Blind Beak and leaned back in his chair. John shot a glance at Mr Jago, who scratched his curly unwigged head with the end of his quill. 'Fire away,' he mouthed.

Nodding, the Apothecary cleared his throat and began an account of everywhere that he had been and all that he had learned.

There was no noise in the room except for his voice and the scratching of the clerk's pen, and even while he spoke John wondered at the intensity of the Blind Beak's powers of concentration. Not a muscle twitched, nor was there a cough or splutter. Every ounce of John Fielding's attention was concentrated on what his newly recruited Runner had to say.

'So,' the Magistrate commented at last, 'it seems you have made considerable progress.'

'I thought quite the opposite, Sir,' John answered in some confusion. 'I am not at all certain how I should proceed from here.'

Mr Jago looked up and grinned widely, resembling one of the more sardonic types of gargoyle. He had a gap between his two front bottom teeth and through it he now emitted a whistle. This was obviously a sign that something amused him, for the Blind Beak rumbled a responsive laugh.

'Do any of us, ever? Eh, Joe?' he said, turning his bandaged eyes in the clerk's direction.

'Never, Sir,' Joseph Jago answered, and whistled low once more.

'Come now, Mr Rawlings,' Mr Fielding continued briskly, 'there's no call for despondency. You've done as well as any of my regular fellows.'

'But how do I...?'

'Simple,' the Magistrate cut across. 'The boy with the country accent won't have ended his search for Lizzie at the first failure. If he discovered that she worked in a brothel he will have gone there, for sure. As for the Comte de Vignolles, you say that his wife is ailing. Call without an appointment – they live at number twelve, Hanover Square, by the way – and offer to treat her with physic. Say the story of her suffering has touched you to the heart or some such flam. If she seeks attention, as is popularly believed, then she'll welcome you with open arms.'

'But how do I ever discover the true identity of the Masked Lady when the whole of London has failed?'

'Ah, now there's a rum doxy if ever there was one,' put in Joe Jago, raising a bushy brow.

'You've obviously heard of her.'

'I know *of* her, but then who doesn't?' the clerk answered.

'The Lady has of late become something of a legend,' John Fielding added. 'Take my advice, Mr Rawlings, and go to Marybone tomorrow night. You may well kill two birds with one stone, for I hear that not only can she often be discovered at play there but it is likely Henry Fox will also be present.'

John turned to the Blind Beak. 'Have you any idea who the Lady is, Sir?'

'None whatsoever. You see, she has done nothing illegal, Mr Rawlings. Her only crime is to fleece some of the greatest gamesters alive, and for that I can do nothing but respect her. She has entered a man's world and now appears to be in the process of conquering it.'

A slight movement from the clerk drew John's attention back to him. 'A morte of mystery, that one,' Joe Jago said, shaking his ginger curls from side to side, obviously lost in admiration and wonder at the very thought of so remarkable a woman.

'Talking of mystery,' said the Blind Beak, smiling in the direction of his assistant, of whom he was clearly fond, 'there's one new piece of information which needs to be looked into.'

'And what is that, Sir?'

'The fact that, according to the woman Hannah, Elizabeth Harper came from Midhurst. Combine this with the knowledge that her former keeper is Duke of that very place and some interesting questions pose themselves, do they not?'

'Where is the Duke at present, Mr Fielding?'

'He has returned to his country seat much shaken, or so I am told, by the death of his mistress.'

'Should I go there to question him?'

'After you have finished in London, yes. Yet first of all you must track down those who were known to be in Vaux Hall on that fatal night.'

John shook his head. 'But that's impossible. Obviously there were several hundred present.'

The Magistrate nodded. 'Indeed there were. So concentrate first on those who knew her. If the girl moved in high circles it is likely her murderer came from the *beau monde.*'

'But what,' said John, 'if this is the work of a madman? A lunatic with a grudge against whores – or even against women in general?'

Fielding shook his head. 'I have a feeling, call it my sixth sense, that Elizabeth's death is somehow connected with her past. But whether it is or whether it isn't, I want you to watch yourself Mr Rawlings. I believe Mr Tyers might well be right. The killer may possibly have seen you and think that you know more than you do.

Therefore, if you believe that someone is following you in the street or watching your home, you are to tell me at once. Is that understood?'

'Perfectly.'

'Then go to it, Mr Rawlings. Talk to everyone who could possibly have known the girl. Somewhere, somehow, our man will reveal himself. I feel sure of it.'

He rose to his feet to indicate that the meeting was at an end and Joe Jago, catching the Apothecary's eye, dipped his head to one side to confirm this. John, too, stood up, feeling not only confused but also decidedly nervous.

'One moment more, Sir,' he said pleadingly.

'Yes?' answered the Blind Beak, his cane tapping before him as he made for the door.

'To whom should I dissemble and to whom should I announce myself as your man?'

'The list, Jago,' the Magistrate answered shortly, and went out.

The clerk, grinning enormously, thrust a piece of paper in John's direction. 'There you are, Sir, bless your worried phiz. It's a bit of a plan for you to follow.'

'Were you writing that while I was speaking?'

'It's my job to make lists, Mr Rawlings. I was only doing my duty.'

'This is most comprehensive,' said John, casting his eyes over the neatly written instructions.

Joe Jago's foxy face creased into a million lines. 'I have my uses for one born a rum cove. Good day to you, Sir. And just you take care of yourself, d'ye hear?' And with that he followed his master out of the room.

Over the cold collation which had been left out for him in the dining room, John read Joe Jago's plan in detail. People he had yet to interview were written in one column, those whose identities were still to be discovered in another. There were only four entries in this last: The Apprentice Lad at Vaux Hall, the Country Boy, the Masked Lady (you will win many a wager should you manage to solve this mystery!) and Those Visitors to the Pleasure Gardens not known to Mr Tyers (this will best be done by dredging the memories of others present).

Underneath these two lists was a rough itinerary —Most Adaptable to Your Own Convenience and Wishes but written with the Geographical Intent of Saving you Travelling Time and Labour. The final entry was a suggestion as to those in front of whom John should appear formally, and others amongst whose number he might insinuate himself.

'Remarkable,' thought John, and made a note to discover the origins of Joseph Jago, Register Clerk to the principal Justice of the Peace for London, amongst his many other tasks.

His supper done, the Apothecary descended the curving staircase which ran through the heart of the house and went to his father's study where ink, pens and other writing materials always stood available. Here, he added some of his own notes to those of Joe: Urgently visit Samuel and ask him to Recount *All* He Saw. Take Hannah her Ointment and Discover what She has found.

But this last, John realised, might present certain difficulties. Having left his Master's premises and not having had time to find any of his own, he had nowhere to mix and compound, to distil and brew, even to store his herbs. Temporarily, he was that somewhat useless figure, a qualified apothecary without a place to practise his calling.

The next day sending down as big a deluge as John could remember on a May morning, he stayed in bed for an extra hour and rose to find that Sir Gabriel Kent had already left the house, not saying where he was going. Rather surprised by this, the Apothecary had just gone into the study to re-read Joe Jago's instructions when Samuel was let into the hall after knocking thunderously on the front door.

'John,' he gasped, 'I have run all the way here! I've remembered something, you see!'

As he had journeyed from West Cheap, the first statement was, to say the least, an enormous exaggeration, but pandering to Sam's apparent state of exhaustion, John immediately ordered him coffee and a restorative brandy.

'Now what's all this?' he said, as soon as they were seated on either side of the library fire, lit to fend off the chills of the dismal day.

Samuel gulped his drink. 'You will recall me telling you that I observed poor Lizzie arguing with a man in a black cloak.'

'Whom I now have every reason to believe, having heard Mr Tyers's description, was her former lover, the Comte de Vignolles.'

'Was it, by God! Then that makes things even stranger. You see, I've remembered there was another man giving her the eye at just that moment. He winked and nodded at her then disappeared into The Dark Walk, and mighty furtive he was acting too. Glancing all about as if he did not wish to be detected. And not to keep you in suspense, I'll tell you straightway who it was.' Samuel paused and swallowed noisily.

'Well?'

'That rampant young blade, the Duke of Richmond.'

'And he winked at Lizzie? You're positive?'

'I most certainly am.'

John's brows leapt. 'Then perhaps she went to meet him...'

'And he strangled her in passion.'

The Apothecary shook his head. 'We can't jump to such a conclusion even though Richmond must obviously be implicated in some way.'

'Well, I'm glad my journey was not in vain.' Samuel finished his glass and held it out for a refill. 'There's something else too. You know that mysterious woman who wore a mask?'

'Yes?'

'Odds life, if she wasn't standing near me too. In fact she was so close I could have touched her.'

'I don't suppose her disguise slipped by any chance?'

'Not a hope of that. But she wore a distinctive scent. It filled my nostrils.'

'What was it?'

'Now how would I know that?'

The Apothecary clicked impatiently. 'Because every perfume is unique.'

Samuel shifted his broad shoulders. 'It is in your line of business to identify smells – though I can't say I envy you some of 'em! So don't blame me if I've no knowledge of such things. It was lovely, though. By God, it was.'

John grinned. 'Now don't start hankering after its wearer. She is unobtainable in every way.'

Samuel sighed. 'I suppose you're right.' He finished his brandy and brightened again. 'So what's next?'

'First and foremost, I visit the Comte de Vignolles and his ailing wife. Then, if I've time, Lucy Pink. And tonight, my friend, if you're game, we go to Marybone to watch the gamblers. The Masked Lady will probably be there,' John added casually.

'Then I'll join you,' answered Samuel.

'I thought you might.'

'Do you think I could borrow those clothes of your father's again? I did not come prepared for a social occasion.'

'I've got the feeling that these days a visit to Nassau Street means being prepared for anything,' John answered ruefully.

'It would certainly seem that way,' agreed Samuel as the two of them made their way in to breakfast.

An hour later the friends left the house together, and proceeded on foot down the length of Piccadilly where they parted company, John turning right into Old Bond Street and thence to Evans Row. Here he called into the shop of his former Master, Richard Purefoy, and stood as he had for so many years looking outwards through the two bow-fronted windows with their shelves containing jars and bottles, all tall and elegant, the latter swollen with bulbous bases. It seemed strange to be buying a mixture which he himself had not compounded, but for the moment John had no choice in the matter. Wishing Master Purefoy good day, making some excuse about his father wanting the physick urgently, John hurried out again, glad not to have been drawn into conversation, anxious to get the next part of his mission over and done. Substituting a label that he had written at home for the bottle's original, John strode towards Hanover Square, wondering what kind of reception he would receive from the sickly Comtesse de Vignolles and her wayward husband when he called upon them unannounced.

Chapter Eight

The area between Piccadilly and Oxford Street was indeed one of the most fashionable in London, for here could be found two of the great squares, Hanover and Berkeley. The former was unashamedly a Whig enclave, its inhabitants supporters of the German Kings of England. And just as St James's Square boasted its own church, so, too, dwellers in Hanover Square worshipped at St George's. In fact the great Mr Handel maintained his own pew there, into which the blind old man, the most celebrated composer of his time, had to be guided every Sunday. Dwelling on this fact and thinking how depressing were the rigours of old age, John turned into Hanover Square from Great George Street and set about looking for number twelve.

He found it almost at once, so quickly in fact that he stood for a moment or two gathering his wits before daring to approach, for the exterior spoke of the sort of moneyed people who would not care to be bothered by a passing tradesman, albeit an apothecary bearing physic. Above the fine doorway, with its pilasters and carved pendants, was a resplendent hood bursting with moulded foliage and amorini. While the house itself, though constrained by being part of a terrace, rose to an elevation of four floors below a parapet and stood three windows wide. Feeling decidedly nervous, John climbed the flight of steps leading to the front door and raised the elegant knocker.

A footman answered the summons and, explaining that he had come to see the Comtesse de Vignolles bearing medicament and making it sound very much as if he had an appointment, John found himself being ushered into a narrow hallway dominated by a monumental double staircase. This entrance hall, though small, was lightly decorated in pale green and salmon pink, and such graceful colours, combined with the delicate mouldings, instantly revealed not only that it had been chosen by a woman of taste but also one of considerable charm.

'If you will wait in the library, Sir,' the footman intoned plummily, 'I will see if the Comtesse is able to receive you.'

And that said, John was shown down a slim passageway next to the great staircase to a small comfortable book-lined room beyond. Always of the opinion that books reveal a great deal about the characters of their owners, the Apothecary gazed at the titles. There was a good selection of volumes by Defoe and Swift, together with *The Works of Mr Alexander Pope*, published by Bernard Lintot of Between the Temple Gates, in 1717. There were also several examples of the chief literary innovation of the period, the novel; these included Richardson's *Pamela, Clarissa* and *Sir Charles Grandison,* together with Henry Fielding's *The History of the Adventures of Joseph Andrews and His Friend Parson Adams* and *The History of Tom Jones, A Foundling.* Also on the shelves stood *The History of the Life of the Late Mr Jonathan Wild the Great,* a mock biography of an actual criminal, but in truth Fielding's bitingly satirical portrait of Sir Robert Walpole. John found it hard to believe that the author of these works was not only the Blind Beak's half-brother, but the man who had actually founded the band of law enforcement officers who currently fought against crime in the metropolis.

A noise in the doorway had him wheeling round sharply to see that the footman had returned, grandly announcing, 'The Comtesse de Vignolles will see you now, Sir.' Congratulating himself on getting over the first and most difficult hurdle, the Apothecary followed the servant up the imposing staircase to a drawing room on the first floor. Situated at the back of the house, he was instantly stunned by its beauty, for it was graceful, intricately moulded, having a barrel ceiling and semi-domes decorated with a minute fragility that was breathtaking. And in the middle of all this splendour, lying on a Louis XV *duchesse en bateau,* placed before the windows so that its occupant could gaze wistfully out, was the Comtesse herself.

'Madam,' said John Rawlings, and gave an old fashioned bow, very low and very deep and utterly without artifice.

'Well?' answered the Comtesse.

'Madam,' he repeated, taking a step forward, 'forgive my temerity in calling unbidden. The truth of the matter is that I am a newly fledged apothecary who, until recently, was working with my Master on an Elixir of Health. Having heard of your unfortunate indisposition I took the liberty of bringing a bottle for you to try.'

'How?' asked the invalid disconcertingly.

'I beg your pardon?' John replied, nonplussed.

'I said how.'

'Well, by mouth, Madam. It is an elixir, a physic.'

The Comtesse sighed impatiently. 'No, I meant how did you hear of my illness? Am I a byword in the neighbourhood?'

'My Master's shop was in Evans Row, Madam, not far away. And as cases of suffering are always of interest to the medical profession, your health was discussed, yes,' John answered smoothly.

'Ah ha!' said the Comtesse, and made a little sound that could have been a cough or a muffled laugh. 'Step closer, young man.'

The Apothecary obeyed with alacrity, anxious to get a better look at this supposed malingerer, but with the light behind her it was not easy to see the woman's features distinctly. However, he did get the impression of good bone structure, a mouth that could have been beautiful had not the corners been drawn petulantly downwards, and a pair of eyes that gleamed intelligence before their owner drooped opalescent lids to conceal their expression.

The Comtesse fluttered a white hand. 'So where is this cure-all of yours?'

'Here, Madam,' and John produced the elixir from deep within his pocket.

'Pray pass it to me.'

The Apothecary did so and, stepping even closer, detected an overwhelming scent of roses with an underlay of something else. John felt a quiver of amusement as he recognised the smell of gin. Was this, then, the lady's problem? Was this why she preferred to remain at home couched supine? Was it to her secret vice that the Comtesse had sacrificed her good health?

He came abruptly back to the present as she spoke again. 'How much?'

'I would like you to accept it with my compliments. If it does you good I can arrange to deliver further supplies. The cost would then be sixpence.'

'Not cheap.'

'It is made from the finest ingredients,' John answered solemnly.

For a second a flicker crossed the Comtesse's mouth, though whether she was smiling or simply irritated, John was not absolutely certain. But it was at that moment, just as he was trying to make up his mind about her, that he heard a door open behind him and turned to see that a man had come into the room, a man whom he instantly recognised as the wearer of the black cloak in Vaux Hall Pleasure Gardens.

'Louis,' said the Comtesse, feebly leaning back against the cushions, 'our visitor is an apothecary who has called with some medicine for me.'

John bowed low, 'My name Is Rawlings, Monsieur le Comte. John Rawlings.'

'Have we met before?' asked the newcomer, narrowing an eye.

John hesitated, wondering whether to broach the subject of the Pleasure Gardens quite so soon in their acquaintanceship. Eventually he said, 'I have recently been freed from my indentures, Sir, and have been out and about a great deal since. Perhaps that is why my face seems familiar.'

The Comte looked bored. 'I doubt we would have been at the same assemblies,' he answered in supercilious tones, and walking past the Apothecary went, without any marked enthusiasm, to kiss his wife's hand.

He was an attractive creature with the dark hair and eyes typical of his race; in fact it was only too easy to visualise him as a lady's man of prodigious charm. Enormously irritated by him, John decided to fire the opening shot and wipe the smile from the Comte de Vignolles's handsome face. He made for the door, then turned as if he had forgotten something.

'How observant you are, Monsieur!' he exclaimed. 'I would never have remembered if you had not said. Of course I saw you the other night at Vaux Hall. I was there with a friend and together we studied the *beau monde* with interest. How sad it was that such an enjoyable evening should have ended in so terrible a tragedy.'

'Tragedy?' said the Comtesse, propping herself up on one elbow. 'What tragedy?'

'Ah, Madam, I hardly know how to speak of it,' John gushed on, aware that de Vignolles's brown velvet eyes were glaring in his direction. 'You see, there was a fatality. A lady of the night, a kept creature so it is said, was cruelly done to death by an unknown hand. Though, strangely, the friend who accompanied me saw her arguing with a man and has made a statement to that effect to the Public Office.'

'What man?' asked the Comte abruptly.

John gave him a radiant smile. 'Oh, it was no-one he knew, merely a fellow in a black cloak. A dark foreign-looking chap, so my friend said.'

'Sounds like you, Louis,' said the Comtesse drily.

'There are hundreds of foreigners in London,' de Vignolles answered, yawning, and John mentally awarded him a point for coolness.

'Well, I must take my leave,' he said, giving the invalid another bow. 'Let it be hoped that the Elixir will serve its purpose. I am resident at number two Nassau Street should you require any further supplies.'

'And should you decide to speak to me privately,' he thought, as he followed the footman down the stairs and left the home of the Comte Louis de Vignolles.

As Vigo Lane was on his route home, John decided that now was the moment to call on Hannah and present her with the jar of ointment which he had purchased in Evans Row. Somewhat guilty that he had made none of these preparations personally, he consoled himself with the thought that he was investigating a murder and all was fair in the circumstances. Yet, despite that, the Apothecary made a mental promise to explain his deceit to Master Purefoy in the near future and somehow try to make amends. But passing beside the wall and high trees which protected the beautiful gardens of Burlington House from the common herd, John put such thoughts from his mind as he entered the quiet surroundings of Vigo Lane.

Exactly as on the previous occasion, the door of number twenty-four stood invitingly open but this time the Apothecary unhesitatingly stepped inside, only to find that the house was not empty. A large fair lady, well rouged and painted, stood in the hallway passing the time of day with Hannah, who was half-heartedly swishing the floor with a tattered mop.

'Excuse me,' said John and turned to go, afraid that the caretaker might be on the point of saying something tactless about the murder.

'It's no trouble,' rejoined the buxom creature boldly. 'How may I help you?'

'Well, er, it is Hannah I came to see actually. I have some ointment for her rheumatism.'

The woman's eyes lit. 'Are you a physician, Sir?'

John smiled crookedly. 'No Ma'am, I am an apothecary.'

'And I am Mrs Cole, widow of the late Mr Cole, milliner. Allow me to present you with my credentials.'

And from nowhere she produced a trade card which she thrust into John's unwilling hand. Bewilderedly he read, 'Mrs Candace Cole, Artist in the Treatment of Feathers, Flowers, Muslins, Gauzes, Crapes and Velvets. At the Sun in St Paul's Church Yard. Wholesale or Retail at Reasonable Rates.'

'Pray step inside for a glass of Rhenish and sugar,' Mrs Cole continued. 'Wine is so refreshing in the heat of the day, is it not?'

'Nothing would give me greater pleasure,' answered John, frantically seeking an excuse, 'but, alas, I have an urgent visit to make. I merely called to see Hannah *en passant* as it were.'

Mrs Cole waved a waggish finger. 'Five minutes will make little difference, surely.'

The Apothecary, horridly aware of the gleam in her eye, decided on desperate action. 'Madam, I have only told you half the truth. I am an apothecary as I said. But I am also here to enquire into the death of your neighbour, Elizabeth Harper. I am one of Mr Fielding's Fellows.'

'Are you now?' she answered, surveying him with even greater interest. 'Then you must indeed come in, You see, Hannah found a letter when she searched the girl's apartment and, as she could not read, brought it to me. So now what do you say?'

'I say that a glass of Rhenish would be delightful,' John answered manfully, and allowed himself to be led into the downstairs suite of rooms, well aware that Hannah was giving him a knowing leer as the front door was closed firmly behind him.

'Now do sit down and make yourself comfortable Mr...?'

'Rawlings. John Rawlings.'

'...while I slip into something cooler. The afternoons are tedious hot, are they not?'

'Er...' answered John,

But she had already vanished and he was left alone except for the presence of a particularly repellent dog which bared its teeth at him and growled.

'Be quiet,' whispered John commandingly, at which it growled all the more, getting up from its cushion and approaching his leg in a speculative manner.

'One move nearer and I'll cane you, so I will,' he hissed again, but was saved by the return of Mrs Cole who swept the creature up in her arms and deposited it on her lap. She was now wearing a flowing robe made of some diaphanous material which revealed that she did not have a great deal on underneath. Averting his eyes from a pair of breasts the size of pumpkins, John cleared his throat.

'Now, Ma'am, you have something to tell me I believe.'

She brushed a straying curl with a plump hand. 'I could certainly tell you many things, Mr Rawlings, and indeed would like to.' She smiled winsomely. 'But I take it you refer to Hannah's finding?'

'Yes, I do.'

Mrs Cole stood up again and the dog crashed to the floor, yelping. 'But I forget my manners. I asked you in to take wine with me and take wine you shall.'

And with that she swept to a side table, her garment trailing, and poured out two glasses of Rhenish.

'No sugar for me,' said John. 'It rots the teeth.'

Mrs Cole, who had been about to give herself a generous helping, stopped with the spoon in mid-air. 'Just so,' she replied.

'And now I really must get down to business,' the Apothecary said determinedly. 'Tell me about the letter Hannah found.'

His hostess rearranged herself in her chair, breasts wobbling as she took a sip of wine. Staring at the floor, John felt himself break into a sweat.

'Well, it was a communication of sorts, though the most ill-spelt, ill-educated thing it has ever been my misfortune to observe.'

'May I see it?'

Mrs Cole made a little moue. 'There now, I've just settled comfortably – and little Quin-Quin too.' She patted the dog which growled again. 'Be a sweet fellow and fetch it for me. It's over there in my writing box.'

Longing desperately for a quick escape, John opened the lid and saw lying on top a grubby piece of paper. 'Is this it?'

'Most certainly. I trust you do not think that any of *my* correspondence would look like that.'

John unfolded the scrap and gazed on a scrawling, unformed hand which had obviously cost its author dear to write as much as it had.

'My swet Lizie,' he read. 'Yew have Broke Mi Hart. I canot Live Wit Yew Gon. If Yew do not Reetun I shalle Kil Miselfe. Cum home for the Love of God. Jem.'

'How tragic!' exclaimed John involuntarily.

'Tragic indeed,' responded Mrs Cole, misunderstanding. 'The ignorance of the labouring classes is quite reprehensible. I employ them in my workrooms, you know, and, believe me, can vouch for their stupidity.'

'It is hardly their fault if they have not received the benefits of a good education,' John answered reasonably. 'What is more reprehensible is the lack of schools for the poor, I believe.' He cleared his throat, determined not to get involved in deep discussion. 'Anyway, meagre though it is, this letter is enlightening enough.'

'In what way?'

'It reveals that Elizabeth Harper had a sweetheart when she left to come to London, someone who felt so deeply about her that he threatened suicide.'

Mrs Cole drained her wine glass and gave a contemptuous laugh. 'Then more fool him. The girl was a thoroughly bad lot. I've never seen such a little schemer in all my born days. Small wonder that she came to a violent end.'

'You knew her well?'

The widow looked indignant. 'Certainly not! Respectable folk do not associate with a creature of that sort.'

'Then there is nothing of interest you can tell me about her?'

A look of cunning crossed Mrs Cole's countenance. 'Well, I'm sure if I put my mind to it I could recall something. Why don't you stay awhile and see what I can remember? I feel certain I could be of service to you.'

And with this last remark she thrust the pumpkins forward until they were only an inch or so from John's nose.

Gulping audibly, he got to his feet. 'No, really, I must be on my way. Duty calls and all that.'

'Men who work and never play are dull fellows,' she replied sulkily.

'Alas, that is very true,' he answered, edging away.

Brightening, Mrs Cole stood up once more, yet again ignoring the dog which cascaded downwards, howling as it went. 'You could come back tomorrow, surely Mr Rawlings? There is much for us to talk about, I feel certain of it.'

'I'll do my best,' he said, hastening to the entrance. 'Thank you for the wine.'

'Are you going to keep the letter?'

'Oh yes, that is evidence which Mr Fielding will most certainly want to have.' He paused as an idea came to him. 'If you think of anything further perhaps you could contact him at the Public Office. Good day to you.' And with that the Apothecary was out of the door before she could utter another word, only stopping to thrust the jar of ointment into Hannah's hand, where she stood eavesdropping in the passageway, as he hurried out into the street.

No sooner had John set foot inside his own premises than he knew something unusual had taken place. The very air breathed it and he was not in the least surprised when, even while relieving him of his hat, the footman murmured, 'There is a gentleman to see you, Master John. He arrived just now and I have shown him into the library.'

'Is he French by any chance?' John asked, gleaming with triumph.

'Yes, Sir. He gave his name as the Comte de Vignolles.'

'Well, well,' said the Apothecary. 'Even sooner than I expected. Tell him that I will join him shortly.'

Five minutes later he strode into Sir Gabriel's fine book room in an exact reverse of the situation which had been acted out earlier that day, to find the Comte staring moodily out of the window.

'I believe you have tried to trick me,' said de Vignolles abruptly, without turning round. 'Who the devil are you, pray, to live in a town house yet act like some common blackmailer off the streets?'

'I am exactly what I say,' John replied calmly. 'I am an apothecary who served his apprenticeship in Evans Row. This house belongs to my father, Sir Gabriel Kent, under whose roof I am again dwelling now that my indentures are over. What I did not tell you, Monsieur, is that not only did I see you at Vaux Hall the other night, but that I am also assisting Mr John Fielding in his hunt for the killer of Elizabeth Harper.'

'So you bluffed your way into my home and would, no doubt, have told my wife everything had I not interrupted you.' And the Comte wheeled round and stared at John furiously.

'And that is where you are completely wrong. I went to visit her only because I wanted to understand you better. I am not a married man, Monsieur, so I needed to know why you took the dead girl as mistress.'

'And now you do, I imagine. Having met the sickly creature that my lively wife turned into, perhaps all is clear.'

John sighed. 'Monsieur, Mr Fielding has asked me to question all those who were in the Pleasure Gardens on the night of the murder. Indeed, he has instructed me to treat every one of them with suspicion. Therefore I have to point out that you could have had a motive for killing Elizabeth. Is it not the case that, although you set her up in comfortable apartments in Vigo Lane, she deserted you and went to live with another man? Could not the quarrel you had with her – to which we have a witness – have led to something far more violent?'

'By God,' the Comte cursed furiously. 'It could have done, but it most certainly did not. Of course I was angry, hurt too. But by all that is holy, I swear I walked away and left her for the cheap slut she was.'

John nodded silently. 'And this quarrel, this quarrel from which you strode away, exactly where did it take place?'

'In the Grand Cross Walk.'

'And where did you go after it was over?'

'To the Grand Walk.'

'So according to you Elizabeth made her way across to The Dark Walk alone and there met her death?'

'Yes.'

'Monsieur le Comte,' said John gently. 'I pray you sit down and briefly tell me the whole story. Everything you can remember about Lizzie, with particular reference to anything that could shed light on this matter.'

De Vignolles shot him a penetrating glance. 'For a young man you have a very soothing manner. I suppose it comes from working amongst the sick.'

'Possibly. Now please continue.'

'There is not a great deal to tell. My wife changed completely not long after we were married...'

'Because you started a love affair with another?' John guessed shrewdly.

The Comte looked uncomfortable. 'Yes, that is true.' He spread his arms wide, palms uppermost. 'I am a Frenchman.'

The Apothecary gave a small chuckle. 'Go on.'

'Well, I began to frequent the brothel in Leicester Fields and there I met Elizabeth Harper, as bright and saucy a being as any man could ever wish for.' He gave John a tragic look. 'I confess I fell in love with her, old fool that I am.'

'But surely you are only in your thirties.'

'And she not eighteen. I could have been her father, and yet I was totally infatuated. Then along came Midhurst, who had youth as well as money, and she upped and abandoned me without a word.'

'Simply moved out?'

'Yes. I expect you know about Vigo Lane and the fact that she left all her things behind her.'

John nodded. 'So you went to the Pleasure Gardens on the off chance, and at last had the opportunity to air your grievances?'

'Yes, but that is all I did do. I adored the cruel bitch. Even though she had betrayed me, I would never have harmed her.'

And with that the Comte, quite suddenly and without warning thrust his head into his hands, his shoulders heaving. If it was an act it was a fine one indeed, and John could do nothing but stare uncertainly before ringing for a servant to fetch brandy. Then he, too, took his place at the window until de Vignolles had once more controlled himself.

'Love's a damnable thing,' gasped the Frenchman.

'Perhaps your wife also thinks so,' John answered quietly.

'Alas, she does not. She long ago ceased to care about me and now is totally preoccupied with her health. It really isn't easy living with her, you know.'

'I'm sure of that.' John turned round as a footman came in bearing a tray which he set down on a side table. 'Thank you, Perkins. I'll pour for our visitor.' He handed the Comte a generous measure. 'There is just one more question I would like to ask you, if I may.'

'And what is that?'

'At Vaux Hall that night, you were present at the lighting of the Cascade?'

'Yes, I was.'

'Did you by chance notice a boy, quite a small young fellow whom I would have taken for an apprentice had he not been so elegantly dressed?'

Louis frowned. 'No, I can't say that I did.'

'He was crouching quite near you, having crept through the crowd to get a better view.'

'Oh yes, I vaguely remember someone now you come to mention it.'

'You don't know who he was by any chance?'

The Comte shook his head. 'I have absolutely no idea.'

John smiled wryly. 'I was rather afraid you might say that.'

De Vignolles looked interested. 'Why? Is he connected with this affair in some way?'

'That,' said the Apothecary, 'is what I am most anxious to find out.'

Chapter Nine

Just as darkness fell over London, Samuel Swann returned to Nassau Street with a smile on his face, so broad a smile, in fact, that it took no great act of clairvoyance on John's part for him to guess where his friend had gone after they had parted company earlier that day.

'You've been to Leicester Fields, haven't you, you sly old fox?'

Samuel attempted to look serious. 'But on your behalf, my friend.'

'*My* behalf? Odds my life, now I've heard every excuse known to man!'

'I went to observe,' Samuel replied, with an attempt at dignity. 'And to ask questions.'

'Did you now? Well, you can tell me all about it in the hackney to Marybone. Now hurry and get changed.'

'Did Sir Gabriel give permission for me to borrow his clothes?'

'I have not seen my father all day,' John answered with just the slightest note of asperity. 'He left the house early, then returned while I was gone, changed into evening dress and went out again.'

'I wonder what he's up to.'

The Apothecary's crooked smile appeared. 'Something or other, I'll warrant. This is odd behaviour for my parent. Anyway, there's no time to think about it. We must get to Marybone. So, in his absence, I give you permission to wear what you like. Within reason,' he added.

An hour later, finely arrayed, the friends stepped forth and hailed hackney coach number 44 in which they set out for the village of Marybone, lying some distance from London's heart, the name deriving from the old church of St Mary le Burn, much favoured for illicit and runaway marriages, which had once stood on the banks of the River Tyburn. Fourteen years earlier, in 1740, a new church had been built further up the village High Street, but the old title had gone with it and the entire district had thus been given the name of Marybone.

It was a flawless night, the moon coming up over rolling fields, casting long and extraordinary shadows over the winding contours of Marybone Lane. High above the small dark dot of the carriage, the star-filled sky hung like the spangled canopy of an exotic tent from Araby, and the lights of the Pleasure Gardens, resembling a cluster of terrestrial stars, enhanced the glow and added to the splendour of the evening's enchanting vistas. For having left the town behind, the carriage was passing through pastoral land, cattle grazing in the moonlight and pretty rivers flowing like quicksilver amongst the verdant grasses.

The village of Marybone itself was much favoured by London families of good position, who had country houses in its High Street. It was these gentry folk who had become the principal patrons of the Gardens, availing themselves of subscription tickets for its balls and concerts. For Marybone Gardens, even more than those of Vaux Hall, had a strong musical tradition, together with a reputation for providing supreme cakes of rich seed and plum, made by the manager's daughter, Miss Trusler. All this, added to Miss Trusler's almond cheesecake, meant that visitors from town would also make the journey to this rural retreat. Yet there was another, far less innocent, reason why the *beau monde* set forth for the village, risking attack from highwaymen and footpads.

In the seventeenth century a little group of Huguenot immigrants from France had settled in Marybone and, in recognition of their presence, a tavern called The Rose of Normandy had been built in the High Street. At the back of this rural inn there had been bowling greens and gardens, and these had become the origin of the Pleasure Gardens, entrance to which eight-acre site was currently reached through the tavern. But The Rose of Normandy itself had undergone a change and had now become notorious as a gaming house where deep play was commonplace. And it was to these gaming rooms, rather than to the less innocent pastimes, that John and Samuel now made their way, determined to play yet not to wager beyond their limited means.

There were several raffling shops, as the gaming rooms were known, and passing through them watching how the cards flew and the dice rattled and fine gentlemen lost their money with ease and negligence, John drew in his breath at the size of the stakes. Rouleaus of guineas, some many inches high, were stacked before the players, who chanced all on raffle, a game of dice in which the stakes went to the gamester who threw a pair-royal. And it was here, resplendent in black, her mask a shimmer of stiffened gold tissue, that the Lady he sought was seated.

Naturally, the most enigmatic woman in London had a crowd round her, watching as her elegant hands seized the dice box and nonchalantly rattled it before she threw two queens upon the green cloth before her. Joining the throng, John and Samuel, drinking the punch they had obtained on the way in, moved to a more advantageous position, observing the faces of the other players, some striving hard to maintain the cool facade that was *de rigeur* when losing a fortune.

Henry Fox, the politician, of course merely smiled affably. But there were others, some who leant back so that the shadows would mask their expressions, betraying by the tightening of their fingers or the way they shifted in their chairs the strain that they were under. John let his eyes rove round the table, studying the assembled company, enjoying the sight as much as he had done the lighting of the Cascade. Then a tall figure seated at the end of the table drew his attention. Resplendent in ebony breeches and silver waistcoat, together with a black coat lavishly embroidered, and wearing a heavily powdered nine-storey wig, its long curls flowing over his shoulders, sat Sir Gabriel Kent.

'Father!' exclaimed John, and received a very cool look for his pains. For the dice box had come round to his parent's place and everyone in the room had grown still.

Sir Gabriel inclined his head to the Masked Lady, who bowed back graciously, her lovely mouth curved in its amused and amusing smile.

'Good luck, Sir,' called someone who was not playing. Elegantly, John's father shook back the lace from his wrists and picked up the dice box, giving it a careless shake before he rolled the contents out towards the centre of the table. Two kings gleamed in the candlelight and there was a momentary gasp before the other players began to push their rouleaus in Sir Gabriel's direction.

'God's life!' whispered Samuel, very impressed.

John remained silent, breathing in the Masked Lady's perfume and identifying it as spirit of ambergris, musk, bergamot and Oil of Rhodium, probably from the shop of Charles Lillie, the perfumer.

'Well done, Sir,' she called to Sir Gabriel, who smiled and, leaning across, offered her his box of snuff. It was his finest, made of silver with a Moco stone in the lid.

'Why, thank you,' she said and took a good pinch, placing it on the back of her hand and inhaling just as deeply as any man.

'You played well, Madam,' he answered.

'Nonsense, that was but a game of chance, a lucky throw and there's an end to it. No, I prefer cards where one's skill and wit is pitted to the full against that of an opponent.'

'Then perhaps you will move with me to the room in which whist is being dealt?'

The Masked Lady shook her head. 'I thank you, Sir, but I fear I have another appointment. I am engaged to play at White's before the night is out.'

'Then allow me to accompany you,' said Sir Gabriel, rising to his feet. 'No Lady should travel alone along these perilous ways once dark has fallen.'

John was filled with admiration, aware that his father had, at his son's behest, joined the quest to discover the Lady's true identity. And, or so he guessed, she too had some inkling of it, for she let out her rather husky laugh and answered, 'Fiddlesticks! A woman such as I long ago learned how to protect herself. Not only do I travel armed but so does my black boy. A sweet child, to be sure, but a deadly shot.'

Sir Gabriel gave an elaborate bow. 'Then I hope, Madam, that I will soon be granted the pleasure of conceding you a victory.'

'You are very gallant, Sir,' said the Masked Lady, rising to her feet.

At once, every other gamester at the table sprang up, for whether they admired or detested her, she was a creature of such fascination that all felt bound to pay her respect. With a smile she acknowledged the salutations of her fellow gamblers then turned to go, making her way through the crowd which had gathered round her chair. Yet as she drew level with John she paused momentarily before sweeping past, leaving nothing but the trace of her perfume hanging in the air for him to remember her by. Very conscious that she had been studying him from behind her mask, he felt the colour come into his cheeks.

So she had seen him at the Pleasure Gardens and recalled him, though why she should have done so John simply could not think. Yet for all that, he felt immensely flattered, almost to the point of elation, that the most mysterious and sought-after woman in town had picked him out of a milling throng and studied him carefully enough to know him again.

'Zounds!' exclaimed Samuel softly, 'did you see the look she gave you?'

'No,' said John, desperately trying to be casual.

'I think she fancies you.'

'Oh don't be silly. A woman like that could have any man she chose.'

'Well, she certainly held you in regard.'

'I think perhaps she recognised me from Vaux Hall.'

'Which compounds my theory. She saw you at the Pleasure Gardens and fell madly in love at first sight.'

'Oh really!' snorted John, but secretly he was delighted that his friend should think him capable of capturing the attention of anyone as attractive, as fascinating and dark a riddle, as the Masked Lady.

'Damme, but she's quite a gal,' commented a rumbling voice beside them, and the Apothecary saw that Henry Fox had left his place and was watching the Lady leave, her little black page, clad all in silver, a turban with three crimson feathers on his head, running behind her.

'Very much so,' answered Sir Gabriel, coming to join the party. He bowed to the politician. 'Sir, I am just about to play a hand at whist in company with my son and his companion. Would you care to make up a four?'

'Gladly,' said Fox, returning the salutation. 'I was just going in to find a partner.'

'Then let us proceed.' And all smiles and nods, they made their way into the room next door.

But though the play was sharp and demanded concentration, John Rawlings laid his cards as if he were in a dream. Again and again in his mind's eye he relived the moment when the Masked Lady paused in her sweeping exit and looked at him. Then somewhere at the back of his mind he heard Henry Fox say, 'Terrible business at Vaux Hall the other night,' and John's attention careered back to the present moment like a racehorse at full gallop.

'I wasn't there,' Sir Gabriel was answering, 'although my son was present. He told me all about it, of course. Did you know the girl, Sir?'

Henry Fox guffawed. 'If I did I wouldn't admit it. She was a whore, no less. But, seriously, I knew nothing of her, though I believe my brother-in-law Richmond – young scampish dog that he is – had sampled her charms. He's a regular tail twitcher as far as women are concerned. He could hardly wait to get in The Dark Walk the other night. Which is where the poor girl was done to death, is it not?' Something of the unfortunate nature of what he had just said must have occurred to him, for he added, 'Young Charles was with Miss Patty Rigby, of course.'

At this, Samuel gave a violent cough and John, focusing on their earlier conversation, recalled his friend's certainty that the Duke of Richmond had not only been alone and acting in a furtive manner, but that he had actually winked at Lizzie as he made his way into The Dark Walk. 'I believe the Public Office at Bow Street are investigating the crime,' John said noncommittally. 'They have already questioned me but I was able to convince them of my innocence.'

'Really?' said Mr Fox, his eyebrows raised almost to the level of his wig. 'Then it's as well young Richmond had a companion. Good heavens, I suppose it won't be long before they seek him out and me too for that matter.'

John could almost have embraced his father who said, laughingly, as he laid a card, 'You'd best try to recall your movements, Sir. Then you'll be ready for that Blind Beak fellow.'

Henry Fox frowned. 'Damme, you're right, you know. Now let me see. Lady Albermarle was with us that evening. We had supper first then Richmond and I went to see the lighting of the Cascade. After that we went back to the box for a while and had a bumper or two of champagne. Then Miss Rigby saw some friends and went to join them for a visit, Richmond went to find her, and Lady Albermarle and I remained together for the rest of the time.'

'Well, I can certainly vouch for you as far as the Cascade is concerned. I saw you there,' John answered quietly.

Fox turned to him. 'Really? Where were you?'

'Standing on the edge of the crowd, looking about me. There was a most varied selection of people present, or so I thought.'

'Indeed there was.'

'Did you by any chance notice a young jackanapes, a 'prentice lad dressed within an inch of his life in a rich blue coat fit for a lord?'

Fox frowned deeper. 'No, I can't say that I did. Why?'

John sighed. 'He interests me, that's all.'

'And me,' Sir Gabriel added urbanely. 'My son asked what such a little rascal might be, no more than a mere boy yet dressed so lavishly.'

'And what did you reply, Sir?'

'That in the City guilds and in the best shops in London, the apprentices are the sons of gentlemen, wearing full-bottomed wigs and good clothes when off duty, just as he did himself.'

Fox turned to John. 'Well, there you have it, my young friend.'

'Yes,' answered the Apothecary, smiling at his father, 'there I have it.' He changed the subject. 'Tell me, Mr Fox, do you get any inkling as to who the

Masked Lady might be?'

'There's a strong rumour that she is the Princess Augusta – you've probably heard it yourself – but her she ain't for sure. No, I reckon she's a titled widow, inheritee of some damnable great estate without the funds to run it, so that is why she started to gamble.'

John looked thoughtful. 'I think you've hit on something there, Sir. For, other than for the thrill of it, why would she indulge in such deep play?'

'Perhaps she wishes to be independent,' Sir Gabriel remarked. 'Perhaps she wishes to have money that is hers and hers alone.'

'I don't care what the reason is,' said Samuel warmly, 'I think she is wonderful. How I would love to know her.'

'And I too,' added John with equal enthusiasm.

'Ah ha,' said Henry Fox playfully. 'I'll wager she's stolen the hearts of these two young gentlemen.'

Sir Gabriel raised a brow, still dark and elegant despite his advanced years. 'Were she not so young she would steal mine as well. For how I like a woman of wit and vivacity.'

'And those qualities,' said the politician, nodding, 'she certainly has a'plenty.'

They travelled back in a small convoy, Mr Fox's coach immediately in front of that of Sir Gabriel, thus lessening the risk of being attacked by the highwaymen and footpads who haunted the road leading to Marybone. It was a known fact that in the in the 1730s Dick Turpin used to rob the Pleasure Gardens' patrons and that once, having publicly kissed a beauty of the time in the Gardens themselves, whispered to the lady, 'Be not alarmed, Madam, for you can now boast that you have been kissed by Dick Turpin. Good morning!' But, whether that last story be true or false, Sir Gabriel and Mr Fox were tonight taking no chances and did not part company until they had reached the safety of the town.

'Well, that was a good evening's work I think,' said John's father as the politician's carriage headed away towards his London residence, Mr Fox's principal home being at Holland House in Kensington village. 'Would you agree, John, that he is not the man you are looking for?'

'I never seriously thought he could be but, yes, if Mr Fox gives the name of Lady Albermarle as she who will vouch for him, then he is clearly innocent.' He gave Sir Gabriel an admiring glance. 'You drew him out very cleverly, Sir.'

His father looked modestly pleased. 'It seemed an opportune moment to do so.'

'Most certainly. I'm sorry I startled you earlier. It was such a very great shock to see you at Marybone and engaged in play with the Masked Lady at that.' John sighed. 'I am following Mr Fielding's instructions to the letter but seem no nearer to the solution of this crime.'

'The victim has already been replaced at the brothel,' Samuel interrupted, also sighing sadly. 'You remember Dorcas, the maid, the one who answered the door to us, John? Well, she has been promoted whore and another country innocent found as servant. No doubt she, too, will be corrupted in her turn. It's a sad world, I think.'

'Very,' said Sir Gabriel. He patted his son on the arm. 'It may seem that you are making little progress, but all the while you are gathering facts and assimilating information. And then the day will come when, just like a puzzle, all the little pieces will fit together and the final picture will emerge.'

'Do you really think so?'

'I do.'

The coach had turned into Nassau Street and, having deposited its passengers, went on to the stables in Dolphin Yard. Yawning, John would have gone to bed at once, following Samuel who, like a guest of long acquaintance, had already made his way upstairs, had not Sir Gabriel beckoned him on one side.

'John, come sit with me in the library a moment. I want to tell you of my day's adventures.'

Forcing his eyes open, his adopted son, feeling though not showing his reluctance, followed the older man into the room where, earlier that day, the Comte de Vignolles had revealed the depths of his unhappiness.

'I wondered what you were about, Sir,' he said as he took his seat beside the fire onto which the footman on duty had hastily put more wood.

'Did you? Well, truth to tell I was out looking for something, something rather particular. And, do you know, I found it.'

The Apothecary could feel himself beginning to doze off. 'I'm so glad,' he answered sleepily.

'I think you will be,' Sir Gabriel said, a smile in his voice, and John felt a metal object placed in his hand. He opened his eyes, awake again, and saw a doorkey, quite large and serious looking. 'What's this?'

'Look on the label.'

John stared at the paper attached to the key, which read, 'Number Three, Shug Lane.'

'But I don't understand.'

Sir Gabriel stood up, his storied wig making him look even taller than he actually was. 'Nor will you at this hour of the night. So off to bed with you.'

'But...'

'No more buts. Simply go to that address tomorrow morning and then report back to me.'

'What will I find there?'

'Something I think you will like. Now, John, you're dropping and will be no good to man nor Beak at this rate.'

'A clever pun, Sir,' said the Apothecary as he helped his father snuff out the candles.

'Ah, there's still a trick or two in the old fellow,' answered Sir Gabriel as he left the darkened room and made his way, yawning just a little, towards the stairs.

Chapter Ten

The delightfully named Shug Lane ran between Piccadilly and Marybone Street, the first turning on the right after the junction of Piccadilly and The Hay Market. Going down Nassau Street and by the gardens of Leicester House, feeling the mysterious key in his pocket, John thought that he could already guess the kind of lock it would fit. He was as certain as he could be without actual knowledge, that his father had bought him a shop in which he could start to practise the profession for which he had undergone his long and serious training. And sure enough, as he turned off Piccadilly – so named after the trade of a Mr Robert Baker who in the early seventeenth century had built a house near the windmill, now remembered as Great Windmill Street, in which he had made pickadills or shirt frills – John glimpsed the bow-fronted windows of an apothecary's shop.

Sir Gabriel had been somewhat economical with the truth, John thought. For as he approached number three he could see that it had been recently renovated and that there was no conceivable way in which his father could have made the purchase the previous day. There were obvious signs that the building had been freshly painted and the windows themselves were new, replacing the old-fashioned sash windows divided by uprights. Smiling to himself at Sir Gabriel's guileless deception, John put the key in the lock.

Inside lay an Aladdin's cave of delight. In the shop itself was a large selection of the usual intriguing bottles and jars, now all standing empty, while the room at the back had been set up as a laboratory, complete with crucibles and alembics, retorts and matrasses, oil lamps, pewter pans and a selection of pestles and mortars. All that was missing were the ingredients which must be obtained before the compounds could be prepared. However, a few visits to the countryside, seeking the plants John had learned about in the Chelsea Physick Garden, and a trip to the warehouses importing the flowers and barks of the New World, would soon put that right. He only hoped that he would have the opportunity to do all this in view of the amount of time his investigations into the murder were taking. Suddenly, highly impatient to catch the killer soon, John locked up the shop and went home.

He spent a comfortable evening ensconced in Sir Gabriel's study, even the notion that the streets of London might hold a killer who not only remembered but was actually seeking him, pushed to the back of his mind. Instead, John thought about the kindness of his father and the fascination of the Masked

Lady. Only the realisation that he must delay the moment when he actually began to run his new shop on a daily basis, spoiled his utter contentment.

'You sighed,' said Sir Gabriel, who was looking at Joe Jago's list through a magnificent pair of ring-end spectacles.

'With happiness. You have given me what I have always wanted, Father. A place where I can put into practice all that I have studied. How can I ever thank you?'

'Just by being yourself,' answered Sir Gabriel, his voice catching in his throat a little. He removed his spectacles and wiped them, then said in business-like tones, 'It seems that you will be off to Sussex soon.'

'Yes. I have to interview the Dukes of Richmond and Midhurst, and also look into the fact that Elizabeth Harper originally came from there. A particular which might be a co-incidence and yet again might not.'

'While you are gone will you gather some simples for your shop?'

This being an apothecary's word for a medicinal plant, John understood at once. 'Indeed I will. The only trouble is I doubt I will have time to get to the warehouses before I go.'

'Would you like me to do so on your behalf?'

'If you could, Sir. I would love to see my shop—' He said the words with enormous pride. '—well stocked on my return.'

'Then sit down now and make a list of the products you need from the importers and I will undertake the commission for you.'

So, with a certain amount of head scratching, John produced a catalogue of his requirements: Peruvian bark, snake-root, sarsaparilla, bark of the sassafras tree, balsam of Peru, cardamoms, camphire (refined), jallop, manna, balsam Coprava, and juice of the white poppy.

'Surely that last is very powerful,' said Sir Gabriel, looking over his shoulder.

'Certainly,' John answered carelessly. 'But from it I can derive opium and laudanum which are both extremely soothing.'

'Yet am I not right in thinking that opium is smoked in the East with very strange effects?'

'I believe that is so, but here in England those properties are known only for their curative abilities,' John stated firmly.

And though Sir Gabriel looked slightly askance, he had no alternative but to accept what his son said and change the subject.

'I gave Samuel one of your potions this morning before he went home, by the way.'

'Oh?' John smiled. 'He was imbibing quite heavily last night, I believe.'

'Partly for that and partly because he's love-sick,' his father answered. 'He dragged the name of the Masked Lady into the conversation at every opportunity.'

John grew strangely silent. 'Well, she *is* very fascinating.'

'And also a suspect in a case of violent death.'

'I really can't see why.'

'Because she was present on the night of the murder.'

'So were a great many other people. No, it's my belief that she just happened to be there.'

'Or was she following Lizzie? Had you thought of that?'

'No,' said John, with an enormous twinge of reluctance, 'I must admit I hadn't.'

He had to confess to himself, as he made his way to The Plume in Old Compton Street where, according to Joe Jago's list, Lucy Pink was employed as a feather worker, that, like Samuel, he was becoming obsessed with the very idea of the Masked Lady. It seemed to John that she had been constantly in his thoughts since he woke up that morning, and though this was something of an exaggeration, the truth was that since the previous night in Marybone he had spent a great deal of time thinking about her.

'Now what a damnable coil,' he said softly as he arrived at the feather shop. 'The last thing I should do now is develop a partiality for one of those involved.'

Yet the fact remained that the woman intrigued him and John felt positive that he would be unable to forget her until he had found out for certain who she truly was.

The owner of The Plume being a hard businesswoman, it took Mr Fielding's letter to persuade her that one of her employees should be granted a few free moments to talk to him. Eventually though, and with some reluctance, John found himself shown into a small room no bigger than a cupboard, leading off the main work room. Peering through the open door, the Apothecary stared at row upon row of feathers, hanging from the ceiling like some bizarre festoon, at girls wrestling with Court headdresses almost as big as they were, at others crouched before dummies, stitching furbelows to the fronts of dresses. In a further room, just visible, were other workers, less well dressed, struggling along with arms full of feathers, stuffing them into mattress covers for beds. Despite the glamorous nature of the product, the whole place had a decidedly depressing atmosphere and John was glad when Lucy came through the door, somewhat breathlessly, then closed it behind her.

'How nice to see you again Mistress Pink,' he said, rising to his feet and bowing.

She went the colour of her name and bobbed a curtsey. 'I was wondering if you would call, Mr Rawlings. I heard a rumour from a friend who knows one of the Runners that Mr Fielding had asked for your assistance and thought you might want to question me.'

'The rumour's true enough,' John answered dourly. 'Having convinced the great man by the simple expedient of shuddering at the right moment that I was not guilty of the crime, he enlisted my help to find the owner of this.' And he produced the fragment of material from out of his pocket.

'What is it?' asked Lucy, staring curiously.

'I found it in the dead girl's hand. It obviously comes from her murderer's coat.' John paused, then said, 'I know you will have gone through all this already for Mr Fielding but I wonder if, just once again, you would mind telling me exactly what you did at Vaux Hall that night, including a description of everyone you noticed, up until the moment you found me kneeling by the body.'

Lucy drew in her breath. 'I'll do my best, Mr Rawlings. Talking to the Blind Beak made me realise how unobservant I am, but I'll try to recall what I can. For a start, Giles and I arrived early that evening and secured a box and ordered our supper.'

'Did you notice anyone in particular?'

'Well, I saw the Beauty and the Duke – I only remarked them because they were such a fine young couple – and I saw a woman in a mask. She was surrounded by a horde of gallants all paying court to her.'

'Go on,' said John with resignation.

'I didn't pay attention to anyone after that until the lighting of the Cascade. We were a little late for that event and had to stand on the very edges of the crowd.'

'So whom did you notice there?'

'You,' Lucy answered, blushing even more deeply, 'I noticed you.'

'Anyone else?'

'A young boy pushed past me to get a better view.'

'A boy?' said John, all attention. 'What was he like?'

'Quite small and slender, a handsome enough young fellow. I thought him remarkably well dressed.'

'In this perhaps?' asked John, handing her the piece of material.

Lucy examined it. 'He could have been, it was a bit too dark to tell. But, strangely, he *was* in The Dark Walk. I saw him there as well. He was skipping along in a world of his own. I thought it incongruous that such a young creature should be playing in a place where only lovers go.'

'Did you notice anyone else there? Please try to remember.'

'I saw the Duke of Midhurst. He came striding by me in a fury and went into the Grand Cross Walk.'

'Yes, my friend Samuel observed him too. Anyone else?'

'Two others. A handsome young blood, very prosperous looking. And a plump pretty girl with a veritable mane of red hair.'

'Were they together?'

'No, they both seemed to be searching for someone.'

'And the victim?'

'I did not see her at all.'

John sunk his chin into his hand. 'But neither did you see me, which means that anyone could have slipped by you in the darkness.'

Lucy looked at him with startled eyes. 'Gracious me, I hadn't thought of it like that. Yes, I suppose it does, doesn't it.'

There was the usual wait in the library before he was ushered into the presence of the Comtesse de Vignolles who, this day, lay on a couch with a gauze veil over her face.

'Merciful Heaven, Madam!' said John and, purely instinctively, went to take her pulse.

She motioned him away feebly. 'No, no, Mr Rawlings, pray do not bother yourself. I have the vapours, that is all.'

'I came to enquire if my physick had done you any good but, though I am loath to say it, you seem a great deal worse to me,' he answered anxiously.

The Comtesse waved a hand in the direction of a chair. 'Sit there, if you will. I cannot bear anyone directly in front of me. It strains my eyes too greatly.'

And she turned away, coughing a little. There was a faint smell of gin in the air and, behind her back, John gave a sudden grin.

'I'm wondering how best I can treat you,' he remarked in a highly serious tone, thinking to himself that a good dose of tartar emetic would probably do the trick.

'I don't believe a physician ever could,' the Comtesse answered softly. 'You see, Mr Rawlings, I consider my condition was brought on by a broken heart.' Before he could comment on this she continued falteringly, 'We women are but frail creatures, blown about like storm-torn vessels at the whims of men.'

'Good God!' John exclaimed, his manners forgotten.

'Oh yes, you might wonder. But you are young yet and a bachelor no doubt. You probably know nothing of the vagaries of those such as my husband.'

'Well, it's true I'm not very experienced in the ways of the world,' John answered forthrightly. 'But could you not fight back, Madam? I don't believe I could ever allow another human being to spoil my life. I have too much anger in me.'

The Comtesse gave a sad little laugh. 'I am too weak to fight, as you put it, Mr Rawlings.'

'Then I'll prescribe something to restore your lost energy. But there's only one thing...'

'Yes?'

'If you were to take strong liquor with this compound it could make you very ill.'

The veiled face turned in his direction and just for a second John saw the flash of the Comtesse's eyes as she regarded him. Then she said, 'And would this magical pick-me-up enable me to go out again? It seems such an age since I set my foot out of doors.'

'That and your own determination, Madam. If you want to get well, you will, mark my words.'

She was silent for a moment, then said quietly, 'I once loved my husband very much, you know.'

'One should never love anyone so greatly that you allow them to take control of your destiny,' John replied with conviction.

'How knowing you are for such a boy.'

'I am not far off my twenty-third birthday,' John answered with a certain dignity.

The veiled head nodded. 'Then go, my wise young friend, and mix your compounds. I'll pay you well if you can bring about my reawakening to life.'

'Only you can do that,' he repeated levelly. And then he stopped, determined to progress in the matter of Elizabeth's death even if it meant lying to the Comtesse to do so. 'Oh, I almost forgot,' John added. 'I found this piece of material lying on the pavings outside your house. I thought it might be torn from one of your husband's coats and could be useful when it comes to making repairs.'

The thin hand he had seen before emerged from the floating materials in which the Comtesse lay déshabillée, and took the fragment.

'Where did you say you found this?'

'Just outside.'

'Well, I have never seen it before,' the Comtesse said quietly, so quietly that John wondered if she were controlling a shake in her voice. 'The Comte most certainly does not have a garment made of such material.'

'Ah well, it must have been dropped by a passer by,' he answered nonchalantly, retrieving the piece and putting it back in his pocket. 'So I'll say adieu, Madam. I shall return tomorrow with your medicaments, for after that I shall be out of London for a few days. I am going into the country to gather some simples.'

'How well I like that word,' the Comtesse answered, and for the first time there was a smile in her voice. 'It conjures up a picture of such unwordly innocence, of the guileless apothecary gathering his plants and herbs.' The concealed face turned in his direction once more. 'But, somehow, I do not feel that description quite fits you, Mr Rawlings. On the contrary, I would guess you are in fact quite a clever young man.'

'It is kind of you to say so,' answered John, starting to bow his way out.

'Yes, yes,' said the Comtesse with a sigh. 'Until tomorrow.'

Chapter Eleven

The court at Bow Street was in full session. Seated in a high chair on a raised dais, his hands folded in front of him, his bandaged eyes turned towards the prisoner under examination, John Fielding loomed large. To his left, almost unrecognisable in a smart white wig, sat Joe Jago, while directly in front of the Magistrate and almost at his feet, the clerk of the court was ensconced at a desk, busily taking notes.

The sides of the courtroom and the gallery above were packed with finely dressed people, those members of the public who came daily to watch the remarkable Blind Beak, who had succeeded his half brother Henry only in April of that year, 1754, but who in that short time had already become something of a legend. For it was said by those who knew him that John Fielding could recognise over three thousand villains by their voices alone. Further, that the man could learn the entire contents of books, newspapers, letters and reports simply from hearing them read out to him.

It was also said that the Beak was hideously underfunded by the government, who treated his job lightly, more concerned with funding themselves. But short of money or no, the Justice for Westminster and Middlesex, the Metropolitan Magistrate, had already gained a reputation so fierce that the courtroom was packed with spectators every time it was in session.

Arriving late, John was obliged to squeeze into the back of the gallery, where he sat wedged between a fair fat lady and a small thin beau, this last complete with face smothered in plaster of Paris to conceal time's ravages, a cane dangling from his top button and one eye completely tucked beneath his hat. Pressed rather too close to them for comfort, John attempted to concentrate on the cases being heard below.

First came a gentleman accused of intending to do grievous bodily harm to a pretty young woman. Mr Fielding found the defendant guilty only of pursuing her with amorous intent and merely bound him over to keep the peace in the surety of forty guineas. At this the girl's attorney volubly protested how unfair it was that his client should pay the costs of the accused's arrest, and John was just thinking that fact to be perfectly true when the beau whispered in his ear that the plaintiff came from a well-known family of bawds and harpies. It was obvious that Mr Fielding, with his prodigious memory, had recognised the girl's name and acted accordingly. Very impressed by the acuteness of the Blind Beak's mind, John stared down into the hall of justice as two further prisoners came to the bar together.

Aged ten and twelve respectively, the boys had been arrested for assaulting and robbing a cabinet maker on the highway. Despite their youth they were committed to Newgate awaiting trial by jury, upon whose findings it was quite possible they would receive the death sentence, though it was unlikely that this would be carried out as both were under fourteen.

'Transportation for life, I expect,' said the large lady with satisfaction.

Her voice was drowned, however, by that of the Blind Beak, who was passing judgement.

'I have no alternative but to send you both for trial. Yet it is a melancholy truth that, if you could avoid prison, you might be of some use to society before you become hardened criminals.'

John, listening intently, thought that Mr Fielding might well be right, for in gaol men, women and children were herded together indiscriminately, prey to vice and disease, helpless to fight against either and therefore only too easy to corrupt.

The last case to be heard that day was particularly unpleasant, and the harshness in the Magistrate's voice as he sent the miscreant for trial at the Old Bailey revealed the strength of his feelings. A woman stood at the bar accused of beating her female apprentice to death, a hapless child who had been sent to her from the workhouse. It was further revealed that the murderess had treated the tragic girl most cruelly while she still lived. Even in that courtroom, packed with those powdered and patched creatures who had nothing better to do than while away an hour or two watching a blind man administering justice, there were cries of 'Hang the bitch!' and 'Put her down.'

The fat lady sitting next to John affected to faint at all the excitement, and he was forced to revive her by means of the salts he always carried in his pocket. Thus occupied, he missed John Fielding's dramatic exit from court, flicking his switch in front of him to feel his way. In fact, by the time the Apothecary had helped his patient from the courtroom there was no sign of the man he had come especially to see. However, Joe Jago was still visible amongst the throng, his wig – in defiance of convention – already snatched from his head which he was busily scratching. He grinned as John hurried over.

'Ah, Mr Rawlings, have you found our murderer for us yet?'

The Apothecary rolled his eyes heavenward. 'I've found nothing except, perhaps, who it isn't.'

'Well, that's a step forward, I suppose.' Joe Jago tapped his nose. 'By the way, Mr Fielding requires you to dine with him, if that would be convenient.'

John looked thoroughly startled. 'How did he know I was here?'

'I saw you and whispered the information in his ear. I think he would like a progress report.'

'Progress, huh!' answered John bitterly.

'Ah well,' said the clerk, scratching hard. 'Now, if you will make your way upstairs, Sir, you'll find Mr Fielding in the parlour.'

The ground floor of the house in Bow Street being entirely devoted to the Public Office and its affairs, the Principal Magistrate and his family had made their home in the upper storeys, four in all, including the attic in which the servants were housed. Ascending the steep stairs, wishing that he had some really relevant information to impart, John found himself on the first floor, which consisted of a narrow landing with three doors leading off it. Knocking tentatively on the one facing him, he heard Mr Fielding answer, 'Come,' and stepped inside.

The room which John had entered stretched the entire width of the house and had three large sash windows, two of which stood slightly open to let in the afternoon air. The general effect was one of light and space, and John thought what a pleasant scene it made to see the Blind Beak and his family seated in comfortable chairs by those very windows, engaged in conversation. Before Mr Fielding was set a small table on which stood a glass of cool punch which he was sipping as John came into the room, picking up the glass with as much dexterity as a sighted man. The two females who sat with the Blind Beak looked up curiously as their visitor entered.

Elizabeth Fielding, John's wife, was just on the verge of prettiness but missed being so because of the commonplace cast of her features. Ordinary was the word John would have used to describe her and yet, taken individually, her facial characteristics were pleasant enough. The child with her though, whom John took at first to be the Magistrate's daughter, was a stunning little thing, her dark hair tied with a red ribbon and her pert nose not detracting in any way from her lovely rosebud lips. John imagined her to be about nine years old and momentarily allowed his mind to wander on to what she would look like in ten years' time.

'Ah, welcome Mr Rawlings,' said the Beak, and the black bandage turned in John's direction.

'How did you know?' he asked amazed.

'Your personal aroma, Sir, as individual to any man as the very air he breathes. Now may I present my wife and niece?'

'Delighted to make your acquaintance,' said Elizabeth Fielding, curtseying neatly, an action which the child copied.

John bowed. 'My pleasure entirely, Madam.' He turned to the little girl. 'How nice to meet you, Miss...

'Whittingham. Mary Ann Whittingham. How dee do?'

She was such a perfect adult in miniature that John found himself smiling, then he remembered that he had come to report not to enjoy himself, and he turned to John Fielding.

'Sir, I have little to tell you, I fear. I seek people out and ask them questions but all to no avail. If there is a murderer amongst them he is cunningly concealing himself.'

'Then we must look elsewhere,' the Magistrate answered simply.

'What do you mean?'

'You should remove yourself to Midhurst as soon as possible. The key lies there, albeit not directly, I feel sure of it.'

'But what of the Masked Lady and that damned boy – or boys?'

'You can forget them for the moment. I'll set one of my men the task of following her and another to search for the lad.' The Blind Beak paused, then said, 'As you know we are not a large force and your help is therefore invaluable to me. Yet perhaps I was wrong to give you so much responsibility. Would you like a Brave Fellow seconded to you? If so, you must say so.'

'But if I answered yes, would it not take him from other duties?'

John Fielding sighed. 'Indeed it would.'

'Then let me continue alone for as long as I can.'

Elizabeth joined in the conversation. 'There speaks a good citizen. Mr Rawlings, I cannot tell you how overstretched the Public Office is. In taking on this enquiry you have, indirectly, assisted in the control and apprehension of London's other criminals.'

He bowed his head. 'Thank you, Madam.'

She smiled charmingly, then stood up. 'Gentlemen, if you will excuse me, I must check the arrangements for dinner. Mary Ann, do you want to come with me?'

'No,' said her niece, bright-eyed. 'If you have no objection, Aunt, I am enjoying listening to the revelations of Mr Rawlings.'

Mrs Fielding suddenly looked rather fetching. 'What a bundle of mischief it is to be sure. Does she bother you, John?'

'No,' chorused the Blind Beak and the Apothecary in unison. With that they both laughed and, for the very first time, John Rawlings felt his feelings of awe for the older man tinged by a certain warmth and empathy.

Chapter Twelve

By tradition the various forms of transportation which plied between the capital and the Southern Counties set forth from that part of London known as The Borough. Here, in the yards of the many inns that stood on the main thoroughfare – The Ship, The King's Head, The White Hart and The George, to name but a few – the public carriages drew up every day to receive their passengers. Beside the carriers' wagons, responsible for the conveyance of goods and the more humble type of traveller, there were two other forms of public transport on offer, namely the postchaise and the stage coach. The chaise was fast, smart and expensive and lived up to its nickname, The Flying Coach. The stage, by contrast, was slow and lumbering, could be more sociable, but was decidedly cheaper. On the rare occasions that John had used it, he had rather enjoyed himself despite the jolting and general discomfort. This morning, however, time being of the essence, he fastened his eyes on a four-seater postchaise, drawn up beside a notice saying, 'For the Better Conveyance of Travellers, the Chichester fast coach. Dines at Guildford. Horses changed, Leatherhead and Midhurst'.

Seeing three passengers clambering aboard, two older people and a pale-looking girl whom John took to be their daughter, he called out to the man, 'I'm going to Midhurst, Sir. May I share your conveyance and the cost?'

'Certainly,' the other replied with alacrity. 'We are being charged £4.8s. to make Chichester by nightfall. If you will contribute one pound, Sir, you may gladly join us.'

'Delighted to do so,' answered John, and handing his luggage to the hostler, who clambered up like a monkey and stowed it on the roof, he climbed aboard.

The chaise was obviously new, there being windows all the way round for observation, while the body was well though somewhat swayingly sprung. There was no coachman as such, this role being taken by two postillions, smartly arrayed in riding clothes and caps, who rode, one behind the other, a pair of the team of four horses.

'A smart rig this,' the Apothecary observed, bowing to the ladies before he took his seat.

'So I should think,' responded the father. 'The cost is iniquitous.'

'But the service good,' John responded reasonably.

The face of one of the postillions appeared at the window. 'All stowed, ladies and gentlemen?' There was a general murmur of assent. 'Right then.

As day is breaking, we'll be off. First stop, the posthouse at Leatherhead.'

'But what if nature...' the girl protested to her mother, only to be stared at reprovingly as the postchaise vibrated into action, its wheels clattering over the cobbles of The Black Swan inn yard, before the equipage turned left into The Borough and headed south.

John, staring out with interest, looked longingly at the great shape of St Thomas's Hospital, promising himself that one day he would discourse on healing properties with the physicians who worked there. Then his attention was drawn elsewhere as the postillions cut a swathe through the stallholders of Borough market, held daily for the benefit of the population south of the river and consequently enjoying a bad reputation for severely disrupting the traffic. However, with many oaths and cracking whips, the postchaise hurtled through this obstacle and Southwark's two terrible prisons, the King's Bench and the Marshalsea, came into view. Knowing something of their ghastly reputation, indeed having heard Marshalsea described as 'a picture of hell upon earth', the Apothecary's face became grim, his thoughts going off at a tangent as he dwelled on crime and punishment, and the horrors endured by both victims and perpetrators alike. Then, with a start, he came back to reality as he realised the other man was addressing him.

'May I introduce myself, Sir? I am Ralph Briggs of Chichester and these ladies are my wife and daughter. We have been in town for the sights and shopping, and a very good time we've had of it, too.'

John bowed his head to the two women and shook Mr Briggs's hand. 'John Rawlings, Sir.'

'Of London?'

'Yes.'

'Ah! And what takes you out of the capital, if I may enquire?'

John fought off a wild desire to say, 'The investigation of a murder', and instead answered, 'I am an apothecary, Sir, and am going into the country to collect some simples. Herbs and flowers, you know, from which I make my various medicaments.' He accompanied this statement by assuming what he thought of as his honest countenance, beaming upon his fellow travellers as if he were the most uncomplicated soul in Christendom.

'A medical man, eh?' said Mrs Briggs, her interest obviously quickening. 'Why, I'll have you know, Sir, that I've been plagued with a delicate constitution all my life. Now, what I need to find is a really good strengthening medicine. Of the many I have sampled none has ever proved powerful enough. Could you perhaps recommend something?'

'Well, I...er...' John answered.

'Splendid. You must tell me more about it over dinner. Mustn't he, Mr Briggs?'

But her husband's reply was drowned by the voice of her daughter, who was frantically screeching, 'Mama, I feel sick. I do, I truly do.'

'Oh, la!' Mrs Briggs exclaimed irritably. 'You're not fit to be out in company, Lettice. One simply can't take you anywhere.'

'I think,' said John, eyeing the girl's greenish countenance, 'that we had better stop the coach.'

This was hastily accomplished and the hapless Lettice thrust behind a bush by her fuming mother to do whatever she must do, discreetly hidden from the public gaze. John, meanwhile, sent one of the postillions to collect his bag from the carriage roof and from it produced some pills, guaranteed to bind the constitution of a giant.

'Take one of these,' he said, offering the returning girl the box together with a cup of bottled water.

'How very kind,' simpered Mrs Briggs, while Lettice attempted a miserable smile. 'Do you always travel so well equipped, Mr Rawlings?'

'I usually carry a few carriage sickness pills, yes. Not that I suffer from it personally. It's more for the benefit of my fellow passengers.'

'I can see that you are a young person of many parts,' Mrs Briggs said admiringly. 'I do hope that we can become better acquainted.' She paused, regarding him with a calculating eye. 'Are you a married man, Mr Rawlings?'

'No, not as yet, Ma'am. I have only recently completed my apprenticeship.'

She looked roguish. 'And made no pledge to your Master's daughter, I take it?'

'He had none, alas.'

'There now!' She tugged at Lettice's crumpled clothing and pinched the poor girl's cheeks, hard. 'My, what a state you are in, child. I see that you'll have to make a toilette when we stop to dine. What a dishevelled creature it is, to be sure. But a lovely disposition. Mr Rawlings, truly lovely.'

Lettice, who had turned from green to white, now went vermilion. 'Oh, Mama,' she protested weakly.

'We are not addressing you,' Mrs Briggs answered tartly, and with that extolled her daughter's virtues for the next fifteen minutes, pausing only to draw in breath.

At one o'clock, having had only one brief stop at Leatherhead when the horses had been changed, they arrived at The Angel in Guildford. Here the travellers alighted, making their way to the dining room, though poor Lettice was banished upstairs with strict instructions to restore her ravaged appearance. She returned some forty minutes later looking a great deal fresher but declining any offer of food, and shortly afterwards the journey was resumed with new horses and a change of postillions.

They reached the town of Midhurst just as the sun began to dip, the chaise heading straight for the posthouse, a hostelry of ancient origins called The Spread Eagle. The moment to part company with the Briggs had now arrived and Lettice, somewhat to John's alarm, was instructed to make her farewells to her fellow traveller by taking a turn with him round the market square.

'For the benefit of your health, girl,' Mrs Brigg boomed as she and her husband took advantage of the few minutes' break while the horses were changed once more, by going inside to sample the inn's hospitality.

'Yes, Mama,' her daughter answered dutifully, after which she relapsed into an uncomfortable silence, her eyes cast shyly downwards.

'I hope you get to Chichester safely,' said John, gallantly trying to make conversation.

'I'd like to stay here,' Lettice murmured wistfully, still not looking up.

'Why?' he asked, surprised.

'Because yours is pleasant company, Mr Rawlings. More pleasant, you see, than that of my parents.'

'Well, I am somewhat younger,' John said, stating the obvious.

'That's just the point.' Lettice stopped in her tracks and at last wheeled round to gaze at him. 'I'm with old people all the time. I've no friends of my own age. My days are spent ministering to Mama, indulging her every whim.'

'She looks strong enough to me.'

'Not she! Her entire life revolves round strengthening medicines.'

'I wonder why it is,' the Apothecary remarked thoughtfully, 'that certain women make such an enjoyable pastime of feeling poorly.'

And he thought of the Comtesse de Vignolles, whose physick he had delivered to her house before dawn, on his way to The Borough.

'You know as well as I,' Lettice answered with more spirit than he would have thought she possessed, 'that they get attention that way.'

John nodded. 'Yes, you're right.' He smiled at her crookedly. 'Listen, as soon as I've collected some simples and returned to my shop, I'll send Mrs Briggs a preparation that should set her dancing.'

Lettice went extremely pink. 'Could you really do so?'

'Well, if we can persuade her that my potion is more potent than any other, it *will* work. It's a matter of convincing her, that's all.'

His companion blushed even more deeply. 'Mr Rawlings, would it not be possible for you to bring the physick to Chichester yourself? You would be made very welcome.'

John hesitated. 'At the moment it's out of the question. I have a great deal to do in Midhurst. But perhaps at some time in the future.'

Lettice looked sad and answered flatly, 'Oh, it was just a thought, that's all.'

The Apothecary gently touched her arm. 'Miss Briggs, I really *am* busy. It was not an excuse. And if ever I do find myself in the vicinity of Chichester I promise to call.'

She looked at him radiantly. 'Oh, how happy that makes me.'

'Then all's well,' he said, firmly propelling her towards The Spread Eagle. 'Now I really believe you'd best be getting on. I think I can see fresh horses in the shafts.'

'Yes,' Lettice answered softly. 'I think I observe them too.'

A few minutes later, amidst a great flurry of fluttering handkerchiefs, the postchaise set off again, the postillions determined to reach Chichester before nightfall and thus avoid the dangers of travelling in the dark. Seeing Lettice's frantically waving hand and thinking how different were all women, John made his way inside the posthouse and booked himself a room for a stay of several days.

And it was only then, envisaging a welcoming bed on which he might throw himself full length and stretch his cramped bones, that the Apothecary realised how tired he was. With a yawn, he lay down and closed his eyes.

When he awoke again it was dark, only a faint shaft of moonlight illuminating the small chamber which he occupied. Drawing the curtains across the leaded light window, John lit a candle and looked at his watch. As it was past eight o'clock and many hours since he had dined, the Apothecary removed the marks of travel as best he could with cold water, and went downstairs.

The Spread Eagle being an inn of substance, he saw as he reached the ground floor that there were several public rooms leading off the hall. To the right lay the coffee room, to the left, the dining parlour. There was also a further parlour reserved for travellers of quality and a downstairs kitchen for the rest, and it was to this last that John now made his way. For here, round the fireside, he knew he would find assembled the men of the town, the rural gaffers who knew more about their neighbours than they knew themselves. Certain that this was where he would get all the gossip, John went down a flight of steps and in through an arched doorway to where the kitchen lay.

It was a cosy room, giving an impression of warmth and comfort even though on such a sultry night as this the fire had not been lit. The floor was paved with red bricks, which were quite remarkably clean, while a large dresser was adorned with shining pewter plates and copper saucepans, scoured until they shone. Before the fireplace stood an array of carver chairs and in these, smoking their pipes and supping ale, sat the locals, their number swelled by one or two travellers of the poorer kind. Calling for a pipe and some home brew, John went to join them.

As he had much expected, he was greeted with little more than stares of curiosity and a few mumbled words, and he was just wondering how to break in on the general conversation when a man sitting to the Apothecary's left started to laugh and wheeze simultaneously. Putting his head on one side, John made a great show of cupping his ear to listen.

'And what might you be after?' asked the sufferer, who was by now coughing painfully.

John put on his contrite face. 'My dear Sir, do forgive me, an unwarrantable intrusion. The fact of the matter is I'm a medical man, an apothecary by trade, and I was just thinking how greatly a jar of my liniment would ease your condition.'

A pair of suspicious blue eyes regarded him from beneath a tangle of flaxen hair, giving John a strong impression of Viking ancestry. 'What condition?' asked the man in an unfriendly voice.

'Why, your wheezing of course. I would imagine you to be a martyr to it in the colder months.'

'Well, I can't see how that could be any of your business.'

'I was merely trying to help,' John answered with dignity, and turned away.

Another fellow spoke up. 'Oh, don't you take no notice of Dickon, Master. He's a rude son of Sodom and prides himself on being fitter an' stronger than all the rest of us put together. The day he's dying, the silly old fart catcher will declare he's never felt better, like as not.'

'Now that b'aint true,' Dickon answered angrily. 'I'm as fair minded as the next man.'

There were several contemptuous laughs. 'Well, prove it then. Give the young chap a hearing. Reckon your wife'd come out and kiss 'im if he could cure you of all the terrible noises you make.'

The assembled company guffawed and Dickon's eyes took on a mean glint. 'Well, go on then, pill pusher. Tell me about your cure-alls.'

John assumed a serious air. 'I could not and would not claim to compound those. All I'm saying is that my physicks and ointments can indeed help the sick. In fact I was going to offer you a jar of liniment entirely free of charge and with no obligation to buy anything further.'

A young man put a word in. 'My wife, Sir, she be awful prey to morning sickness with our first child. Could you help her?'

'Certainly,' answered John with conviction. 'I have a bag of preparations in my room. I'll go and fetch it.'

'Mind out for the Green Lady,' said Dickon nastily.

'And who might she be?' John asked, surprised.

'Someone who's beyond your skills.'

'I take it you're talking about a ghost?' he answered lightly.

'I certainly am. And she's a soft spot for gentlemen, so they say.'

'Then I must watch myself,' the Apothecary said as he made his way upstairs.

The jars and bottles he had brought with him, envisaging very much the sort of situation in which he now found himself, had survived the journey well. A box of pills had come apart, scattering its contents all round his bag, but other than for that everything else was intact. Taking his portmanteau by the handles, John carried it back down to the kitchen with an air of triumph.

'Now, gentlemen,' he said, and smiled engagingly.

The landlord's wife, who had been hovering in the background and now introduced herself as Anne Pruet, came forward at once to enquire after a complexion whitener. With a flourish, John presented her with a large bottle for which he would accept no payment. She, in return, insisted that he enjoy a free supper.

'... though it's not fitting you should eat down here, Sir. Let me serve you in the dining parlour.'

'I beg you not' John answered. 'I prefer to be amongst the folk of Midhurst rather than in the company of my fellow travellers.'

Looking round at the circle of bucolic faces, many of them still unfriendly despite his manful efforts, John thought himself a blatant liar, but one who was prepared to go to almost any lengths to get information. He lowered his lashes at Anne Pruet.

'So The Spread Eagle is haunted, is it, Ma'am?'

'Oh yes, we have two ghosts. A Golden Lady walks in what used to be the medieval hall and the Green Lady, she wears Tudor dress, appears in the parlour during the small hours.'

'Well, well,' answered John, determined to lead the conversation towards local gossip. 'Do you think they were crossed in love?'

'Who knows?' answered Mrs Pruet, and bustled away to serve the humbler travellers a simple repast of roast fowl with sauce, potatoes and melted butter, poached eggs and a hunk of cheese.

'Why did you ask that?' put in Dickon. 'About ghosts who were crossed in love?'

'I don't really know,' said John carefully, a sudden pricking at his spine telling him that something was about to be revealed. 'Because that is one of the most common causes of suicide, I suppose.'

The man drained his pot of ale which John signalled to the boy should be refilled. 'Do you come from round these parts?' Dickon asked, staring at the Apothecary narrowly.

'No, from London. I've made the journey to collect plants and herbs for my various medicines.'

'Oh, so you just took a good guess.'

'What do you mean?'

'That we *do* have a ghost, no more than five mile distant, who died for love. He drowned in the millpond when his sweetheart upped and left him.'

'How extraordinary!' said John, certain that he was on the point of discovery. 'I must make a point of visiting the spot.'

'Aye,' Dickon answered taciturnly.

As the conversation appeared to be about to dry up, John asked desperately, 'What happened exactly?'

'I told you. The miller's daughter had a sweetheart, one Jemmy Groves. And when she went to London to make her way in the world...' Dickon laughed meaningfully. '... he jumped into the millpond and killed himself. Another death came out of that incident, as well. She has a lot to answer for, has Lizzie Harper.'

Barely able to control his triumph, John said, 'What other death was that?'

Dickon looked over his shoulder. 'I've said enough. There's folk round here don't like to hear it talked about. She breaks hearts, does Lizzie.'

'You mean...?'

'Yes, I do. There's some in this very kitchen who fancied themselves smitten with her.'

'Is she very beautiful, then?'

'No,' said Dickon surprisingly. 'She has a black heart and that will never make up for a pretty face.'

'You are a very perceptive man,' commented John. 'Now, will you take a jar of my liniment or does your perception not stretch that far?'

The other man smiled for the first time, revealing a mouthful of wildly craggy teeth. 'I'll try it,' he said, and held out his hand.

A call to supper, coming at that very moment, provided a welcome excuse to sit alone and think. Chewing his leg of fowl, John set his pictorial memory to work and up came a copy of the scarcely literate note that Hannah had found in Elizabeth Harper's apartments. The words 'If Yew do not Reetun I shalle Kil Miselfe. Cum home for the Love of God, Jem' ran before his eyes. Jem and Jemmy Groves, then, must be one and the same, which led to the obvious conclusion that Elizabeth Harper had been the miller's daughter. It seemed that the hunt for her murderer was beginning to grow warm at last.

'And are you off to gather simples tomorrow, Sir?' asked Anne Pruet as she cleared away the main course and served John a portion of cheese that was a meal in itself.

'Yes, but I shall need to hire a horse. The particular thing I'm looking for can only be found at Goodwood.'

'Goodwood?' she echoed. 'But there's nothing there except the Duke of Richmond's place.'

'That is where I am going to seek,' said John, childishly enjoying his play on words. He lowered his voice. 'Mrs Pruet, Dickon told me such an intriguing thing.'

'And what was that?'

'That the mill nearby is haunted by a young man, Jemmy Groves, who killed himself for love of a girl called Lizzie. He also said that *two* deaths resulted from the tragedy. What did he mean by that?'

Anne glanced round cautiously. 'That after Jemmy's death, Eleanor Benbow vanished without trace and has never been heard of since.'

'Eleanor Benbow? But who is she?'

'The miller's only daughter, of flesh and of blood.'

'You mean that Lizzie was adopted?'

'Aye, the traitorous little bitch.'

'Why do you say that?'

But another customer was calling and Mrs Pruet was turning away, and there was nothing left for John to do but consume his cheese and quietly ponder the evening's interesting revelations.

Chapter Thirteen

The Spread Eagle inn had been in the hands of the Pruet family since 1716, so John learned the next morning when, after breakfast, he set about hiring himself a horse. First in line had been Henry Pruet, knacker, succeeded by his son John, a tallow chandler, who had now passed the lease on to *his* son William. John Pruet, however, had not retired completely and was in charge of the stables where, with much pride, he cared for his string of beasts, some of which were very fine indeed. Leading out a chestnut mare of rippling proportions, the old man insisted on pointing out her good qualities to the Apothecary who stood somewhat impatiently, ready to tie his herb and flower baskets on to the saddle.

'This is Blade, Sir; very fast but very even-tempered, an exceptional animal in every way. Now how many days might you be wanting her for?'

'Two or three, I imagine. Perhaps more.'

'But you'll be bringing her back at night? For though she is of impeccable temperament, she does prefer her own stable.'

'I certainly will. I have a room here.'

'Then cherish her well. They are all like children to me.'

And with this admonition, the business was transacted and John clattered out of the yard, somewhat nervously for he had not ridden for quite a while, and headed south towards Goodwood House, the country seat of that naughty young rake, the Duke of Richmond.

He had decided earlier that morning to make his first task a visit to the two Dukes, Richmond and Midhurst, in order to question them about their activities in Vaux Hall on that fateful night. For much as he longed to investigate the strange story of the mill and the suicide of Jemmy Groves, to say nothing of the disappearance of Eleanor Benbow, a new character in the drama, there could be no escaping the fact that the young noblemen were high on the list of suspects. Obviously, of the pair of them, Richmond appeared to have no motive for killing Elizabeth Harper though, John thought, a well-heeled blade such as he, known to have patronised the house in Leicester Fields, might well have been one of the girl's clients and fallen out with her for some reason not, as yet, revealed. As he rode along, the Apothecary summoned into his mind everything he knew about Charles Lennox, Duke of Richmond.

The first thing he recalled was that the Duke was the great grandson of

Charles II, this particular line of royal bastards having sprung from the King's liaison with his French mistress, Louise de Queronaille. From these two accomplished lovers, the family of Lennox had inherited a certain wildness as well as their dark good looks, both these characteristics never more prevalent than in the present holder of the title who, still aged under twenty, was enjoying life to the full before custom insisted that he wed. Stopping before the great gates of Goodwood House and showing the lodge keeper John Fielding's letter, the means to gain admittance, John started up the long drive to the house, deciding that in order to handle such an ebullient young scamp as this, serious formality must be the keynote.

The Duke received his visitor in the library, standing before one of the room's many windows so that the light of the June morning shone directly in John's face. Whether he had had time to prepare especially, the Apothecary was not certain, but Charles Lennox, youthful as he was, certainly looked imposing. Elegantly dressed and wearing a neat white wig with a queue tied back in a bow, he was every inch the aristocrat, the privileged young being in whom flowed the blood of kings, the boy to whom the squandering of money must mean very little indeed.

'How can I help you?' Richmond asked disdainfully and without the flicker of a smile.

John bowed respectfully. 'By answering a few questions, if you will, your Grace. I take it you have already seen my letter and know that I represent Mr Fielding, Principal Magistrate of the Public Office in Bow Street.'

'Yes,' said Charles, affecting a yawn.

'Well, on his behalf I have come to enquire as to your movements when you were last in Vaux Hall Pleasure Gardens. That was the night, just in case your memory fails you, when a young woman named Elizabeth Harper was done to death in The Dark Walk.'

'Really?' said the Duke, yawning again.

'Yes, really,' John replied, an edge in his voice. 'Come, Sir, let us not shilly shally. It is a known fact that you frequented the brothel in Leicester Fields and would, therefore, most likely have known the girl – well. It is also known that you were in The Dark Walk at the time, that you winked at the deceased and gave her the eye, and that you also appeared to be searching for someone. Now what do you say to that, remembering that you are as much obliged to answer for yourself as any man in the kingdom?'

'I say damn you,' answered Richmond, and sat down, rather fast.

'May I?' asked John, and on the Duke's nod took a seat directly opposite him.

'I'd also say,' Richmond continued, recovering himself, 'that your precious Mr Fielding – is it true that the mob call him the Blind Beak? – is remarkably well informed.'

'Then that being the case,' John said in a reasonable voice, 'why don't we discuss the matter sensibly? We are of an age, Sir, you and I, and can speak to one another without barriers I believe.'

There was a pause and John saw the Duke's saturnine face tighten as he gave the matter his consideration. He caught himself thinking that the young man looked terribly like his royal great-grandfather at such a moment of intense concentration.

Then Richmond spoke. 'If I trust you, will everything I say be kept in confidence?'

'It will be my duty to report back to Mr Fielding but, sentence for sentence, I shall not repeat what you tell me.'

'Do I have your word on it?'

'Yes, you do.'

'Then I'll make a clean breast. I knew Elizabeth Harper, of course I did. Why, I'd taken my measure with her several times, you know the way it is?'

'Yes,' said John, thinking of Diana. 'I know.'

'Well, I'd heard rumours that she'd been set up by a fancy man but thought no more about it. And then, that night at Vaux Hall, I saw her in company with Midhurst – a right Miss Molly that fellow, in my view – so was startled, to say the least. Anyway, the long and the short of it is that I got damnably drunk. Truth to tell, I sank six half-pint bumpers of champagne and some super numeral bumpers into the bargain. Anyway, not being at the stupid stage, the drink made me desirous of female company and I went in search of Miss Patty Rigby, whom I had escorted to the Pleasure Gardens but who had gone to visit friends in another box. They told me she was looking for *me* and, guessing her mind, I went off to The Dark Walk.'

'And what about Lizzie?'

'I saw her, strange to say and, yes, I did ogle her up, thinking that if Miss Rigby didn't appear, she would do equally well.'

In the face of such unbridled naughtiness it was impossible to maintain formality, and John found a crooked grin creeping over his features. 'Your Grace, I beg leave to tell you that you are a rampant young blood,' he said, and burst out laughing.

'Yes,' said Richmond, grinning back. 'I know.'

'So what happened then?'

'I went into The Dark Walk and found Miss Rigby and we disappeared for a while about our business. By the time we'd finished, the cry was up that a girl had been murdered and, discretion being the best course, or so I believe, we went back to our box.'

'Um,' John answered thoughtfully. 'Tell me, did you see anyone as you made your way to your trysting place?'

'I saw several people, none of whom I knew.'

'Could you describe them? This might be vitally important.'

'They were all members of the *mobile vulgus*,' stated the Duke, waving a languid hand.

'But that didn't stop you noticing them, surely?'

'It most certainly did,' the nobleman answered, grinning again, and then he frowned. 'But now you come to mention it, one of their number did momentarily attract my attention. You see, the little beast actually had the temerity to bump into me.'

'Little beast?' repeated John, convinced he knew what was coming next.

'Yes. Some vile child, all prinked up in blue, ran headlong into my path and we collided. I clipped his ear for him, I can tell you.'

The Apothecary shook his head in resignation. 'The boy again!'

Richmond looked astonished. 'You know about him?'

'I most certainly do. He runs through the tale of poor Lizzie's murder like a persistent thread.'

'So who is he?'

'That I have yet to discover.'

'But you're not saying he killed her, surely?'

'He might well have done.'

'I should hardly think so,' the Duke contradicted. 'He was only small, you know. His head didn't come up much above my waist.'

'And I presume he was fair-haired and blue-eyed?'

'Yes. The collision knocked his wig off and I particularly noticed that his hair was light.'

'If only I could trace his identity,' John muttered.

'Ask Patty,' answered the Duke surprisingly. 'She knows everyone.'

'Miss Rigby? Is she here?'

'Indeed she is. I can't abide the boredom of country life so I am usually accompanied by a lively companion. She's in the garden, sketching. Shall we go and find her? I'll get some champagne brought out.'

John stood up and bowed politely. 'I would enjoy that, Sir. But there's just one thing more before we leave the house. A mere formality, I assure you.'

'And what might that be?'

'I seek permission to look at your coats. You see, the dead girl had a piece of torn material in her hand which I believe came from her murderer's garments.'

The Duke turned a little pale. 'What a ghastly thought. But please feel free to do so. I have nothing to hide in that or any other regard.'

A quarter of an hour later, having searched through two large and elaborate presses, John knew that Charles Lennox was telling the truth. Amongst his dazzling display of splendid clothes, several of which were of the colour blue, there was not a single item that matched the ripped fragment.

'Satisfied?' asked Richmond, who had hovered over John in rather an unnerving fashion.

'Perfectly, Sir.'

'Thank God for that. However innocent one is, one always manages to feel guilty in the face of officialdom, though I must confess you don't look at all like a dignitary to me. Now, shall we seek out Patty and have a bumper or two?'

'It would be a pleasure.'

And with that the two young men, a great empathy between them despite their very different stations in life, sauntered into the gracious grounds of Goodwood House.

The girl they sought was not far away, for Miss Rigby, buxom and beautiful, a big creature in every way, was sitting beneath a nearby elm tree, sketching a rather rude piece of statuary which stood guarding the entrance to one of the long walks. She looked up as they approached and John saw that on her flaming head, as bright and vivid as a bowl of oranges, she wore a shady hat, while her dress, over its wide panniers, was of cool striped silk, trimmed with taffeta bows and a long apron edged with lace He also could not help but observe that her neckline was cut very low, revealing extremely ample breasts.

'Ah, Charlie,' she called out as the Duke approached, and the Apothecary hid a smile at the familiarity. For despite all Richmond's assertions that he never regarded a member of the lower orders, Miss Rigby's accent definitely revealed somewhat humble origins.

'This is Mr Rawlings,' Lennox said now, coming to stand by his light-of-love's side and looking over her shoulder at her sketch. ''Zounds,' he added, 'trust you to draw that.'

She grinned at him. 'Too realistic?'

'I should certainly say so. Anyway, you must behave with decorum in Mr Rawlings's company. He represents that powerful man, John Fielding, I'll have you know.'

'The Blind Beak?' Patty surveyed the newcomer closely. 'Well, I never thought one of his runners would look like you.'

'Is that a compliment?' asked John, bowing.

'It most certainly is.'

'Mr Rawlings,' said the Duke severely, 'is here to enquire about the death of that girl at the Pleasure Gardens. Now, there's no need to look nervous, sweetheart. He's a civilised chap and that's for sure. He knows we were in The Dark Walk at the time and he also knows what we were about, so there's no call for falsehoods.'

'What I really would like to find out, Miss Rigby,' John put in, 'is whether you saw anyone in the Walk and, if so, whether you knew who they were.'

Patty frowned thoughtfully but was stopped by the arrival of two footmen who appeared from the house, one bearing a silver tray and glasses, the other three bottles of champagne in buckets of ice. It was not until they had gone and she had downed a rapid glass that she finally answered.

'In truth I saw several people, Sir, but none of them of any consequence. They were people from the country, if you understand me, sightseers and that type of person.'

'And unlikely to know Elizabeth Harper?'

'Yes, indeed.'

'What about the boy,' asked Richmond, 'the child who bumped into me? Had you ever seen him before?'

Patty shook her head. 'Only earlier in the evening, creeping in to watch the lighting of the Cascade. I remarked him then because I thought what a pretty little thing he was, and so finely dressed. I wondered what he could be doing out on his own like that.'

'Did you take him to be an apprentice?' asked John.

Miss Rigby shook her head again. 'No. I thought him to be a nobleman's son who had slipped out of the house without his father knowing.'

'How old did you reckon he was?'

'About thirteen or fourteen.'

John looked grim. 'Too young to be infatuated with Lizzie then.'

'Oh, I don't know,' answered Richmond, cheerfully. 'I was seduced by a maid when I was that age.'

'Well, *you* are unusually scandalous,' Patty replied promptly. 'Not all males are as bad. Are they, Mr Rawlings?'

'Well, er…'

'There you are,' she said triumphantly.

John regained his composure. 'Miss Rigby, just for my sake, could you tell me who you *did* see that night? People with whom you were acquainted, I mean.'

Patty drank another glassful. 'Well, I saw Midhurst leaving The Dark Walk in a regular pet. I saw the Comte de Vignolles, with a face like a thundercloud. And, of course, I saw his wife.'

'His wife?' John exclaimed. 'Was *she* there?'

Miss Rigby frowned. 'Well, yes, I thought I spied her, though not with her husband, it's true.'

'Where was she?'

'Making her way towards the Wildernesses, quite on her own.'

'Are you positive it was her?'

Miss Rigby frowned even more deeply. 'No, that's just the point, I'm not. I only glimpsed her from the back and had a momentary impression it was the Comtesse. I know her a little, you see, having been engaged to play whist with her from time to time.'

John did not answer, staring out over the formal gardens towards the parkland. Then he said, 'But if she *was* there it could alter everything.'

'What do you mean?'

'That she had a stronger motive than most to kill Elizabeth Harper and if she were actually present instead of lying on her sick bed…' He paused and turned to the Duke, who was listening intently. 'I saw the Comtesse only a few days ago, you see. She made a great show of knowing nothing about the murder whatsoever. I even called again and showed her the torn material, pretending I had found it in the street and asking whether it belonged to her husband.'

'Damme,' said Richmond, refilling everyone's glass. 'What a yarn! Will you stay to dinner, Rawlings? I'd like to hear more of this.' He turned to his sweetheart. '*Was* it her you saw, d'you think?'

Patty looked thoroughly perplexed. 'I just don't know. Mr Rawlings, I wouldn't like you to accuse the Comtesse because of what was no more than a fleeting glimpse.'

John shook his head. 'I'll be a little more subtle than that, I assure you. But thank you for the information; it certainly sheds a new light on the entire evening.' He got to his feet. 'Your Grace, much as I would enjoy dining with you I regret that I must be on my way. I would like to see the Duke of Midhurst before evening.'

'His place is near West Lavington, a bare ten miles. You'll cover that in an hour. Do stay. We like company here.'

'Yes, we do,' said Patty, collecting together her sketching things. 'Now, I simply won't take no for an answer. Will you dine?'

'I'll have to attend you as I am,' answered John, indicating his riding clothes.

'Informality shall be *de rigeur*.'

'Then I would be delighted.'

'La, here's amusement!' exclaimed the Duke, and opened yet another bottle of champagne.

By the time he left Goodwood House, John Rawlings was the worse for drink, though not wretchedly so, but rather in a way that had his spirits bubbling like the bumpers of wine he had just consumed. The redoubtable Blade, who had also enjoyed the hospitality of the Duke of Richmond's stabling, trotted through the Sussex countryside as if aware that the singing individual astride her was only too pleased to let his horse take him the ten miles that separated the two great estates. The estates belonging to the two young noblemen who had not only been lovers of Elizabeth Harper but, equally, had also been present on the night she met her death.

Chapter Fourteen

The afternoon sun had dipped low in the heavens, bathing the parkland of Midhurst Place with a roseate glow which transformed the somewhat forbidding mansion that lay at the end of the long drive into a warm and welcoming domain. Built in the reign of James I in an architectural style typical of the period, the Duke's ancestral home, with its multiplication of gables, its vases and heraldic animals, its mullioned and transomed windows, its many towers, obviously would, in the harshness of normal daylight, have a sinister air. Indeed it was, in the opinion of John Rawlings, just the sort of place in which a murderer might dwell.

And as he approached the house, the Apothecary almost found himself wishing that this impression might prove correct. For, so far, everyone connected with the killing seemed to be perfectly pleasant and reasonable and quite incapable of committing such a brutal act. Yet Patty Rigby's assertion that she had seen the Comtesse de Vignolles at Vaux Hall had given him much food for thought. Could the lady's apparent illness be masking a heart so jealous its owner was capable of violence? John wondered, as he arrived at his destination and dismounted, staring about, somewhat overawed, for the entrance to Midhurst Place vied with that of Goodwood House in terms of sheer grandeur.

A mighty front door, set within ornate pillars which supported a double-gabled roof, reared before him, and grasping Mr Fielding's letter in one hand in order to give him confidence, John announced his arrival by knocking firmly. Almost immediately, as if there had been some forewarning from the lodge keeper, a liveried footman answered, and the Apothecary found himself ushered through an enormous Great Hall and into a contrastingly cosy parlour situated in the west wing.

'His Grace will join you presently,' the man said haughtily and, giving a slightly supercilious bow, left the room. John, delighted to have a few further moments in which to recover from the effects of Richmond's champagne, sat down on a satin-covered chair and closed his eyes. A second later, though, a slight sound from the doorway disturbed his rest and he jumped to his feet as he saw that Henry Wilton, Duke of Midhurst had come quietly into the parlour.

In the shadows of the Pleasure Gardens, John had thought him handsome, but now the Apothecary understood what Tyers and Richmond had meant by calling Midhurst a Miss Molly. For it was an effeminate youth who stood in the entrance, a pallid creature, slim almost to the point of undernourishment, whose large blue eyes gazed out at the world sadly from beneath an elegantly curled white wig.

'Mr Rawlings?' asked the Duke of Midhurst huskily.

'Yes, your Grace,' answered John, and bowed.

Henry Wilton nodded his head. 'Then pray take a seat and tell me why you have called here. My steward said something about you representing Mr John Fielding.'

'That is correct, Sir. I am here on his authority to ask you some questions regarding the death of Elizabeth Harper.'

The pale face flushed uncomfortably. 'But I have already given a full account of that night at the Public Office. Mr Fielding questioned me personally. I have nothing to add to my original statement.'

Unmasculine he might be but centuries of good breeding had given the Duke a certain hauteur which now made him appear almost formidable.

'Your Grace,' John replied with as much authority as he could muster, 'new evidence has subsequently come to light and I must ask if I might search amongst your coats.'

'My coats?' repeated Midhurst, obviously startled.

'Yes, Sir. It has now been revealed that the murdered girl had a piece of material clutched in her fingers; a fragment which, or so it is believed, was torn from the garment of her assailant. Every person involved with the affair has therefore been asked to cooperate in this matter.'

'I see,' said the Duke and bleached of colour again, so rapidly that he looked almost ill. After a pause during which he swallowed several times, he added, 'Am I under suspicion of this crime?'

'No more and no less than any other man connected with the dead girl. However, you were seen striding away from The Dark Walk round about the time she was killed. A fact you omitted to tell Mr Fielding, I believe.'

'Oh God!' exclaimed the Duke and rolled his eyes, showing a great deal of white, before slumping out of his chair and on to the floor, an act which happened so quickly that it caught John completely unawares. Just for a second the Apothecary sat staring at Midhurst's unconscious body before he shot to his feet, snatching his smelling salts from an innermost pocket and simultaneously pulling the bell rope. Then, heaving the slight figure into a sitting position, John pushed the nobleman's head between his knees. All this activity unseated the unfortunate Duke's wig and the Apothecary found himself gazing at a sad little head covered with long, straight fair hair, the whole effect somehow rather vulnerable and childlike.

'Oh dear,' sighed John resignedly, thinking that the wretched young man hardly looked capable of choking a chicken, let alone a healthy female. 'Not another innocent party!'

But the Duke was moaning and fluttering his lids which, after a deep inhalation of the salts, he finally opened. 'What happened?' he gasped, pitifully clutching at his rescuer.

'You fainted, Sir,' John stated tartly. 'I was telling you that further evidence had been found regarding the murder of Lizzie Harper and you lost consciousness.'

The great blue eyes brimmed. 'It was the shock,' answered Midhurst, starting to sob. 'That, and the thought of her lying dead, a piece of material clutched in her lifeless hand.'

'Did you then love her so greatly?' asked John in a kindlier tone.

'On the contrary,' said the Duke surprisingly, attempting to struggle into his chair, 'I didn't love her at all.'

'Then why...?

At that moment, however, the door opened to reveal the footman.

'His Grace has been taken ill,' said John, delighting in the look on the servant's superior face. 'Fetch some brandy and ice and a towel, if you please.'

'Yes, go along, Stokes,' the Duke added, nodding. 'And don't stare, man.' He turned to John. 'You seem very accomplished in medicine, if I may comment.

'I am an apothecary, Sir,' John answered, and did not elaborate further. 'Now, tell me what it was you were going to say.'

The nobleman's eyes welled again. 'That I didn't care for her in the least, she was just someone to be seen with, a beautiful being who demanded nothing more of me than to provide her with clothes and money and luxuries.'

John frowned. 'Do you mean she was just a kind of ornament?'

'Precisely that,' Midhurst answered eagerly. He gulped. 'If you must know the truth, I do not find women easy to get on with, particularly those of my own class.'

'Are you saying that you prefer men?' the Apothecary asked levelly.

'Yes...no,' the miserable boy replied. 'The fact is that I feel easier in male company but yet I am not...' His voice died away and he added quietly, 'At least, not as far as I know.'

'So you took Lizzie as mistress in order to quell the gossips?'

'Partly that, partly to reassure myself. Do you understand?'

'I think I do. So there *was a* physical side to your liaison?'

Midhurst blushed violently. 'Actually, I'm not really too keen on that sort of thing, probably because I'm not very good at it. But Lizzie was teaching me.'

'Ah ha,' said John, putting on his physician's face. 'I know of certain properties that might be able to help you there.'

The Duke brightened. 'Really?'

'Oh yes, there are various creams and tonics which can be most effective. But enough of that. What were relations like between you and Elizabeth? Obviously you had quarrelled with her that night. After all, she got up and left you.'

The Duke blew his nose. 'The fact is that she said she was bored with me. That my lack of manly prowess was too much for her to cope with.'

'Why in heaven's name did she do that? After all, you were keeping her.'

'She'd clapped her eyes on some former lover of hers. A formidable Frenchman. I think she'd a fancy to go back to him.'

'Oh, I see,' said John, and thought to himself that if the Comtesse *had* been present and had noticed Elizabeth's renewed interest in her husband, it might well have been the final factor in driving her to murder. He turned his attention back to the Duke. 'So what were you doing in The Dark Walk if your lover had abandoned you?'

The Duke of Midhurst looked so desperately uncomfortable that John wondered if he might be about to faint again. However, the poor fellow was saved by the arrival of the footman bearing a decanter and glasses and the various other items ordered. Wrapping some ice in the towel, John rapidly strapped the makeshift cooler round Midhurst's head, and saw to it that the servant poured his master a generous tot. Then the Apothecary sat patiently, waiting until they were alone once more.

'You were saying, Sir,' he prompted as the door closed quietly.

'Well, I may be a Molly Milksop but the girl's remarks had stung me. I intended to follow her into The Dark Walk and...er...'

'Take her by force? Show her who was master?'

'Precisely,' said the Duke in a muffled voice, and gulped his brandy.

'Then why didn't you?'

'Because, Mr Rawlings, she laughed at me. I caught up with her, tried to be rough, and she just giggled at my pathetic efforts. If ever a man were given motive for murder, it was I. But I didn't lay a finger on her, I swear it before God.'

John sighed deeply. 'I am beginning to think that no one committed this crime. Everyone I question seems alarmingly innocent.'

'*Cherchez la femme,*' said Midhurst meaningfully.

'What makes you say that?'

'Woman are traitorous beasts, all of them.'

'That is a very sweeping statement, your Grace, if I may make so bold. Yet perhaps you may be right in believing there is a female hand behind all this. Tell me what you know of the Comtesse de Vignolles.'

'Very little really. I believe I met her once or twice in the distant past but, of course, Lizzie told me of her illness when she moved into my town house and out of her apartment in Vigo Lane. Yet surely, Mr Rawlings, you cannot equate such a feeble creature as the Comtesse with murder?'

'I have still to make up my mind as to exactly how feeble she really is. I suppose you did not see her when you were in The Dark Walk by any chance? Or anyone else for that matter?'

Midhurst bit his lip in concentration. 'I saw Richmond and the pretty Miss Rigby. I also saw several people who were strangers to me. Oh, and of course, there was young Leagrave.'

'Young Leagrave?'

'A youth of my acquaintance. I thought I saw him there and wondered what he was doing out so late without the Squire.'

The Apothecary stared at him. 'And who *is* young Leagrave?'

'His father's a local landowner. The family has been prominent in this area for centuries. He has a son of about fifteen and I thought at the time that that was who it was. Yet now I'm not so sure.'

'Why?'

'There was something not quite right about the boy.'

'What?'

But the Duke would not be drawn further, shaking his head and saying he was not certain, to the point where John was forced to change his line of questioning.

'Tell me if you will, Sir, how long you were acquainted with the dead woman.'

'Three months. I saw her at the theatre and was greatly smitten with her beauty. Shortly afterwards I offered to put her under my protection. Why do you ask?'

'Because she came from the mill just outside the very town from which you derive your title. In other words she was a local girl, your Grace, and because of that I wondered if you and she had had a friendship that went back into the past.'

The Duke stared at the Apothecary, wide-eyed. 'Lizzie came from round here?'

'Yes.'

'Well, let me assure you this is the first I've heard of it. I had no idea at all.'

John nodded, not certain whether to believe him, and Midhurst continued to speak.

'Do you mean she came from Miller Benbow's place? Where there was a suicide? Are you telling me that Elizabeth was one of his daughters?'

'I believe so, yes.'

'To think,' said the Duke reflectively, 'I could have had a tumble with her all those years ago. It might have done me the world of good.'

John smiled. 'Indeed, it might.' The shadows were beginning to lengthen in that comfortable room as he asked his final question. 'Is it possible, even if *you* did not know her, that the Leagrave family did?'

'I would have thought it more than likely. The mill stood on Leagrave land and was rented off the Squire.'

'And this boy in The Dark Walk reminded you of his son?'

'Mr Rawlings,' answered the Duke, just a trifle tetchily, 'there was a similarity, yes. Yet I simply would not go so far as to say that they were one and the same. I hope that is clear.'

'Perfectly,' John answered calmly, 'but none the less, Sir, you must realise that this is the strongest indication I have had so far as to the identity of a young man who might well prove to be a vital witness.'

'Just so,' said Midhurst, but would make no further comment.

Chapter Fifteen

Riding back through the summer's evening, listening to Blade's measured breathing, his nostrils full of the reassuring smell of horseflesh, John cleared his mind of all thoughts and allowed himself the luxury of revelling in the loveliness of the night. High above his head, the moon was full in a rook-dark sky, its radiant circle filled with shadows and mysterious patches of shade. And to accompany its piercing silver light, it seemed as if every star in the firmament was glittering crystal. The landscape through which he rode was bleached to the point where it looked almost blue, and the mysterious outlines of the great trees threw deep pools of purple on the ground around their feet. It was a night for dreaming, for dwelling on the beauties of nature, and it was almost with reluctance that John finally turned into the yard of The Spread Eagle, Blade's hooves clattering on the cobbles, then dismounted somewhat stiffly, not used to riding quite so energetically or for so many hours.

This time he supped late and alone, sitting solitary in the parlour, trying to assemble his thoughts into some sort of order, though with no particular success. Constantly flitting through his mind, like half-glimpsed ghosts or creatures from a dream, were the shadowy figures of the dead Jemmy Groves, the vanished Eleanor Benbow and the mysterious young Master Leagrave. Feeling certain that the key to the death of Elizabeth Harper lay somewhere amongst all the people he had met or heard about, and was not the work of a mindless' assassin, the Apothecary eventually retired to bed.

Sleep would not come, though, and he spent a wretched night tossing and turning and dreaming wildly on the odd occasion when he managed to drift off. Yet strangely, despite his lack of rest, John woke feeling cheerful and alert and ready for anything that might come his way. His high spirits were lifted even further by the arrival of a letter from Samuel, brought by the post boy who rode into the inn yard with a bulging sack.

'My dear Friend,' John read as he tackled a large dish of ham. 'I have done as you bid Me at our Last Meeting and written to you at your Lodging in Midhurst in the Hope that you were able to find suitable Accommodation at The Spread Eagle.

'First let Me Apprise you of the fact that I have Acted on your Behalf as best I can. I did call at the House in Leicester Fields as you wished and There saw Diana.' There was a slight smudge round the word 'saw' which made John chortle. 'She informed Me that the Comte de Vignolles has Appeared, most Suspiciously She did add, amongst the Patrons. She wondered – and so do I – why He Should do so after his Argument with the Madames but added that, strangely, all now appeared Peaceable Between Them. Could It be, John, that He is there to Spy upon Someone? Diana did Say that he asked Questions about You. Who you Really Were and So On.

'You will Remember that I told You of the New Servant who has Come There? Well, I have Spoken with Her and a Pretty Little Spark She is. Fresh from the Country and as Fair as Day. She is Sore Afraid of Being Forced into a Life of Degradation and I have a Mind to Rescue her from This by asking Someone of Influence if they would take her for Maid. She really is Quite a Beauty in her Rustic Way.'

'Oh Samuel!' said John, laughing to himself. 'Not smitten again!' And then he remembered his own fixation about the Masked Lady and stopped smiling.

'As for the Others,' his friend continued, 'there is Not a Great Deal of News. Matt Tyler, who lives near Hanover Square, tells Me that the Comtesse has been Seen sitting Most Feebly in the Gardens, too Exhausted even to Read, or so it Appeared to the Onlooker. Meanwhile, the Masked Lady was Observed Playing Deep at White's where She lost a Considerable Sum, so it is Said. A Rumour now Sweeps Town that she Is a Bastard of the Duke of Devonshire. Business at Vaux Hall is Picking Up but has not Restored to what it was before the Killing, much to the Chagrin of the Redoubtable Mr Tyers. I fear that I have Seen Neither Sir Gabriel nor Mr Fielding so Cannot Report on their Welfare.

'If All Fails I had thought of Approaching Your Father as to whether he might Require another Servant, on Behalf of Little Millie, the Girl mentioned Above. Would You Consider that Sir Gabriel would Consider this a Great Imposition? Her Case is Truly a Sad One.

'With the Ardent Hope that All Your Ventures prove Successful. I Remain Your Friend, Samuel Swann.'

Despite the somewhat ingenuous tone of the letter, it was none the less descriptive and John could vividly picture all that had happened in London since he'd left. With a twinge of apprehension he wondered why the Comte had been enquiring about him, and remembered John Fielding's warning that the murderer had probably got a better look at John than John had at him.

'I hope he doesn't know where I am now,' he muttered to himself, and then considered that even though de Vignolles might not there were several who did, including, of course, the two Dukes and the vivacious Miss Rigby. Very thoughtfully, John went into the stable yard, mounted his horse, then cantered briskly away towards the home that had once been occupied by Elizabeth Harper.

Benbow's mill lay a mile outside Midhurst, back along the road to Goodwood, a sturdy set of buildings beside a sheet of water, still as glass beneath the rising sun. Close to the attractive cottage, built about a hundred years earlier, or so John reckoned, stood the mill, its wheel motionless, the sluice above it shut, the overflow pouring into the tail-race which flowed out into the centre of the mill pool. The pool in which, if rumour were to be believed, a man had died for love of a girl destined to meet a violent end herself. Hardly able to credit that it was from rural surroundings as humble as these that the beautiful Lizzie had set forth to capture herself a place in London society, however scandalous, John stared about him.

The place did indeed have a haunted air, as quiet as the grave with the great mill wheel silent. Proceeding cautiously, John removed his herb baskets from his saddle and slowly made his way round the pond to the little wooden bridge which spanned the mill race just where it flowed into the gushing brook which fed the pool. Stooping now and then to pluck the wild flowers, John left the bank and crossed the bridge, making his way towards the cottage. The door, which had been closed as he had stared at it across the pond, suddenly flew open as he approached, startling him, and at the same time a voice called out, 'And what's your business?' in a menacing tone. Blinking slightly, John put on his studious face, screwing up his eyes as if he were somewhat short-sighted.

'Forgive me, good Master,' he called back. 'I should have asked your permission to gather some simples but as your door was closed, I did not wish to disturb you.'

'Who are you?' the miller answered, taking a step outside.

John held out his hand. 'Rawlings, Master. John Rawlings, apothecary of London, come to this lovely part of the country to pick plants for my medicines. Forgive me my trespasses...' He beamed as if delighted at this terrible joke. '...but I do need a certain variety of willow bark – for the treatment of fever, you know and just such a thing grows upon the banks of your pool.'

He smiled again, widely, an ingenuous look beaming from his countenance.

Miller Benbow narrowed his eyes. 'From London, you say?'

'Yes,' answered John, certain he knew what was coming next.

'I had a daughter went there,' the man went on, heaving a sigh and displaying all the signs of a truly lonely individual, glad to converse with anyone. 'She thought to make her way in the world, find some fancy man to marry her. Yet she had a good strong chap for sweet-heart hereabouts. I'll never understand the ways of womankind.' He sighed again, then peered at John even more closely. 'You didn't know her, I suppose? Her name was Elizabeth Harper.'

There was a moment of agonising choice whilst the Apothecary hovered between the roles of friendly stranger and keen official, then answered, 'No.'

'It was just a hope,' the miller replied, and relapsed into moody silence.

He was not the sort of man, John thought, observing him covertly, of whom he would like to fall foul. For Jacob Benbow stood over six feet in height and was built like a bull. A mass of curling dark hair, heavily streaked with grey, covered his head and chest, and dark brown eyes which held an angry, molten look in their depths, glared out from beneath his mat of curls. The miller also boasted a vast pair of shoulders and arms shaped like legs of mutton. Staring at him, the Apothecary felt positively slight in build in comparison.

'Of course,' John went on, his voice pleasant, 'so many country girls come to town looking for work. One wonders why they do it, particularly when they have a comfortable home.' He let his eyes sweep over the mill cottage with an expression of approval.

'You're right there, Sir, she has a good place here. And I dote on that girl, love her as if she were my own.'

John looked perplexed. 'But I thought you said...'

'I have *two* daughters – leastwise I call them so. But only one was my child of flesh and blood, that was Eleanor. The other, Elizabeth, is my wife's sister's girl, orphaned young, and taken into our household out of the kindness of our hearts. Little did we know what a viper we were welcoming into our nest.'

'Dear me!' said John sympathetically.

'Aye. She grew up lovely as a rose, that child did. Even more beautiful than my own sweet girl. Anyway, it happened that they'd both played since childhood with Jemmy Groves, old widow Groves's son from the nearest cottage. You can guess the rest I suppose?'

John shook his head.

'Well, my poor Eleanor fell in love with him, in the way that young females do at a certain age. But he only wanted Lizzie, besotted to foolery with her he was, truly mad. Anyway, when she ups and leaves him to make her way in London, he kills himself, here in this very pond.'

'That was a little extreme, surely.'

'I think she wrote him that she wasn't coming back. He could read and write a little, could Jem.'

John nodded, seeing yet again the words of the poor man's tragic note. 'So what happened exactly?'

'He came here one winter's night and jumped in. I found him next morning, all icy. I'd have spared Eleanor the sight but she rushed out of the cottage and took her beloved in her arms. I'll never forget the expression on her face till the day I die.' The miller's great chest heaved, 'Anyway, she had gone to join her sweetheart by nightfall.'

'What do you mean?'

'That Eleanor wandered away as soon as darkness came. It's my guess she went down to the sea and threw herself off the cliffs.'

'What a terrible tale,' John said, a sense of horror beginning to consume him. 'So have you been left all alone ever since? Have you no wife to keep you company?'

Miller Benbow shook his head. 'She went to her rest when those two girls were naught more than children. I brought the pair of 'em up single handed.'

There was a feeling in the air which John could sense but not identify. 'No easy task for a man,' he answered slowly.

'No,' Benbow agreed shortly. 'You know, it's said in these parts that the mill is cursed, haunted, evil. Perhaps it would be best not to gather your plants hereabouts.'

John gave a short laugh. 'I am a man of science, Master. You can't expect me to believe in such superstition.'

Benbow shook his head. 'I tell you there's something strange about this place. How else could a man be so ill-used by fate?'

It was on the tip of John's tongue to say that people are often parent to their own misfortune but he thought better of it. Instead, he answered, 'Ah well, who knows?' and turned to look back at the cottage. 'I wonder, Master, if I might just step inside for a glass of water? I've been out since dawn and am parched dry.'

Benbow looked as pleased as was possible for a man of his stamp. 'Yes, by all means. We'll have a pint of ale together. I'll be glad of the company.'

John gulped, thinking he had had quite enough to drink the day before but accepting the offer for all that, longing to get a look at the place in which Lizzie, to say nothing of the doomed Eleanor Benbow, had formerly dwelled. Yet there was no clue in the downstairs room that two young females had once lived there, for the place had the general air of spartan untidiness always associated with a man who fended for himself. But added to this there was an extraordinary atmosphere, not only of sadness but of brooding tension. It seemed to John, man of medicine though he might be, that something terrible had happened within those walls, though whether this was simply the miller's anguish over the loss of his daughters, he could not be altogether certain.

Accepting the ale and downing a draught, somehow refraining from pulling a face at its sharpness, John stared round and said, 'What a pleasant home you have here. Do you own the mill and cottage?'

Benbow shook his head. 'No, I'm a tenant of Squire Leagrave, just as my father was of his father. It's an arrangement that goes back well over a century.'

John looked interested. 'Leagrave? I'm sure I've heard that name before.'

'They are the most prominent family hereabouts, along with the Wiltons and the Brownes, and employ many local people. My Lizzie was in service with the Squire before she left home.'

John gaped and gave the game away. 'Elizabeth used to work for Squire Leagrave! Then, by God, she must have known his son.'

The miller stared at him suspiciously. 'Why do you say that? Of course she knew him. But of what interest is that to you?'

John's face rapidly became unreadable. 'My medical training has given me a lively interest in human behaviour. I just wondered whether your adopted daughter had eloped with the Squire's son, that's all.'

Miller Benbow looked entirely askance. 'Whatever next? I've never heard such foolishness. Young James is just a boy and still here in Midhurst, as upset by everything that happened as anyone else.'

John downed his ale and got to his feet. 'I've taken up enough of your time, I fear. So I'll just collect a few plants and be on my way.

'You don't think they might be accursed then?'

John smiled. 'No, I'll risk it. Thank you so much for your hospitality.'

The miller nodded dourly and poured himself another draught of ale as John stepped out into the sunshine.

It was the sight of a stage coach, its passengers gone into The Spread Eagle to dine, that made John do what he did next. Before going inside to have a midday break, the Apothecary booked himself a seat on the Chichester to London postchaise which would be passing through Midhurst the following morning. It had been a spontaneous decision, yet behind it lay the urgent need to confer not only with the Blind Beak but also with Sir Gabriel Kent. For it seemed to John that the investigation had now reached a critical stage.

He had eaten his midday repast in the kitchen in order to get a word with Anne Pruet but almost immediately afterwards set out for Court Green, the house at the bottom of Castle Hill, upon which had once stood the castle of the de Bohuns, who had held the barony of Midhurst. It was in this grand domain, so the landlady had informed him, that he would find Squire Leagrave and his family. So, taking his simples basket with him and adopting his earnest face, John made his way.

The house was very old in parts, obviously having been added to over the centuries, but the new part of the building dated from the reigns of William and Mary, and Queen Anne, and the Apothecary found himself looking at a home that combined both grace and dignity with charm and comfort. Delighted to see that it had not only a formal but also a wild garden, he knocked on the front door and was relieved when a fresh-faced maid rather than an overbearing footman answered him.

'Good afternoon,' John said cheerfully, doffing his hat. 'I wondered if I might have a word with your master.'

The girl shook her head. 'He's out riding, Sir. But would Miss Edith do?'

Not quite certain who this might be, John made his eyes look bewildered. 'Er...'

'She's the master's sister. The lady of the house. Who shall I say is calling?'

'My name is Rawlings, John Rawlings, but I must tell you that she doesn't know me and I haven't an appointment. In fact I've called to ask whether I might gather a few flowers and herbs from her wilderness. I am an apothecary, you see, and could not help but notice the very interesting selection of plants there.'

The maid frowned. 'Well, I'm not sure about that, Sir. Neither the master nor the mistress are very fond of strangers about the place.'

'Indeed, I understand,' answered John. 'One cannot be too careful in these violent times. But perhaps you would inform the good lady that I visited and sought permission to see her garden. Tell her that I will return in a day or two that I might know her mind.'

The maid misunderstood. 'I can't do that, Sir. She's lying down at the moment and I've orders not to disturb her.'

'No, of course not. I trust she is not ill?' he added slyly.

The maid grinned. 'Not ill, Sir. But the poor soul is a martyr to wind.'

John guffawed uncontrollably. 'What did you say?'

The girl joined in, clapping her hands over her mouth. 'Not of the farty kind, young Sir. I meant heartburn. The mistress has been its victim for years.'

The Apothecary wiped his sleeve across his eyes. 'Well, that's a relief at least.'

'Oh don't,' said his companion, giggling loudly. And it was at that moment an inner door was thrown open and a grim-faced female appeared in the hall.

'Really! What is the meaning of this outrageous noise?'

Struggling desperately to keep a straight face, John bowed. 'A thousand pardons, Madam. The last thing I wished to do was disturb your repose.'

'Who are you?' asked the newcomer, peering suspiciously.

'John Rawlings, apothecary of London. I am in the Midhurst area to collect simples for my medicines and was drawn, as if by a lure, to beg a closer look at your lovely gardens. I cannot remember when I have seen such a fine selection of herbs and flowers.'

Looking not the least mollified, Miss Leagrave glared at him. 'And do you make a habit of snooping round other people's property?'

John became extremely dignified. 'No, Madam, I never snoop, as you put it. Were it not for the fact that I believe you to be in poor health, I would have to take exception to that remark and leave at once.'

She stared, somewhat surprised. 'Why do you say that?'

'Because you have called my honour into disrepute.'

'No, I meant about my health.'

'Why, your suffering is written on your face,' lied John vigorously, studying her countenance and thinking that the woman looked as if she'd just consumed a pint of vinegar, so sharp and unfriendly was her expression.

Miss Leagrave continued to gaze at him narrowly. 'You say you are an apothecary?'

'Yes, Madam, fully qualified and trained. D'you know, I'd hazard a guess that your problem is caused by dyspepsia. I would imagine that you suffer agonies from heartburn.'

There was a muffled snort from the maid which turned into a cough.

'It's true,' answered the Squire's sister, her voice slightly less harsh. 'I do.'

'Then I think I may be able to help you. I am returning to London, a mere flying visit you understand, but will be back in a day or so. While I am there allow me to compound for you a strong physick that should cure you not only of the pain but also of the melancholy attached thereto.'

'And how much money would this cost me?'

'Why none,' said John, drawing himself up. 'I would present it to you as a token of my goodwill.'

'I see,' said Miss Leagrave. When she spoke again her tone was less abrasive. 'Perhaps I have misjudged you, Mr Rawlings.'

He maintained a steadfast silence.

'I thank you for considering my health and I will gratefully receive a bottle of your physick. In return I promise to show you the wilderness.'

The Apothecary bowed. 'Then I'll bid you good day.' And with that he turned to go and would have done so had the front door not been flung open, almost knocking him over. Somewhat startled, John stared at the person who had come in so precipitously and found himself looking at a boy, a boy with fair hair and blue eyes, somewhat taller than John had imagined, whose features already had about them the square-jawed look of determination. So this, it would seem, was Master James Leagrave who, quite possibly, had ruthlessly done Elizabeth Harper to death.

'Charmed!' said John, and inclined his head, amazed to be finally face to face with the elusive young wretch.

'Who are you?' asked the newcomer rudely.

'James!' remonstrated his aunt. 'This is Mr John Rawlings, an apothecary from London.'

'London?' the boy repeated, and just for a moment a slightly wary expression crept across his face.

'Yes London,' said John firmly. He stared James Leagrave in the eye. 'Do you know, Sir, there is something familiar about you. Is it possible that we could have met when you were last in town?'

James flushed uncomfortably. 'I doubt it. I am hardly ever there.'

'That is not quite true,' Edith put in. 'James enjoys going to the capital to study the fashions and to mix with young bloods of his own age. Why, I'd swear he'd move there if he had half the chance.'

'That is an exaggeration,' answered her nephew sulkily.

John looked urbane. 'I could not blame you if it were so. The excitements of town life are many indeed. Though, of course they are not all pleasurable. Why, danger even stalks in paradise. Do you know, Mam there was a murder at Vaux Hall Pleasure Gardens the other night.'

'Oh how dreadful!' Miss Leagrave exclaimed, clutching her breast.

'It was, utterly,' answered John, and he turned his head to stare straight at James Leagrave who, he was interested but not surprised to see, had turned white as frost, and had sat down on the hall seat so fast it would appear his legs had buckled under him.

Chapter Sixteen

John's journey back to London, shared with an elderly couple who slept most of the way, heads lolling and mouths wide, was fast and uneventful and he arrived back at The Borough as dusk fell. Hailing one of the many hackneys that waited nearby to take passengers alighting from the stage coaches and postchaises on to their final destination, John proceeded straight to number two, Nassau Street, where it pleased him to see that candles had been lit and every window gleamed a welcome. Running swiftly up the steps, he knocked at the door, then swept into the hall as if he had been away for a month.

Sir Gabriel Kent was at that delicate stage of preparation to go out during which he allowed no one to disturb him. So, John had no option but to hastily organise himself a bath and to dress as finely as he could, in fact in the clothes he had worn on the night of the murder, determined to accompany his father on whatever diversion he had planned. Yet despite all this, he was ready first and awaited Sir Gabriel in the library, his mulberry satin coat, gleaming in the firelight, reflected in the glass of sherry which he sipped pensively.

And then John stopped, his glass halfway to his mouth, arrested in sudden thought. 'Um,' he said slowly, and was standing thus, still thinking, when Sir Gabriel came through the door.

Tonight his father walked very mincingly, in black shoes with pinchbeck heels and silver buckles, his full-skirted coat, heavily laced with silver, thrown back to reveal a dark waistcoat of silver-flowered silk. His shirt and cravat were faultless and there was a flaunting of jewels about him that John found quite breathtaking.

'Oh Sir, I shall never be as fine as you,' he found himself exclaiming, and was rewarded with a smile so wise that he caught his breath.

'My son,' said Sir Gabriel, his eyes twinkling, 'old age brings few compensations, but one of them is the ability to be exactly who one desires without a care as to what the next man thinks. It is my choice to dress as I do, eccentrically, and thus I do so boldly. When you come to my age, perhaps even before, you may follow suit.' He kissed John on the cheek. 'You should have sent word that you were returning. I would have arranged a celebration.'

'But I've only been away a few days.'

'Another trick of old age; celebrate all life's small festivities to the full, remembering that they are growing increasingly precious.'

'I intend to emulate you in everything, have no fear about that. So, may I celebrate with you at whatever place you have chosen for your evening's diversion?'

'White's,' answered Sir Gabriel succinctly. 'I had intended to take a chair there, but if we travel by hackney you can tell me all that has befallen you.'

'Excellent,' said John, 'for I need the benefit of your advice.'

The journey from Nassau Street to St James's Street, where the great gambling club was situated, being one of quite short duration, John found himself talking non-stop while Sir Gabriel listened in silence. And it was not until they had drawn up before the former chocolate house that the older man held the hackney a few minutes before alighting, in order to ask a question.

'So do you believe the apprentice and James Leagrave might be one and the same person? And, if so, it is possible that James assumed a country accent and came to London looking for Lizzie?' He paused, then provided the answer himself. 'Of course a youth could well become smitten with a beautiful servant somewhat older than he is. It has happened many times before and, no doubt, will continue as long as time itself. Yet there is something that bothers you, isn't there?'

'Yes,' said John, and told his father what it was.

Stepping through the somewhat commonplace doorway – the proprietor of the former White's Chocolate House was anxiously seeking new premises – John Rawlings and Sir Gabriel Kent found themselves in a room from which all evidence of its previous usage had long ago been removed. Elegant chandeliers hung from a moulded ceiling and the many tables at which the gamesters sat each had their own individual candelabra to light the play. Conversation in these most gracious surroundings was hushed and, as at Marybone, John stood for a moment looking at those who sat absorbed. He saw fists clenched in anguish, grins of malicious exultation and the white faces of despair. He also saw the frenzy of those who had risked all upon a game of chance. For it was true to say that enormous sums of money, vast estates and fabulous jewels could be staked, lost and won, in a night.

This was a male preserve, that was for certain, for only gentlemen of rank or position sat at the gaming tables. And yet John knew by the very fragrance in the air that she was there. Turning his head to the table at which there was deep play at hazard, he saw her and his heart quickened its beat. Clad in claret velvet, her face covered in a matching domino, was the most fascinating representative of womankind, the Masked Lady.

Following his son's gaze, Sir Gabriel said with a certain wry amusement, 'I would gladly join them, knowing that you are investigating her, but, alas, the stakes are too high for me.'

And indeed they were. For as far as John could see from where he stood, rouleaus of a thousand guineas were being staked on each throw of the dice.

''Zounds and life!' he exclaimed to his father. 'How can anyone sustain it?'

'They gamble their all,' Sir Gabriel answered. 'Quite literally.'

'But the Masked Lady...'

'She must have accumulated a fortune already and now no longer cares whether she wins or loses.'

'But how could any woman be strong enough to endure such pressure yet remain so calm?'

'My dear John,' said Sir Gabriel, laughing, 'women are the strongest creatures of all. Look at her now.'

For there had been an audible gasp in the room as the stakes were raised at the Masked Lady's table, followed by the murmur that she stood to win £50,000 if the dice fell her way. Yet to see her, it was almost impossible to credit that fact, for she sipped her glass of champagne and smiled as serenely as any lady of fashion at a levée.

'I must get closer,' said John urgently.

'There are two places being vacated at the table next to hers. I'll take them.' And Sir Gabriel slipped into one of the empty chairs, bowing to the Lady as he did so.

She recognised him from Marybone, that much was obvious, for she inclined her head in return. Trembling slightly, John took his seat beside his father, his eyes fixed firmly on the Lady's face. She must have felt his admiring stare, for she momentarily lost concentration and rolled the dice without thinking, gleaming a glance in his direction as she did so.

A second later there was a cry of triumph from old Lord Stavordale. 'You're beaten, Madam. I've thrown three sixes to your fives. Now what say you?'

'That I'll play you one great throw, my Lord,' the Masked Lady answered in her husky voice.

'On what terms?'

'For all that you have just won plus another ten thousand pounds.'

'You are saying this before witnesses, you realise?'

The Masked Lady made a noise of contempt. 'Of course I do – and I'll repeat it louder. The fifty thousand you've just won from me plus another ten. Is that acceptable to you, my Lord?'

The elderly nobleman cleared his throat. 'Yes. Yes, it is indeed.'

'Then pass me the dice box, if you please.'

John had never seen anything like it. Cool as an April shower, the creature about whose true identity the whole of London speculated, dropped a swift kiss upon the box in her hand then threw the contents on to the green baize cloth before her. He could not bear to look and turned his eyes away, gripping his father's arm as the assembled company drew its breath. Then there was a gasp as Lord Stavordale made his play, followed by a cry and the sound of the Masked Lady's laugh.

'She's won,' gasped Sir Gabriel. 'By God's fair fingers, she's won.'

Relief swept through the Apothecary so strongly that he could have wept. 'You're enthralled by her, aren't you?' asked his father softly.

'Is it written all over my face?'

Sir Gabriel smiled his worldly smile. 'Let me simply say that your interest seems somewhat more than professional.'

But the Lady was rising and addressing the company as she did so. 'Now if I had been playing *deep* I might have won millions. Good night to you, gentlemen.'

There was a burst of laughter and the scrape of chairs as, in the manner of Marybone, every person present stood up. And it was at that moment that John turned to his father, his manner urgent. 'Sir, I am going to follow her. Forgive me for leaving you but it is something I have to do. I will see you at home, at what hour I do not know.' Then before Sir Gabriel could argue, the Apothecary had sauntered from the room in as nonchalant a manner as he could possibly manage.

A flunky helped him into his cloak and from his vantage point in the hall John could see that the porter was calling a chair from the street, while the Masked Lady stood in the doorway, her black boy beside her. Drawing as close as he dared, John tried to hear what it was she murmured to the two chairmen who came running to do her bidding, their empty sedan swaying on its poles between them. But to no avail. She had entered the conveyance and rapped on the door that she was ready to leave before he had even come into earshot. Moving swiftly, John did the only thing possible and followed the sedan up St James's Street towards Piccadilly.

At the junction of the two thoroughfares, the chairmen hesitated, and John was forced to draw into a doorway as one of them looked back over his shoulder. But after a second in hiding, the Apothecary realised that they only were checking the whereabouts of the black slave, who was running a yard or so behind his mistress's conveyance, the butt of the pistol he carried in his belt gleaming in the light cast by the torch of the linkboy who walked ahead. Having satisfied themselves that the page was keeping up, the small procession moved on, John slipping out of concealment to follow it once more.

The sedan chair crossed Piccadilly and went directly ahead, down Albermarle Street. And then, when it reached the top and the junction with Evans Row, in fact almost outside John's old Master's shop, the procession halted. Once again John drew out of sight and watched as the Masked Lady alighted and paid the chairmen off.

'By God, she *can't* live here,' he murmured. 'Not right under my nose for all these years!' And he was just about to dwell on the extraordinary coincidences in life when his quarry vanished into the dark lane that ran between Bruton Mews and the alleyway opposite. The Apothecary quickened his pace, determined not to lose sight of her, only to find as he turned out of the mews and into Bruton Street, staring all around him, that there was not a soul to be seen. And then he heard a light footfall and wheeled round, just in time to observe the Lady's black boy disappearing like a shadow towards Conduit Street. In his anxiety, John made his first mistake and ran into view. The page turned his head and there was a glimpse of the whites of his eyes before he took to his heels and was gone, leaving the Apothecary no choice but to give chase.

Of course he should have known that a child of that ancestry, so fast and lithe and light, could lose him in a moment. Yet not before John had been subjected to the indignity of pushing through groups of people, still out and about, making himself look a total fool and drawing the unwelcome attention of the Watch. Eventually, sweating and panting, he gave up. That most enigmatic of all women had defeated him once more. Kicking the cobbles and swearing under his breath, John made his way down Piccadilly and then, instead of going home, headed for the house in Leicester Fields and the solace of a little female company.

A girl he had not seen before answered the door, a girl yawning with fatigue, the dark smudges under her eyes betraying the fact that she was utterly exhausted. Looking at her, taking in her delicate beauty, John guessed at once that this must be Millie, the female for whom Samuel so obviously had a soft spot. A wave of his friend's kindness swept over him making him, too, feel compassion for her.

'Good evening,' he murmured in a quiet voice, not wishing to attract the attention of her employers. 'My name is John Rawlings and I am a great friend of Samuel Swann, with whom I believe you are acquainted.'

Millie looked thoroughly startled, almost to the point of total confusion. 'Are you, Sir?' she managed to gasp.

'Don't be afraid, my girl,' John went on gently, 'I know he has offered to help you should you so desire it and I can assure you that if Samuel says such a thing he will carry it out.'

Astonished eyes, blue as cornflowers, stared into his. 'Oh thank you, Sir,' the girl said breathlessly.

'Be calm,' the Apothecary added encouragingly.

Millie recovered herself. 'If you see Master Swann can you tell him that I might be forced to take up his offer soon. You see, if it is a case of becoming a whore or being turned out to starve, I shall have little choice.'

It was a plight so common that John felt a stab of fury as he reflected on the savagery of a society that brought innocent country girls to London in the hope of bettering themselves, and then rewarded them with squalor and corruption.

'I am also on your side,' he whispered.

Millie shot him a stricken glance and said, 'Thank you kindly, Sir. I'll not forget that.'

'And now I'll have a word with Diana if she is available.'

'Her last client has just gone, Sir. You'll find her in the coffee house.'

Millie gave a tentative smile and turned away but not before John noticed how white and haggard she looked.

'Are you quite well?' he asked.

'Just weary, Sir,' she answered. 'Oh, so weary.'

The beautiful Diana, voluptuous in a diaphanous gown that left little to the imagination, was sitting alone at one of the tables. For a moment, John had a mental picture of her with the man who had just received her favours, and felt sickened.

'I believe that the Frenchman has returned here,' he said without preamble, and took a seat opposite hers.

Diana looked slightly surprised and the Apothecary instantly regretted the abruptness of his tone, thinking that the poor girl was only earning a living after all, and had probably once been as innocent and vulnerable as Millie.

'How did you know?' she said.

'Because Samuel wrote and told me. I have been out of town, you see.'

'Visiting your kinsman?' asked Diana, narrowing her eyes.

'My kinsman?' John repeated, not understanding.

'Yes, the kinsman who thought so highly of Elizabeth Harper.' Diana's voice changed and she leant forward over the table in a conspiratorial manner. 'You are not all that you seem, are you?'

'Why do you say that?'

'Because any other young man would have been back to see me after such an enjoyable occasion as last time. This made me think that you were genuinely busy with something or other. And then when the Comte asked me if you had been here, and what you had talked about, and whether I knew anything further about you, I began to suspect that your connection with Lizzie was something very different from what you made it out to be.'

'Did you now?'

'Yes, Sir, I did. So are you going to tell me who you really are?'

John smiled. 'I told you the truth. I am John Rawlings, apothecary of London. But, as you have correctly guessed, I lied about my connection with Elizabeth's death, news of which has obviously reached you.'

Diana smiled bitterly. 'It has not only reached us but has been the source of all conversation since. You are out to catch her murderer, aren't you?'

'Yes,' said John, 'I am.'

Diana looked thoughtful. 'You know she came from the country, don't you?'

The Apothecary nodded.

'Well, here's something you might not have heard. One of them came here once, looking for her.'

'What do you mean?'

'One of those country people. A boy it was, very softly spoken and rural. Said he was her brother.'

'Did Lizzie receive him?'

'No, she'd gone by then, to Vigo Lane. One of the girls gave him the address and he went on his way.'

'The boy who called on Hannah!' John exclaimed softly. 'So the Blind Beak was right. He *did* come here.' He turned his attention back to Diana. 'Did you see him by any chance?'

Diana shook her head. 'No, I was working at the time. But I do know what he looked like because Ella told me.'

'Shortish and fair haired?' asked John.

She stared at him. 'Yes, he was, as it happened. Why, do you know who he is?'

The Apothecary made a rueful face. 'I'm not sure. Does the name Leagrave mean anything to you?'

Diana frowned. 'Yes, I have heard it before somewhere. But be that as it may, I can tell you who that boy wasn't.'

'Go on then.'

'He couldn't have been Lizzie's brother. You see, my dear Mr Rawlings, even though she was brought up with an adopted sister, Elizabeth was an only child. She told me so herself.'

John's crooked smile appeared fleetingly. 'Out of all the confusion one thing now becomes crystal clear.'

'And what is that?'

'That the time has come for James Leagrave to answer for himself.'

Chapter Seventeen

Even from a distance of several yards away, it was perfectly obvious that the window nearest to the door of John Rawlings's shop in Shug Lane had been neatly broken. Hurrying forward, the Apothecary's suspicions were all too horribly confirmed. The glass lay on the cobbles below, two of the panes smashed, the fragments picked out to allow a gloved hand to slip through and open the door from inside. With a sinking heart, John put the key in the lock and went within.

Sir Gabriel had obviously been as good as his word and in John's absence had visited the warehouses with his son's list of required products. Yet the chests in which these had been delivered now stood open, the contents spilling upon the floor. Somebody had clearly been in and riffled through the entire stock.

John stood, staring at the damage, wondering if this was just the work of young rips, not unknown to raid an apothecary's shop in search of aphrodisiacs or a cure for clap, or if he should read something more sinister into it. Could it, he asked himself, mean that someone whom he had already interviewed had come searching for something they believed he had found and kept concealed? Or could it simply be a warning? A warning that the murderer was aware of every step he made, even to Sir Gabriel finding him premises in Shug Lane, and that he could not escape his sinister surveillance wherever he went? Shivering with sudden fear, John took off his coat, donned a long apron and set about the task of clearing up the mess, before sending for a glazier and organising the simples he had brought with him from Sussex.

This took him till noon, after which he mixed a pick-me-up for himself, then brewed a strong compound containing common valerian for the malingering Mrs Briggs of Chichester and a blend of lemon balm, well known for driving away melancholy and black choler, for the Comtesse de Vignolles. To this last he added, rather wickedly, an ample measure of a powerful aphrodisiac, hoping that this might solve the Comte's marriage problems for him. Finally, before he reluctantly closed up again, John brewed an elixir of liquorice and meadowsweet to combat the flatulence of Squire Leagrave's sister. Then, with one last pensive look round, he locked his shop securely and proceeded on foot to Hanover Square.

It was a distressing walk, for with every step John agonised over exactly how he should challenge the Comtesse with being at Vaux Hall on the night of the murder. Eventually, though, after formulating and discarding several plans of action, he decided on the light touch, the shocking statement thrown away as a jest, and then a careful observation of the Comtesse's reaction.

For once, or so it seemed, the invalid was not lying on her bed of pain, for, quite clearly, from the first floor drawing room came the sound of a harpsichord and a voice raised in song.

'The Comtesse?' John asked the footman in astonishment.

'Madam is feeling a little better today.'

'It must be my medicine,' the Apothecary replied cheerfully, and was rewarded with an icy stare.

'I will see if my Lady is able to receive you.'

'I should imagine she might do so if I am able to cure her ills.'

The servant did not reply to this bold statement but made his way up the staircase and, after a moment or two, the music stopped abruptly. John smiled to himself as he had rather expected something of the sort, and was not surprised, on being shown into the room, to see the Comtesse sitting on the music stool, one languid hand raised to her forehead.

'Madam, how wonderful to find you in better health,' he said, by way of opening shot, and gave a florid bow.

She looked at him from beneath lowered lids. 'Yes, I believe I have to thank you. The physick you left for me early the other morning certainly seems to have helped. May I ask what was in it?'

'A compound of various unusual herbs,' John answered vaguely. 'Now tell me, when did you first notice an improvement?"

'Why, that very day. At least I think so.'

'And have you been able to get out at all as a result?'

'I ventured into the square gardens and sat for a while in the sunshine.'

'Well, that is a start to be sure. Though really, Madam, I believe a little exercise should now be considered. Nobody ever regained their health by remaining still, you know.'

'Is that so?' said the Comtesse, and John had the horrible feeling that she was laughing at him.

He looked dignified. 'Indeed, it is. But let us speak of other, more congenial, things.'

'By all means.' Again, that faint suggestion of a smile in her voice.

'Have you managed to leave the house on any other occasion? At night, perhaps?'

She stiffened and suddenly became wary, there was no doubt about it. 'Why do you say that?'

'Say what?' asked John, playing the innocent for all he was worth.

'About my going out at night?'

'Idle curiosity, that is all. Though prompted, perhaps, by Miss Rigby, who is, I believe, an acquaintance of yours.'

'Quite true. But what does that have to do with it?'

John gave the Comtesse an ingenuous smile, then laughed. 'Oh, it's just that she told me she thought she saw you at Vaux Hall the other evening. I assured her she must have been mistaken.'

The lowered lids opened wide and the Comtesse gazed at him, her lips slightly parted and her breathing quickened. 'Indeed she must. I have not been to the Pleasure Gardens for some considerable time.'

'As I thought,' answered John, and bowed his head to hide his triumphant smile. There was no doubt in his mind that not only had he shocked the Comtesse considerably, but also that she was lying to cover herself. 'Let it be hoped that soon you will be well enough to brave the evening vapours,' he continued in measured tones, raising his head and giving her another shrewd glance.

She had gone very pale but was in control of herself, though her lips still trembled slightly. 'I presume you have called to bring me some further supplies?' she said at last.

'Yes.'

'Then you really must allow me to pay your fee,' the Comtesse added in an entirely different voice.

So she was going to be formal, he thought. 'Thank you, my Lady. And will you be requiring any more bottles after this one?'

'Yes,' the Comtesse answered, her manner careless now. 'Make me up half a dozen and leave them with one of the servants. I will see to it that you are paid for your trouble.'

She was defending herself by reducing him to the status of tradesman, John realised angrily. 'I shall send my bill in when I deliver the rest of your order,' he replied curtly.

'As you please,' the Comtesse said dismissively and returned her attention to the harpsichord, flexing her fingers over the keys.

She had most cleverly turned the situation round to her advantage, as John was more than aware. He decided on one more attempt at riling her.

'Miss Rigby asks to be remembered to you, by the way.'

'Oh yes?' said the Comtesse, playing a note. 'Are you two then well acquainted?'

'Not really,' said John, as he made his way towards the door. 'It was just that I was dining with her and the Duke of Richmond recently. That is why the subject of Vaux Hall came up. They were both there that night, you see. The night of the murder.'

She had gone pale again, though her voice was calm enough. 'Some poor woman was done to death, was she not?'

'Yes. A girl in keeping, mistress of some rich wretch.'

'Did he do it?' she asked, starting to play.

'He – or his wife,' said John, and bowed his way out.

By the time he arrived at the Public Office, the effects of the previous night were beginning to catch up on him, and John was only too pleased to take a seat in Mr Fielding's first floor room, the air blowing the curtains back from the windows, and avail himself of a glass of cordial.

'So,' said the Blind Beak, 'you have been successful?'

'Yes and no, Sir.'

And John told him everything that had transpired in Sussex, right down to the smallest detail.

The Beak sat in silence for a while, the black bandage turned towards the window just as if he were looking out. 'So it looks as if the Squire's son could be the boy you are seeking.'

'He practically fainted when I mentioned Vaux Hall, as did the Comtesse de Vignolles for that matter.'

'You think that both of them were there?'

'I'm positive of it.'

'You have done well.' The Blind Beak smiled at the Apothecary ruefully. 'But there has been little progress here, I'm afraid. The identity of the Masked Lady still remains a mystery.'

'I must confess that I tried following her from White's last night and got nowhere for my pains.'

'It is her habit to pay off her chairmen and then proceed on foot, I believe.'

'Yes, and she sends her black boy off to act as decoy. She's as cunning as a vixen, that one.'

'Obviously.'

'Her voice is strangely gruff,' John continued pensively. 'Do you think she is disguising an accent of some kind?'

'Perhaps she is a man,' said John Fielding with a laugh. 'She certainly has a masculine character in the way she stays so ruthlessly calm.'

'No, she's a woman,' John protested violently. 'I'm absolutely certain of it. Her very atmosphere breathes femininity.'

Mr Fielding chuckled, a deep melodious sound. 'I bow to your judgement. You have obviously been closer to her than I have.'

'Yes,' said John, and went bright red.

The Blind Beak became business-like. 'Well, you have achieved much on Joe Jago's list, my friend. I must congratulate you.'

'But I am nowhere near solving the crime.'

'On the contrary. You have discovered a great deal. When do you intend to return to Midhurst?'

'Tomorrow morning, early.'

'I imagine you will find out even more on your second visit. You say you have ingratiated yourself with the Squire's spinster sister?'

'I am taking her some medicine for dyspepsia.'

'Excellent, she will no doubt be glad of a new face to look at and a new ear to bend. I am sure that she will be the source of much valuable gossip.'

'I hope so.' John got to his feet. 'I shall come back to London as soon as I have learned something of interest. But, Mr Fielding...

'Yes?'

'Do you think the Masked Lady *is* involved? Do you include her in your list of suspects?'

The bandaged eyes turned towards John. 'Anyone who keeps their true identity so well concealed and was also present on the night of the murder must indeed come under suspicion. I assure you that this Office will continue to watch her with hawk-like alertness.'

Chapter Eighteen

The fine weather vanished in the night and John woke to see pewter skies and deluging rain and soggy, sad trees in the gardens of Nassau Street. Creeping out of the house at daybreak in order to board one of the early flying coaches, he was forced to step through filth and garbage which washed down the streets in a noisome tide, averting his eyes as he did so from a particularly revolting dead dog which came floating slowly past him. Much as he loved London, it was almost a relief on this occasion to get aboard the postchaise and head out to the somewhat cleaner conditions of the Sussex countryside.

Slowed down by mud, the journey took longer than advertised and John did not arrive until after nightfall, bidding farewell to his three fellow passengers who, somewhat nervously, were bound for Chichester in the darkness.

'Good luck,' he called and waved his arm, glad to step into the warm and comfortable confines of The Spread Eagle and, after putting his bag in his room, head for the kitchen.

The fire had been lit on so wretched a night as this and seated before it, as good luck would have it, was Dickon of the wheezing chest. He looked up with a malevolent expression at the sound of a stranger approaching but on seeing John transformed his features into a grimace, as close to a grin as he would ever get.

'Well, that done me some good, that liniment of yours. I reckon I'll have another jar of that,' he said, nodding.

'I'll fetch you some.' And John made to go back upstairs.

Dickon laid a restraining hand on his arm. 'No, sit ye down, Sir. I'll buy you some ale to show my content.'

'Well, thank you,' said John, and took a chair beside him.

It wasn't difficult on this occasion to bring the conversation round to the black-hearted Lizzie, nor was it hard to get Dickon talking, his earlier suspicions of the Apothecary now having been allayed. In fact it seemed almost as if the man wanted to unburden himself in some way, and after a few moments John realised why.

'You remember that girl I told you of, that Lizzie Harper who went to London? You never did meet her, did you, Sir?'

'No, I never met her,' the Apothecary answered truthfully.

'Well, just steer clear if ever you do. She tempts a man, you know, and drags him down to ruin.'

John assumed his sympathetic face. 'Surely she never tried her wiles on you?'

'No, not on me, but on the husband of my poor sister-in-law, God rest her.'

'Your brother, you mean?'

'Bless you, I never did have no brother. No, I meant my dead sister-in-law's husband, Jacob Benbow.'

John's eyebrow's, ever mobile at the best of times, flew across his forehead. 'So Elizabeth Harper was related to you?'

'Aye, she was my niece, as she was Jacob's by marriage. But she led him on, she did, even when she was little more than a child. It broke my sister-in-law's heart to see it and she died of grief.'

John shook his head. "I can't quite work this out. How many sisters were there?'

'Three. Lizzie's mother, my wife and Jacob's wife. Leastways, when the girl's mother passed away it was between Jacob and me which took the child on. I can tell you, she'd have felt my belt about her. I'd never have mooned after her like Jacob did.'

'No wonder you dislike her so much.'

'I'm not the only one. What with the trouble she made in the Leagrave household and breaking poor Jemmy Groves's heart, to say nothing of Eleanor's, why I could have throttled the bitch.'

John took a chance. 'Somebody has,' he said.

Dickon stared at him. 'What was that?'

'Somebody *has* murdered her. It is true that I am an apothecary but I am also here investigating Lizzie's death.'

Dickon's eyes widened further. 'Are you a constable?'

'No, I work for John Fielding, Principal Magistrate of London.'

'Then I'll say no more to you. For I think whoever did it should be rewarded.'

John nodded. 'I respect that view but none the less would like to ask you one final question, not really connected with the killing. It's this. Was Eleanor Benbow's body ever washed ashore?'

Dickon paused reflectively, then downed the contents of his tankard in a single swallow, wiping the back of his hand across his mouth. 'No, Sir, it weren't. And there's some as say that without a body one can never be sure there's been a death.'

'Was she the type of female to do away with herself?'

'No, Sir, she were not,' Dickon answered firmly, and there the matter was allowed to rest.

Despite all John's hopes for a fine day, the next morning was as dark and discouraging as the previous one, and it was with a feeling of trepidation that he set out for Court Green, the home of the Leagrave family. It was hardly the weather for gathering simples from a wild garden and yet he had little other excuse to call, except for the bottle of physick, wrapped in paper and tied neatly with string, a blob of wax sealing the ends, which he carried in his pocket. Onto the bottle itself, John had stuck a label which read, 'Compounded by John Rawlings, Apothecary of Shug Lane.'

The lady of the house, much as he anticipated, was already about the mind-achingly dull tasks which comprised her daily life. Having, no doubt, made it her duty to give her brother and nephew a hearty breakfast in the comfort of the morning room, she was presently overseeing the servants as they followed their many pursuits around the establishment. This last, of course, combined with a stint in the kitchen, to say nothing of checking the menus, providing for her household and working in the still room. In the afternoon, when she could relax, Miss Leagrave would undoubtedly be taken up with her needle or paints, this to be followed perhaps by a little practice on the harpsichord so that the men of the household could be entertained while they slumped in front of the fire, exhausted after a hard day's riding, a decanter at their side. Yet, John supposed, she was probably contented enough in her way.

Miss Leagrave received him in the small parlour, looking extremely flustered, a mobcap on her head to protect her hair from dust.

'Oh la, I had not expected you quite so soon, Mr Rawlings,' she said in somewhat accusatory tones.

He bowed. 'My visit to London did not take as long as I thought. Forgive me, Madam. I was anxious to give you your bottle of physick.' And he produced it with a flourish.

His hostess glanced out of the window at the dismal day. 'And what of your wish to look at the garden?'

John assumed a stoical face. 'Madam, I am used to all kinds of climatic conditions. It will make little difference to me. But, of course, if you desire to accompany me...' He smiled endearingly. '... just to point out those plants that I may not touch, I could not presume to ask you to get your feet wet. I shall call back another time.'

Miss Leagrave's stern features relaxed slightly. 'Perhaps you should wait a while to see if the rain passes. I can offer you some coffee. It may be only London fashion to drink it but my brother, the Squire, is very partial to the beverage.'

'I would be honoured to have a cup,' said John, 'provided that you will take one with me.'

'Well, I am very busy...'

'Then I shall go.'

'But perhaps I could spare a half hour or so. Pray take a seat, Sir, and I will ring the bell.'

'How very kind,' said John, and divesting himself of his cloak, settled himself in a chair by the fire which he felt certain belonged to the Squire.

'Very comfortable,' he said, stretching his legs. 'How I envy you your country life.'

'Really?' responded Miss Leagrave in surprise. 'Why?'

'So peaceful and healthy. The streets of town were stinking with refuse when I left it.'

'But surely one is prepared to endure that for the many compensations.'

'You mean the theatres and assemblies, I take it? Or perhaps you refer to the various pleasure gardens? Or to the balls?'

'All of them really,' Miss Leagrave answered wistfully. 'Of course we do have entertainments here but nothing on the scale of London's gaiety.'

'I must confess,' answered John, taking the coffee which his hostess had just poured from a silver service brought in by a servant, 'that I do have a certain partiality for Vaux Hall. Have you ever been for a visit, Madam?'

'Oh yes, several times. But not for about a year or so.'

John shook his head and looked grim. 'As I mentioned on my last visit, a very nasty incident took place there recently. Some poor wretch was murdered. A girl by the name of Elizabeth Harper.'

Miss Leagrave's cup rattled violently in its saucer. 'Elizabeth Harper? But how extraordinary!'

'Why, surely you do not know her?'

'A girl of that name once worked here as a servant. But that would be too great a coincidence to be believable.'

'They say,' said John, looking gossipy, 'that the victim did indeed come from the country. That she had made her way to town to better herself. She was the mistress of a French nobleman, you know.'

'Was she very beautiful, this murdered woman?'

'Glorious, I believe,' John answered, with an extravagant gesture. 'A regular Helen of Troy.'

'Then it has to be the same girl. How strange.'

'A freakish chance, I'd say. Do tell, what was she like as a person?'

'Cruel,' said Miss Leagrave, tightening her lips. 'Cruel and heartless. Every man was her prize, if you follow me.'

'I do most certainly. How very shocking.'

'She came here from the mill, the miller was her adopted father, you see. Some poor unhappy young man, a labourer called Jemmy Groves, was totally besotted with her, but, not content with that, the little minx set her cap at my own brother.'

'How terrible!'

'Oh yes. Of course he did not respond, being a sensible man of mature years, but the very thought of it was enough to make me dismiss her, though I did allow poor Eleanor to stay.'

'Eleanor?'

'Elizabeth's cousin, who also worked here. The tension between them was enormous because of Jemmy – Eleanor believed herself in love with him – and in the end the situation erupted in the most unseemly manner.'

'What happened?'

'They came to blows in this very house, in the kitchen. Just as I was preparing to entertain guests.'

'How inconsiderate,' said John, his expression pained.

'Lud, Mr Rawlings, it was frightful. The crashing and banging could be heard all over the building and when we rushed to see what it was, they were rolling upon the floor, clawing and biting.'

'What did you do?'

'It was my nephew, James, who separated them, being rather strong for his age. I must confess that I think he thought it amusing. Anyway, I had the wretched girl thrown out of doors and not long afterwards I heard she had gone to London.' Miss Leagrave's expression became earnest. '*Do* you really think it is the same Lizzie Harper, Mr Rawlings?'

'From what you say, it sounds very likely.'

'Then how small is the world.'

'Uncannily so.'

Miss Leagrave gave him a narrowed glance. 'One can hardly credit that fate should bring you, who knows so much about it, here, to the very place in which she worked.'

The lady was no fool and John knew it. None the less he felt unable to take her into his confidence, sensing that the Squire's unmarried elder sister would fiercely protect her brother and nephew against all comers, even if it meant lying in order to do so.

He cleared his throat. 'Life is full of inexplicable events, Miss Leagrave. Who knows what destiny guides our footsteps?' He put down his cup. 'And now I feel I have trespassed upon your time enough. With your permission I shall step into the garden, rain or no rain.'

Still with a look of suspicion about her, his hostess said, 'I shall send one of the gardener's boys to accompany you. He can, perhaps, be of assistance.'

And with that she swept from the room, leaving John in great doubt about whether he had said too much, so that Miss Leagrave had guessed something, if not all, of the truth.

Outside, the rain was falling as hard as ever, though there was in fact something rather beautiful and refreshing about it. Not caring whether he got soaked, John stood stock still, ignoring the boy, who stared at him open-mouthed as the Apothecary listened to the song of a thrush, then tilted his face upwards to be bedewed by drops. He appeared to be even more astonished when John dropped to his knees on the sodden grass and, with fingers quite small and delicate for a man's, started to pluck at the fragile stems of the plants in order to fill his baskets.

'How long are you planning on being out here, Sir?' the boy asked, turning up the collar of his coat.

'Till I've finished,' John answered over his shoulder. 'But you can go in if you like.'

'More than my job's worth, that would be. The Mistress said not to leave your side.'

'I can well imagine,' John said with a cynical smile. He looked up at the boy, sweeping him with a forthright gaze. 'Like gardening, do you?'

'I do, Sir. I've a mind to be head gardener one day.'

'Well, kneel down by me and I'll show you what plants are used to make medicines. That might be useful information for you. It always pays to know more than your elders.' The Apothecary plucked a primrose. 'This flower produces many a good remedy. Were you aware of that?'

'No, Sir.'

'You ought to be, a boy of your age. Tell me, how old *are* you?'

'Sixteen, Sir. One year older than Master James.'

'Known him a long time, I suppose?'

'Six years. I started work here when I was ten.'

'Then you must have met Lizzie Harper.'

An extraordinary expression crossed the boy's face, almost one of furtive excitement. 'We don't talk about her in this house.'

'Oh? Why is that?'

'The Mistress forbade us to.'

'Because she fought with Eleanor?'

'No, not for that. It was for the other thing.'

'What other thing?'

But the boy had closed his mouth firmly, shaking his head. 'No, Sir, I'm forbidden. If I tell I'll be dismissed.'

'I understand,' said John, and turned his full attention to the gathering of his simples.

An hour later he had finished, by now wet through and caked with dirt. Bowing on the front door step, too unkempt to come into the house, John's crooked smile flashed in his grimy face as he took his leave of Miss Leagrave.

'My dear lady, how can I thank you enough? I only hope that my physick brings you relief from your ills. Should you require any more bottles, which I shall be happy to present to you as a gift, please send word to The Spread Eagle. I shall be there for a few more days.'

'Have you found all you were seeking?' asked Miss Leagrave, very pointedly John thought.

He decided to answer in an equally barbed manner. 'Not quite all, Madam. There are still one or two things left to discover.'

She twitched her eyebrows and said nothing, and John had no option but to take his leave, trudging off through the rain, well aware that any further visits to Court Green would probably have to be made in secret.

The next obvious move would appear to be a confrontation with James Leagrave, including a search in his clothes press, seeking the coat from which the piece of material had been torn, even though John was beginning to despair of this line of enquiry. So far, not one of the men in the case had owned a garment even resembling the fragment, and he was fast coming to the conclusion that the killer was aware of what had happened and had disposed of the evidence. However, there was still a chance that the torn coat was being hidden somewhere, and he was not quite ready to give up the search without one further attempt at finding it. Hands in his pockets, John plodded through the rain, marshalling his thoughts.

There was no apparent motive for James wanting to kill Lizzie, despite Sir Gabriel's belief that the boy could well have nursed a youthful passion for her. Yet John's chat with Miss Leagrave had revealed one new and very interesting fact. The murdered girl had thrown herself at the Squire who had, apparently, refused her.

'But I wonder,' thought John, 'I just wonder about that.' Then big mind went on to the task before him and he braced his shoulders.

Before he left London, John Fielding had asked that the Apothecary should take it upon himself to break the news of Elizabeth Harper's death to her adopted father.

'I'm afraid you must act in your official capacity, Mr Rawlings. A most unpleasant duty, but there it is.'

'Then I will have to reveal to him the fact that I lied when we last met,' John had protested.

'Not lied, merely did not tell all the truth,' the Blind Beak had answered urbanely, and there the matter had been allowed to rest. And now the moment had come. Pulling his watch from an inner pocket, John saw that he had spent so long in the wild garden that he had missed dinner completely, and decided there and then to go to the mill and get the awful task over.

It was almost dark by the time he reached his destination, though not so much because of the lateness of the hour as the general gloom of the day. The great wheel was silent once more, the milling having been done that morning, but John gazed anxiously at the swollen pond, thinking how treacherous it would be to miss one's footing in the darkness. Just as uneasy as he had been on the last occasion he had come to this place, he knocked softly on the cottage door.

Jacob Benbow answered almost immediately and stood swaying in the opening, his hair and body as drenched as John's, proving that he, too, had recently been walking in the rain.

'Yes?' he said belligerently, and the Apothecary could tell by his slurred speech and general demeanour that the man was well on the way to being drunk.

'Rawlings, Master,' John answered politely. 'I wonder if I might step inside a moment out of the downpour.'

The miller stared into the gloom. 'Who the devil are you?' he asked unpleasantly.

'John Rawlings, the apothecary who came here the other day.'

'Oh yes, I remember. The flower gatherer. You'd better come in.'

And with that Jacob stepped back to allow John into the cottage, where he stood in the humble room, the water dripping from his clothes forming a puddle round his feet.

The Apothecary cleared his throat, trying to look as solemn as he could with a trickle of water running down his nose. 'Master Benbow, I'm afraid I have some very bad news for you,' he began.

The miller looked at him blankly, as if he hadn't understood a word his visitor said.

'It's about your adopted daughter, Elizabeth Harper,' John continued bravely.

'Elizabeth?' Jacob repeated hoarsely. 'You have word of her? Dear God, I never thought I'd live to see the day.'

'The tidings are not good, I'm afraid. I lied to you previously when I told you I knew nothing of her. The fact is that I *do* have information, quite a good deal of it, but it is not pleasant. The truth, Master Benbow, is that Elizabeth is dead.'

'Bastard!' screamed the miller. 'Blackguard! Knave!' And seizing John's collar in a huge ham of a fist, he swung him into the air, his feet kicking helplessly above the floor.

'For God's sake, man,' John gasped, half choking. 'I am only the messenger. If you kill me you'll have to answer to John Fielding, London's Principal Magistrate. For I am his representative and he'll come looking for me, rest assured.'

'You're a liar and a thief,' Benbow continued, the veins bulging on his forehead. 'Nobody tells me that my girl is dead. Nobody, d'ye hear?'

'Did you love her that much?' panted John, spots swimming before his eyes.

'Aye, I did,' Benbow answered, and then as suddenly as he had picked the Apothecary up, he released him again and sat down hard in the wooden chair beside the rough-hewn table.

Gulping for air, John watched as the miller thrust his head into his hands and heaved with sobs. 'Oh no,' he kept repeating. 'Oh no, oh no.'

'Look,' the Apothecary said as sympathetically as he could in view of the fact that the man had half choked him. 'I know you worshipped the ground she walked on, probably more so than was natural in the circumstances. But the fact remains that somebody hated your adopted daughter enough to kill her. For that's the truth. Elizabeth was murdered, and now you have been told it all.'

Jacob wept bitterly. 'If only you had known her. Her beauty and her grace. No man could resist her, I tell you. I know what I did was wrong but I couldn't control myself.' A dark eye swivelled in John's direction. 'You didn't know her, did you? You're not one of her lovers pretending to represent the law?'

John shook his head. 'No, I'm dealing straight with you, and I apologise that I did not do so on the last occasion we met.'

Benbow did not answer, merely continuing to weep.

'Listen,' John said quietly, 'I am not here to sit in moral judgement of you. I am a man like any other. But for all that I am duty bound to ask you certain questions. Would you prefer me to come back tomorrow when you are more in control of yourself?'

Jacob looked up, his eyes still pouring. 'No, ask away. Let all the filth come out if it must.'

'Right.' John took a seat opposite him and poured out two beakers of ale from the pitcher that stood on the table. 'Firstly, you were her lover, I suppose?'

'Yes, yes,' answered the wretched man brokenly. 'I corrupted her when she was scarce more than a child. I have lived with the shame ever since.'

'Perhaps,' the Apothecary answered in a very quiet voice, 'she wanted you to make love to her. After all, you were not tied by blood.'

'No, but I had the responsibility for her welfare and I grossly betrayed that trust. I am less than the dust and must carry my scar to the grave.'

A thought occurred to John and he asked, 'Did Eleanor know what was going on?'

Jacob's head came up and he looked at his questioner properly for the first time. 'No, I don't think so. Why?'

'It was just an idea I had. And tell me one thing more. Was Eleanor's body ever washed ashore?'

'No, it wasn't. Why are you asking these things?'

'Because I want to assure myself that she really is dead. How do you know that she didn't wander off somewhere? What proof have you?'

'None, except that my daughter wouldn't do that to me.' And then the miller obviously made the connection between John's earlier question and this and gave the Apothecary a startled look.

'Be that as it may, would it be possible for me to visit her room before I go?'

The miller shook his head, the water glistening on his matted curls. 'What good would that do?'

'None, probably. It's simply that I would like to get some idea of what she was like and seeing her things might help me.'

'Very well.' Benbow sighed heavily. 'I'll take you up before you leave. And then will you have done with me, Sir?'

'Almost,' said John soothingly. 'There's one more thing. Confirm for me if you will that Elizabeth's beauty brought its share of enemies.'

'Aye, that it did. Men desired her and women were jealous. A fierce and powerful combination.'

'Indeed it is.'

The miller paused, then said slowly, 'Do you think there's a chance my Eleanor could still be alive, Sir?'

'Who knows?' John answered, as he followed Jacob Benbow up the wooden spiral to the place where both Lizzie and Eleanor had once shared an overcrowded bedroom.

Chapter Nineteen

It stopped raining as night fell. John, glad of the time and the solitude which walking gave him, made his way along the wooded path leading to Midhurst, his mind teeming with ideas, by far the most powerful of which was the extraordinary impression created on him by Eleanor Benbow's few possessions. He had stooped his way into the narrow confines of the little attic room and looked about him, to see that one bed and its accompanying shelf had been stripped, cleared, only the belongings of one girl remaining in evidence. John had turned to Jacob questioningly.

'All Eleanor's,' the girl's father had said. 'What Elizabeth left behind, my daughter burned when Jemmy died.'

The Apothecary had said nothing, letting his eyes wander over the collection of tawdry things that once had been a young woman's treasures. He saw a cheap fan and some laces, a little painted box and a plait of ribbons, a handful of tricks and trinkets of the kind that gypsies sell at fairs. And then, nestling beside them, incongruous and somehow out of place, John had also seen a pack of cards and a pair of dice.

He had turned to Jacob, surprised. 'You did not tell me that Eleanor liked to gamble.'

The miller shook his head. 'She didn't, Sir, not as such. Yet she was the finest card player in the district. She learned up at the Squire's house, you see.'

'Extraordinary,' the Apothecary had said, and had quivered momentarily as just for a second he had felt something of Eleanor's personality.

Thinking about her like that, utterly absorbed through all the journey back, it was almost a shock to John to walk into the light, warmth and noise of The Spread Eagle. A noise which tonight seemed twice as loud as usual. Following the sound, he made his way through the hall towards the parlour and opened the door to see a merry bucolic scene, one, indeed, that could have come straight from a print depicting country life.

Seated round the table near the fire, a table currently groaning beneath a whole assortment of bottles and glasses, were half a dozen or so gentlemen, the state of whose clothes showed that they had just returned from a day's hunting and were now taking liquid refreshment to cure any ailments brought about by damp. At the precise moment that John entered, one of the company had risen to his feet and was proposing a toast.

'Here's to the fox and here's to the hounds and here's to the Squire for giving us grounds.'

It was a meaningless enough rhyme but it brought a roar of approbation from the assembled huntsmen, who chorused, 'The Squire,' and rose to their feet.

'Thank you, gentlemen, thank you,' answered one of them, then turned his head to look at the newcomer who stood framed in the doorway. 'Welcome, Sir, whoever you are. I hope you're a drinking man for we don't like shirkers round here.'

'I'll sink a bumper with you gladly,' John answered in a cheery voice reserved for just such hearty occasions. He held out his hand. 'Rawlings, Sir. John Rawlings.'

'How dee do,' answered the other. 'Ralph Leagrave's the name. I own the house yonder.'

'Ah, *Squire* Leagrave,' John responded respectfully. 'How nice to make your acquaintance, Sir.'

Sir Ralph looked pleased. 'You've heard of me then?' This said amidst a roar of raucous laughter.

'Most certainly,' John answered, endeavouring to look impressed. 'Why, it was said in the kitchen on the very first night I came here that no one could claim to know Midhurst if they did not know the Squire.'

Leagrave roared and slapped his thigh. 'Well said, boy. Take a seat.'

He was a caricature of his type, his face the colour of crisp bacon, his hair sandy, his eyes both blue and bloodshot. Further, Squire Leagrave boasted a set of huge white teeth which sprung over his lips when he smiled. John stared at them, fascinated, wondering if they could possibly be his own.

'Now, Sir, what will you have, you being a drinking man and all?' The Squire winked heavily at his companions.

'A little brandy, I think,' John answered, 'the night being somewhat chill.'

'Good fellow,' roared the other, and poured John a measure so strong that he quailed at the very sight of it. 'Now let's see you get that down,' he added, and slapped the Apothecary on the back.

So here, obviously, lay the initiation rite. Anybody who could remain upright at the end of the session was considered fit for the Squire's company, those who fell to the ground or vomited would be shown the door. Wondering quite how he was going to cope, John took a tentative mouthful.

The liquor burned his throat like fire, causing him to splutter, a fact which sent the assembled company into gales of laughter. Thinking to himself that this was going to be an unforgettable night, John swallowed the lot and held out his glass for a refill.

The Squire bellowed his approval, great teeth flashing. 'I see you're a fellow to be reckoned with, Sir. Whereabouts did you say you come from?'

'London.'

'Ah, now there's a place.'

'I take it you visit our sinful city?'

'Damme, do I look the sort of man who would not?' Ralph Leagrave rumbled a laugh. 'Believe me, I go to taste the town's sweet fruits as often as I can.'

'God preserve us! thought John, only to hear the huntsmen guffaw en masse at the *double entendre*. The Apothecary's mind ran on, wondering how Elizabeth could have brought herself to flirt with such a creature. With a wave of courage brought about by the brandy, he decided to find out.

'I met a girl from Midhurst recently,' he said. 'A beautiful creature she was, name of Elizabeth Harper. Did you know her by any chance?'

The Squire's eyes tightened and his terrible smile disappeared. 'Yes, I did as it happens. She used to work for me. Where did you come across her?'

Wondering just how much the man knew and whether he might possibly be aware by now that Lizzie had been killed, John answered with caution.

'Well, to be honest, Sir, I encountered her in the brothel in Leicester Fields. She was – er – *employed* there, if you take my meaning.'

The Squire hesitated, a man-of-the-world expression hovering but not quite appearing. He downed a vast glass of port and appeared to come to a decision.

'You're a cock sparrow and no mistake,' he said, slapping John on the back with a leathery hand, hard as a hammer. 'Why, we're all chaps together, what?' He looked round at his fellow huntsmen with a confiding leer. 'Of course, it's well known in these parts that Lizzie left for London because I would not take her for my wife.'

'Eh?' said John, totally surprised.

'Ah, you might well look askance, as did my sister. Truth to tell, John my friend, the gal threw herself at me. Hoped I'd make her the next Lady Leagrave, ideas above her station, d'you see. Damme, but that was an awkward situation 'cos I'd been a naughty chap, when all's said and done. Anyway, my sister – God bless her – gave Lizzie notice to quit, so that saved my face.'

'Not just your face!' commented one of the cronies.

Sir Ralph roared with laughter and slapped his thigh. 'Not just my face! 'Zounds, but that's rich. Don't you think so, John?'

The Apothecary, now downing brandies to give himself strength, nodded feebly.

'So she ended up in a brothel, eh? I might have guessed.'

'Then you never saw her after she left Midhurst?' asked John, focusing what was left of his wits.

The Squire narrowed his eyes. 'Strange that you should say that, because I did, just once, though she didn't notice me.'

'Where was this?'

'In Vigo Lane,' Sir Ralph answered surprisingly. 'I was going to visit a little lady of my acquaintance who had an apartment there. And there was Lizzie, mincing along as dainty as you please. I didn't call out in view of the circumstances.'

The brandy was beginning to take effect and John realised that he was slurring very slightly as he said, 'Do you go to the balls and assemblies when you're in town, Sir, or do you prefer the theatre and pleasure gardens?'

'I like Covent Garden best and you can guess why,' Sir Ralph answered, smirking. 'But the pleasure gardens and assemblies are more my meat than theatres. Trouble with them is, you have to listen.'

'Damn shame, that,' answered an associate, slumping forward in his chair.

'Do you prefer Vaux Hall or Ranelagh?' persisted John, gamely trying to make some sense of his line of questioning.

'Love the former, particularly The Dark Walk. Don't like Ranelagh at all. Only visited there twice and went off it straight away. No Dark Walk, that's the damnable trouble. All puff, no blow.'

John consumed yet another brandy, feeling that he had now reached the stage of kill or cure. 'Indeed, sir, indeed. Forgive my saying, but you have a look about you that's familiar, do you know. I wonder if I could have seen you at Vaux Hall. I all but live there in the season.' He concentrated his fast scattering wits and gazed at Squire Leagrave as narrowly as his swivelling eyes would permit.

'Possible, I suppose,' said Sir Ralph, belching a little. 'I was there in April at the start of the season but haven't been since.'

'Then I must be mistaken,' John answered lamely, unable to judge by now whether or not the Squire was lying.

Sir Ralph sank a bumper. 'You're a fine young fellow, so you are. Would you not agree, gentlemen?' There was a groan of assent from the others at the table, 'I've a mind to ask you to the ball I'm giving. In fact, I will. Come on Saturday night and see how we country fellows amuse ourselves.'

John's faculties were still sharp enough to register that here lay the golden opportunity not only to see James Leagrave at close quarters but also to examine the clothes press of both father and son.

'Honoured, Sir,' he said, rising swayingly to his feet. 'However, there is one small difficulty.' His words were falling over one another and he knew it.

'Which is?'

'I have not brought any good garments with me.'

'My tailor will run you something up,' responded Sir Ralph, his expression betraying that he was pleased John should regard rural pastimes so highly he should worry on that account.

'Just so,' the Apothecary answered and, as he fell back into his chair, hoped fervently that Mr Fielding would regard the purchase of a new suit of clothes as a justifiable expense.

For a country tailor, the Squire's man did very well indeed. Clothed entirely in rose red velvet, an unusual choice of both colour and material as far as John was concerned, he felt quite the rake as he set off for the ball with his buckled shoes shining, and his white shirt and hose immaculate, wondering whether there would be any pretty maidens present whom he could impress with his tales of London life. And then he remembered Miss

Edith Leagrave and hoped that she would not put too great a damper on the evening by telling her brother that John was nothing more than an inquisitive young apothecary who had asked too many questions to suit her taste. Therefore, it was with mixed feelings that John arrived on foot at Court Green and announced his presence by a firm knock on the door.

Earlier that afternoon he had tried to picture what such bucolic revels might be like and now John found himself pleasantly surprised. A great effort had been made with the Squire's ballroom, which was brightly decorated with garlands of flowers and many shining candles and even had a little gallery above in which sat a group of musicians, more notable for their enthusiasm than the accuracy of their playing. Down the sides of the room had been placed benches and chairs for those who wished to sit out the dances and, looking along their length, John was pleased to observe several personable young women in pretty dresses. Leading off the ballroom was an alcove in which Miss Leagrave had laid out some lighter refreshments, cakes, syllabubs, lemonade and the like. Another table, standing close by, bore an enormous punch bowl and dozens of bottles of wine, standing in coolers, waiting to be decanted into jugs. Peering into the dining room, John could see yet another board groaning with hams and sides of beef and vast hands of pork. There could be little doubt Squire Leagrave did very well for himself, and his friends and neighbours into the bargain.

The musicians struck up a country dance with a chord of flute, fiddle and drum, and John, turning to the lady on his left in order to invite her to dance, found himself staring straight at Edith Leagrave.

'Oh, it's you,' she said rather coldly. 'I was not aware that you and my brother were acquainted.'

John bowed. 'We met in The Spread Eagle, Madam. May I have the pleasure of this dance?'

She looked fractionally annoyed but none the less gave a small curtsey and John, seizing her round the waist, whirled her away to the jolly tune of Big Breasted Susan. Somewhat flushed, Miss Leagrave gamely kept up as her partner leapt and cavorted in a positive frenzy of steps.

'Heavens,' she exclaimed, as the music ended, 'I had not realised that dance was quite so wild.'

John bowed again. 'May I fetch you a cooling syllabub, perhaps?'

'Thank you, no. I must see to my other guests, if you will excuse me.' And dabbing at her forehead with a lace handkerchief, Miss Leagrave made her escape.

Standing by the punchbowl, dressed in dark green and looking every inch the typical tippling rural squire, was Ralph Leagrave and, there beside him, quite the dandy in powder blue, John spied the youthful figure of James.

'Ah,' said the Squire cheerfully as the Apothecary approached. 'Here's a chap after your own heart, my boy; a bright young sprig from London. Mr Rawlings, may I present to you my son, James.'

'We've already met,' said the young man, colouring up.

'Have you?' exclaimed Sir Ralph, surprised.

I *must* get in quickly, John thought, before the wretched little beast says something.

'Yes, indeed,' he answered, with a polite nod of his head. 'I called at your house the other day, Sir Ralph. You see, I am an apothecary by profession and I wanted to ask Miss Leagrave if I could gather some simples from your garden.'

The Squire looked astonished. 'An apothecary, are you? Well, well! You don't look the dry as dust sort to me. I'd have put you down for a man of fashion.'

John looked apologetic. 'I try to be both, Sir.'

The Squire guffawed and slapped John so hard on the shoulder that he rocked on his feet. 'Well said, boy. Now there's an answer for you. Times are changing and I've been the first to see it. There's nothing to stop those with an honest trade from emulating their betters when they are out and about. Indeed, I'm all for it. 'Zounds, Mr Rawlings, if you ain't an example to us all.'

'Thank you for your generosity, Sir,' answered John, tongue well and truly in cheek, and was aware that James was looking at him suspiciously.

'Not at all, not at all,' Sir Ralph went on, blissfully unaware. 'Now, James, I want you to copy your old father and be as democratic as I. Have a chat with young John here, do. It is the coming trend, mark my words.' And with that he filled his glass to the top and walked away.

But it was obvious, John thought, observing the pinched look round James's nostrils and the two high points of colour which had suddenly flared in his cheeks, that young master Leagrave was alarmed by the very idea. The fact that John had hit him on the raw when he had mentioned London, was more apparent than ever.

'May I introduce somebody with whom you may dance?' James now asked stiffly.

'How kind of you,' John answered, giving a winning smile which clearly fell on stony ground.

'Miss Phoebe Rolands, the curate's daughter, is very charming,' the youth went on, and escorted John to the benches at the side of the room, pointing out the ugliest girl in the entire assembly.

'It will be a pleasure,' the Apothecary said without a flicker, and gallantly bowed to the blushing Miss Phoebe, who accepted his offer of a dance with a great deal of confusion.

It was not so much that she was fat but rather an odd shape and John felt as if he were whirling round the room with a feather bolster, for wherever he laid his hands on the unfortunate girl, she seemed to collapse. Consequently, he found himself half carrying her and was fit to drop when he fiddler finally scraped the last discordant notes of the dance, which had been executed at the breakneck speed of a gallop.

'Syllabub, Miss Phoebe?' he panted, wiping the sweat from his face.

She dimpled pinkly. 'Oh yes, please.'

'My pleasure,' said John, and dragged himself to the refreshment alcove returning with a single glass.

'Are you not having one?' she asked, disappointed.

'I thought perhaps I would just go out for a breath of air.'

She looked wildly discomfited, as if he had mentioned something rude.

'Oh, I see,' she managed to gasp.

Thinking perhaps that he knew the cause of her embarrassment, John made things ten times worse by saying, 'It really *is* in order to cool down.' After which, he hurried away, unable to cope with the abashed Miss Phoebe a second longer.

Swiftly leaving the ballroom, John passed, by way of a small anteroom, into the hall beyond, from which rose a fanciful staircase, dividing on itself at the top. Peering round to make certain that he was not observed, John quietly make his way up, taking the right hand flight and finding himself in a long dark corridor. Very stealthily, he crept along it, silently opening the first door he came to. The room he was gazing into, though clean and aired, was obviously reserved for guests for it had the dull air of a place rarely used. Terrified of discovery, John made his way onwards and opened yet another door.

It would seem that this time he had come upon the Squire's bedroom judging by the great four-poster bed, the large clothes press, the chests-of-drawers and the dressing room beyond, through the open door of which he could glimpse an interesting selection of articles. For on display were several bottles, at least a dozen wig stands, some of them adorned with headpieces of a rather old-fashioned type, a leather bucket full of riding whips and, crowning all, a glass containing a formidable set of false teeth.

'Damme!' said John, and very quietly made his way inside, closing the door behind him.

The clothes press, which stood in one corner, was relatively new, albeit somewhat simple in design. Made of pine, it consisted of a hanging space above three rows of drawers beneath. There was a key halfway down the right-hand door, which John turned warily, almost as if he expected something to leap out at him.

The garments revealed as the door swung open were the most extraordinary mixture he had ever seen, for they ranged from the downright shoddy to suits of fine stuffs. Presumably, John thought, this variety echoed the Squire's life, from the shabby to the over-dressed, from the huntsman to the lady's man. Very much intrigued, he began to search through with deft fingers, looking for anything made of blue. Yet, though there were several items, there was none that matched the torn fragment which John held in his hand, drawn from an inner pocket for the purpose of comparison. It would seem that not only had Sir Ralph Leagrave been telling the truth about his last visit to Vaux Hall but also did not own a coat made of the vital material either – or else had destroyed it.

The other rooms were empty, all kept for guests, and it was not until he had gone to the opposite passageway, leading off the left hand flight of stairs, that John found more inhabited bedrooms. It seemed that Edith Leagrave and her nephew both dwelled in the same wing, perhaps to keep well clear of Sir Ralph. Having taken a cursory glance round the chamber belonging to the Squire's sister, the Apothecary made his way to the next room and found himself in a young man's domain.

There were clothes everywhere, lying in heaps, piled on the bed, some, rather grubby, concealed in a corner. John shuddered, his own quarters constantly kept immaculate, even when he was very young. It had always seemed to him that there could be no such thing as tidiness of thought whilst living in the midst of chaos. Very distastefully, John began his search.

And it was then, with his head in the clothes press and his back to the door, that the Apothecary heard a sound behind him. Spinning round, he saw that the bedroom door was slowly opening and knew that it was too late to try and hide. Bravely, his mind running over a million excuses, John braced himself for whatever was to follow next and drew in a breath of sheer cold panic as he heard a voice say crisply, 'And what the devil, Sir, do you think you're doing in here?'

Chapter Twenty

John froze. Then wheeled round to see that it was James Leagrave who stood in the doorway, his fingers clenched into fists, his features flushed with fury. Staring at him, the Apothecary came to an instant and vital decision.

'What I am doing,' he responded icily, 'is inspecting your room, Sir.'

'How dare you...' James started to blurt out, but John held up his hand in such an authoritative manner that the young man's protests died away.

'James Leagrave,' the Apothecary continued commandingly. 'I am here representing Mr John Fielding, Principal Magistrate of London, and carry his letter of authorisation upon me.' He drew it from an inner pocket. 'So the reason why your bedchamber is being searched is simply this: I am investigating the murder of Elizabeth Harper who was done to death at Vaux Hall Pleasure Gardens on the night of 21 May, 1754.'

James went a livid shade of ash but said nothing.

'The connection between you and the deceased girl is known,' John continued ruthlessly, deciding to take a risk, 'and I have every reason to believe that you were present at the Pleasure Gardens on the night of her killing. So, Sir, I must ask you to answer for yourself.'

James swallowed noisily. 'Can I come into the room?'

'I not only want you to enter, I also want you to shut the door and tell me the truth. Now, were you at Vaux Hall that night? Reply to me.'

'Yes,' said the boy wretchedly, 'yes I was. But that doesn't mean I killed Lizzie, by God it doesn't.'

A certain unscrupulousness that had always been part of the Apothecary's make-up overrode any pity, he might have felt for the unhappy youth who stood before him, chin wobbling defiantly.

'Do you own a coat of this material?' he hissed, and thrust the torn fragment under James's nose.

The young man's eyes widened in amazement. ''Zounds! Where did you get that from?'

'I believe you have a great deal of explaining, to do,' John continued harshly. 'You see, it was found clasped in the dead woman's hand, ripped from the garment of the man who did her to death.'

James clutched his throat, making a ghastly retching sound, then his legs went from under him and he sat down hard on the bed. His bulging eyes and ghastly colour were so piteous that John relented. 'I think,' he said, sitting down on the bed beside him and offering James his hip flask, 'that you had better tell me the whole story from the beginning.'

'You mean starting when Lizzie first came here?'

'Yes, I do. Take your time. And, Master Leagrave...'

'Yes?'

'Don't leave anything out. However small a detail, it could be important.'

James wiped a tear from his eye. 'It began two years ago. Lizzie came to work here initially, before Eleanor, I mean. I was thirteen then and she was the first really beautiful girl I had ever met. Even though she was a few years older than I was, it didn't stop me falling in love with her.' His cheeks blazed. 'I know what you're thinking, that all boys are the same at that age. But I really cared for her, madly in fact. And then my father came on the scene, filthy old lecher, promising her the earth if she would share his bed.'

'And did she?'

'Of course she did. But not before... before...'

'She had introduced you to the delights of passion?'

James hung his head. 'It happened when I became adolescent. I couldn't help myself, you must believe me.'

'I do – truly. Anyway, go on.'

'My father tired of her, naturally. In fact, not so much that, as grew frightened she would make demands on him. I think he encouraged Eleanor, who had joined the staff by that time, to have the fight with Lizzie. He had been looking for an excuse to put the girl out of doors. It nearly destroyed me when she went, because I loved and hated her all at the same time, do you understand me?'

John nodded. 'Perfectly. So what happened next?'

'Lizzie left the house and shortly afterwards we heard that she had gone to London. Her adopted father lamented his lot and so did Jemmy, a great ox of a creature who worked as a blacksmith. I never could stand that fellow.'

A bit of his old confidence was returning and John gave him a reproving glance. 'Never mind about that. Just tell me what occurred.'

James stroked his chin. 'Let me get this right. She'd been gone about ten months when the Groves man committed suicide. I suppose you know about that?'

John took a swig from the flask and passed it back to James. 'I certainly do. Though I wonder why he waited so long.'

'The rumour was he had managed to trace Elizabeth and had begged her to come back, but that she had written him a letter refusing.'

'So her address in London was known to someone,' John said reflectively.

James flushed once more. 'Yes, I suppose it must have been.'

The Apothecary tightened his eyes. '*You* had it, didn't you?'

The youth looked away. 'I can't deceive you. Yes, I got it from Eleanor.'

'So she knew it too!' John changed his voice. 'And did you call on Lizzie during one of your famous visits to town?'

'Yes, I went to see her in Vigo Lane.'

John nodded his head slowly. 'And there you met an old woman called Hannah who told you that Elizabeth Harper had moved on.'

The astonishment on James's face was too spontaneous to be feigned. 'No, I didn't. I saw Lizzie. She used to entertain me in the afternoons.'

John smiled grimly. 'Go on.'

'Then one day she told me not to come any more. Said she was going away and I should cease to call.'

John looked thoughtful. 'I see! Now tell me about the night of the murder. How did you come to be at Vaux Hall?'

James gave a sheepish grin. 'My father and aunt were away, playing whist with some neighbours. I snatched the opportunity of their absence to try and raise my spirits. I went to the Pleasure Gardens with no idea that Elizabeth would be there, then I saw her at the lighting of the Cascade.'

The Apothecary turned on him like a whip. 'So you *were* present! By your own mouth betrayed. And I know exactly where you were located at that moment, too. You were crouching in front of the onlookers, weren't you?'

'No! I was standing on the very edge of the circle. And how would you know where I was?'

'Because I was there as well. And I don't believe a word you're saying. You were kneeling down, passing yourself off as an apprentice lad. And you were wearing this.' And John waved the piece of material under James's nose.

Master Leagrave looked at him, his mouth harsh and his eyes burning. 'No, by God, I wasn't. I would have told you earlier had I not been so shocked. I did indeed have a coat like that but I lost it six months ago. That's a fact.'

'Lost it? Do you take me for a complete fool? The most incriminating piece of evidence of all and you say you lost it!

James looked even more terrible, if such a thing were possible. 'I did, I tell you.'

He was either lying in his teeth or telling the truth, so obvious was the young man's distress.

'And where exactly did this convenient loss take place?'

James shifted his position. 'That's the devil of it, I can't remember exactly. It happened quite some while ago, you see. I got damnably drunk in London and slept most of the way home in the postchaise. A few days after that I looked for my coat and realised it had gone missing, so concluded I had left it in town somewhere.'

John stood up and paced irritably, still not certain whether the youth was a skilled liar or completely honest. And then James added, 'But I did see the boy you're talking about. I noticed him at once.'

John shot him a black look. 'What did you say, you precocious brat?'

'I said I saw the person you mean. I noticed him particularly because I thought he was wearing my lost coat – or at least one very like it. It's got such a distinctive weave with those faint silver threads.'

John stood stock still. 'I cannot make up my mind about you, you know. But, just for a moment supposing you are being truthful, then I urgently need to question that other lad. He is a vital witness. What colour do you maintain you were wearing that night incidentally?'

'Unfashionable green,' answered James, with reluctance.

For the moment, the Apothecary had no choice but to accept what Master Leagrave had said, and he nodded silently. 'Tell me, do you know the Dukes of Midhurst and Richmond?' he added tersely.

'Slightly. Everyone from round here does. When we were younger, Henry Wilton and I used to be quite friendly but we grew apart as we got older.'

'And what about the Comte de Vignolles? Are you acquainted with him?'

'No, but Lizzie spoke of him, of course. He had her in keeping.'

'While you enjoyed her in the afternoons,' the Apothecary commented drily. 'What about his wife?'

'I never met her. I believe she boasted bad health."

'Then I have one final question for you before we rejoin the party. Have you ever heard of the Masked Lady?'

'The most mysterious woman in London? Yes, most certainly. I have even seen her at play,'

John smiled grimly. 'I thought you probably had.' He caught Master Leagrave by the shoulder. 'If you have been lying to me, you forward little hound, I shall find you out, never fear.'

James shook his head. 'I have spoken truly. I *did* lose my coat. You have my word on it.'

'We shall see,' answered John, stony-faced.

Beneath them, the ball was at its height, the room full of whirling couples. The Squire, fiercely drunk, was pursuing Miss Phoebe in a gallop, and even Miss Leagrave was going through the motions with one of her brother's reprobate friends. John, looking around him with wry amusement, turned to James.

'Have you forgiven your father for his transgression with Lizzie?'

The boy pulled a wicked face. 'Well, yes, I have. Because in the end, you see, I won.'

'What do you mean?'

'That it was me who went to visit her in London, not him.'

'But he had finished with Lizzie by then, surely?'

'She was not the sort of woman with whom one could ever finish,' James answered wistfully. 'It was as if she got inside your brain and refused to go away.'

'Are you saying that the Squire still yearned for her?'

'Oh yes,' said James. 'I am absolutely sure he did.'

He needed to leave, to go into the night air and sift his thoughts, but John had reckoned without rural hospitality, which was not content until all the gentlemen were drunk as lords and the ladies swooning or bedded. Halfway to the front door, John felt a hefty arm throw itself around his shoulder and himself forcibly dragged back into the fray.

'Not thinking of going, are you?' Ralph Leagrave breathed moistly into his ear.

'Yes, I feel I should be off, Sir.'

'Nonsense. The party's only just started.'

'It *is* getting rather late.'

The Squire peered into his face, small eyes glistening. 'You ain't a flincher, I hope? I reckon you town chaps have no stamina, by God.'

'Oh, that's not true...' John started.

'But I envy you, y'know,' the Squire interrupted, obviously by now at the terrible sentimental stage of drunkenness. 'I reckon I'd have made a regular blood had I been born in town.'

John made polite noises.

'Fact is, I have a kind of yen for the place, slip up there as often as I can, as I've already told you, I expect.'

Despite the effects of the wine with which the Squire was plying him, a signal sounded in John's mind and he struggled back to full alertness. 'I'm sure you do, a man of your stamp,' he said, nudging Ralph Leagrave boisterously. 'I'll wager not many weeks pass without your paying a visit to town.'

'Ha ha?' said the Squire, and winked a tiny eye.

'I know you haven't been to the Pleasure Gardens since the season began, I remember that,' John continued, throwing caution to the winds. 'So where have you been, I wonder.'

Sir Ralph lowered his voice to a whisper. 'Where do you think?'

A moment of inspiration came to John. 'To the house in Leicester Fields?' he said, the puzzle beginning to fit.

The Squire roared in astonishment. 'By God, you're sharp. Of course, I have. And while I was there recently, in all that throng, d'you know I saw someone who shouldn't have been there at all. Naughty young scamp!'

He was near the answer, John knew it instinctively. 'And who was that?' he said, his voice shaking very slightly.

'Well now,' answered the Squire, putting a thick red finger to his lips, 'that would be telling, wouldn't it?'

Chapter Twenty-One

He did not stop even to wash or change his travelling clothes; instead John took a hackney straight from The Borough to Bow Street, arriving at the Public Office just as darkness fell. The hour being quite late, the Fieldings had obviously eaten their supper and from the family rooms above the official quarters came the sound of a harpsichord. Just for a second, John stood listening to its music, enjoying the counterpoint provided by a blackbird singing in a neighbouring tree, before he climbed the steps and knocked on the front door, delighted at being able once more to discuss the situation with the finest brain in London.

Joe Jago answered the summons almost immediately, a quill pen behind his ear. 'Ah, Mr Rawlings,' he said, grinning his foxy grin. 'Have you had good hunting?'

'I've learned a great deal,' John answered, 'though the answer still eludes me, I fear.'

'Then I'll step aloft and ask Mr Fielding to join you below. Mrs Fielding and Mary Ann are amusing themselves with songs and it would not be his wish to disturb them. Now if you will be kind enough to wait in here, I'll see that some refreshment is brought to you.'

He ushered John into the same room in which he had first encountered the Blind Beak, the chamber used by Sir Thomas de Veil for the purposes of interviewing his pretty female witnesses. Thinking how much had happened in the short space of time since he had first set foot in there, John took a seat on the sofa.

He had not slept at all on the journey back to London. Instead, his mind had gone over and over all the information he had gathered, trying to collate it into a series of linking facts. If James was to be believed it would appear that by some means, not yet clear, the murderer had either stolen or found Master Leagrave's coat and had then used it to disguise himself. So in that case, what was the identity of the elusive boy? Had Elizabeth broken another lad's heart at some time in the past? Or did someone John had already interviewed briefly don the garment in order to mask his true personality?

With a puzzled shake of his head, he was just about to picture the scene at the Cascade yet again when the tap of a stick told him that John Fielding was approaching. Standing up to mark his respect, the Apothecary turned to face the door as it opened to reveal the looming figure of the great man himself. As the blinded eyes turned towards him, John studied the strong feature of the heavy face, realising yet again that Mr Fielding was of no particularly great age, still in his thirties, in fact. Yet it was almost impossible to credit such a thing, in view of the power and force exuded by the awe-inspiring being John was regarding.

'Good evening, Sir,' said the Apothecary, a note of genuine reverence in his voice.

'Mr Rawlings,' rumbled the other, 'take a seat, do. I have ordered a good bottle of claret to come up from the cellars, to be followed by another if that is not sufficient. Now, pray tell me all that you have discovered.' And with those words the Blind Beak felt his way towards the chair opposite John and sat down, the black bandage turning towards the speaker as the Apothecary began his story.

'So,' said John Fielding eventually, 'it would seem that Squire Leagrave holds the key to it all.'

'To be perfectly honest with you, Sir, I find the man utterly confusing. He lies in a very subtle sort of way. First he told me that he was glad when Elizabeth Harper was sent packing because he was afraid that she was growing too demanding, then James assured me his father still lusted after her. Then he said that he had only seen her once since she left his employ, and that by chance in Vigo Lane. Yet the Squire admitted to me just before I left that he frequents the house in Leicester Fields. He has bewildered me so much that I no longer know what to believe, particularly about his not being at Vaux Hall since the beginning of the season.'

'Urn,' said the Blind Beak and relapsed into silence.

John did not dare utter, too afraid of breaking Mr Fielding's train of thought. Thus he sat, tense and mute, until the Magistrate spoke once more.

'I think that the man tells half truths. He may well have seen Lizzie in Vigo Lane but yet I feel certain he had accidentally come across her in the brothel long before that.'

'Because of the fact that Jemmy Groves knew where she was and wrote to her?'

'Precisely. Who else from Midhurst travelled regularly to town? And who else knew the miller and his family? My strong impression is that Sir Ralph went to Leicester Fields as was his wont, there discovered the whereabouts of his ex-servant, and at some time after that, probably in his cups, passed the information on to Jemmy Groves.'

'Who told Eleanor what he knew, thus enabling her to reveal the secret to James. Yes, I believe that must have been how it happened.'

The Blind Beak did not move, the extraordinary stillness which always surrounded him never more apparent. 'So if James Leagrave is telling the truth it seems that there was someone else at the Pleasure Gardens that night, a someone whom we have been referring to as the apprentice lad, who somehow came by James's coat and used it to disguise himself, never thinking for one moment that its true owner would also be present.'

John looked thoughtful. 'But we cannot necessarily presume that this person is the murderer. He might simply have shrouded his identity for another purpose entirely.'

'And there again he might merely have stolen the coat and the fact he wore it on the night of the murder was pure coincidence. But in any event it might possibly explain why the Duke of Midhurst thought he saw young Leagrave in The Dark Walk but was uncertain of the fact when you pressed him. He probably recalled the coat but thought that the face of the owner did not quite fit.'

'It would appear so, yes.'

The Blind Beak shifted slightly. 'How odd that the Squire would not reveal to you the identity of the person he met in the brothel.'

'I don't know about odd, Sir, but it was certainly irritating. It seemed he gave his word of honour, a gentleman's agreement apparently, not to say who it was.'

'Well, let us see if we can flush that person out. Whoever was present at the time of the killing, however innocent they might presently appear, must of necessity fall under suspicion. Therefore, I intend to take the ultimate step.'

John felt a frisson of excitement run the length of his spine. 'What do you mean, Sir?'

'I am going to ask Mr Tyers to close the Gardens to the public and to re-create the scene with all the players in place.'

'But would they all come?' John asked in astonishment.

The Blind Beak made a small sound of amusement. 'They will be ordered to do so by the Court, Mr Rawlings. Failure to comply will be a punishable offence.'

'But what about the Comtesse de Vignolles and Squire Leagrave?'

'I shall invite them to attend as well. I do not think they will refuse.'

At that moment there was a noise in the passageway and John brightened as the door opened to reveal Joe Jago bearing a tray of delicacies. The clerk twitched his brows at his employer, just as if the Magistrate could see him. 'I heard what you said through the door, Sir. Would you like me to draw up one of my lists?'

'I certainly would, Joe. And be so kind as to check it with Mr Rawlings before he leaves in the morning.'

'The morning?' repeated John.

The Blind Beak smiled tolerantly. 'I imagine that the combination of fatigue, excitement and good wine will deter you from going home tonight and I am therefore delighted to offer you my hospitality.'

'And I am equally delighted to accept.' John paused and his face changed. 'But there is one thing that still worries me, Sir. As neither you nor I know who the apprentice is – unless it is James, of course, and all he said is a sham —how are we going to get him there?'

John Fielding took a sip of the wine that Joseph Jago had poured for him. 'I truly believe, Mr Rawlings, that he must have entered the scene by now. That somewhere, unbeknownst to us at the moment, he is lurking. I therefore feel that if we invite everyone connected with the case, he will be present, come what may.'

'And do you still think that the murderer might be a threat to me? I was unnerved by the forced entry of my shop, I can assure you.'

The Blind Beak nodded. 'I think you should continue to be careful. The killer must be aware that the net is tightening and might yet try to silence you. Particularly when the invitations to the re-enactment are issued. For he will know quite clearly then that I will be relying on your sharp eyes to pick him out.'

John took a mouthful of claret from the glass Joe Jago passed him. 'I hope I'm up to the challenge.'

'I have every confidence in your powers of recollection,' the Magistrate replied, and raised his glass in a silent toast.

'And when shall this re-enactment take place?' John asked.

'One week from tonight, if Mr Tyers is willing. That should give us enough time to contact everyone, wouldn't you say, Joe?'

'Just about,' answered the clerk, who seemed not in the least in awe of his brilliant employer. 'Yes, I reckon that will give us the fun we need to nail a rum customer.'

And with those somewhat incomprehensible words, he left the room.

Having imbibed far too much of Mr Fielding's fine wine, it had been a question of the physician healing himself on the following morning. Dragging some compound from the depths of his bag, John had mixed it with water and swallowed the noxious brew in one enormous gulp. Then, somewhat revived, he had partaken of a light breakfast in the company of Mrs Fielding and Mary Ann, before setting out to visit the Comtesse de Vignolles.

It would seem that the Blind Beak and Joe Jago had worked well into the night, for those invitations that had not yet to be endorsed by the Court were already prepared and waiting to be delivered.

'My husband has asked that you hand this over personally, Mr Rawlings,' Elizabeth Fielding had said, passing John a paper as he sat down at the table.

Glancing at the address above the seal, his brows had shot upwards. 'So I am to visit the Comtesse officially?'

'It would appear that that is the intention, yes.'

'But she has always looked upon me as a helpful apothecary.'

'I am sure you will find a way out of the dilemma, Mr Rawlings,' Mrs Fielding had answered cheerfully, and there the matter had been allowed to rest.

Yet it had been difficult to know quite how to change roles at this stage, and John was still considering whether to say he had found the document lying in the street even as he climbed the steps of the house in Hanover Square. However, common sense told him that a woman as shrewd as the Comtesse would not be deceived, and then he wondered to himself why he had used the word shrewd about an invalid.

Today, though, this same invalid seemed much recovered, for the Comtesse stood in the hall, wearing a gown with immense hoops and a striking hat. Seeing John's look of amazed admiration, she said swiftly, 'I was just about to take the air, Mr Rawlings. But I do thank you for calling. As you can see I am improving daily, so I'd be delighted if you could leave some more physick for me on your way out.'

John bowed respectfully. 'I will gladly do so, my Lady. However, there is one small personal matter about which I must see you urgently.'

She swept him with impatient eyes. 'Really! Can't it wait?'

He shook his head. 'I am afraid not. You see, I have been asked to deliver a letter to you.'

The Comtesse raised a graceful shoulder. 'Then deliver it.'

'It is not quite as simple as that,' John answered, hardening his voice.

'And why not?'

'Because the sender wished to know your mind.'

'Oh, la!' said the Comtesse angrily, and tore open the seal.

Her reactions were as quick as they had been when he had asked her about Vaux Hall, John had to grant her that. For after an initial drawing in of breath, the Comtesse merely cleared her throat and read on in silence. Then she said, 'What nonsense is this?' and cast the letter aside.

'It's no nonsense, Madam,' John replied levelly. 'The fact of the matter is that Mr John Fielding, the Principal Magistrate, wishes you to attend him at Vaux Hall Pleasure Gardens.'

'Whatever for? It seems to me that the world's gone crazed about the place. First you ask me if I've been for a visit when you know I've lain at death's door for weeks. And now the Blind Beak wants me to meet him there. Well I'm damned if I will.'

John shrugged his shoulders. 'The choice is yours, of course.'

The Comtesse pursed her lips. 'And what is the connection between yourself and John Fielding, pray? I thought you were an apothecary and now it appears you are his paid lackey.'

'Lackey, yes. Paid, no,' John replied shortly. 'The fact of the matter is the Beak asked me to assist him with the investigation, to be his eyes, as it were.'

'And is that why you came here? Under false pretences?'

'In a way. Though it was true I had heard about your illness and wanted to help you. That much was genuine.

'You're a fraud, Mr Rawlings,' said the Comtesse furiously, and snapped her fingers under his unsuspecting nose.

They were very lovely fingers, strong, white and supple, and John found himself staring at them intently before he impetuously pulled them towards his mouth and kissed them, smiling crookedly as he did so.

'Fraudster, trickster, call me what you will,' he said. 'Is there a single member of the human race who can claim to be exactly what they seem?'

And, with that, he flourished his way out of the front door before the Comtesse de Vignolles had had a chance to say another word.

The moment John set foot in his home in Nassau Street he sensed a stir of excitement in the atmosphere, and voices coming from the direction of Sir Gabriel's study told him that indeed there was a visitor. Handing his hat to the footman, the Apothecary made his way straight there, pausing only to knock at the door politely.

'Come in,' said his father, and John walked into the room to discover, much to his surprise, that the guest was none other than his friend Samuel Swann, pink with importance and looking excessively earnest.

'What's to do?' asked the Apothecary, astonished that his companion should be there during the day when he should by rights be in his Master's workroom, where he was continuing as a journeyman until such time as he could afford to set up on his own.

'It's Millie,' said Samuel in doom-laden tones. 'She is in peril, I fear.'

Resisting a terrible urge to laugh, John took a seat, not daring to catch Sir Gabriel's eye. His father, however, seemed more than capable of coping with the situation. Pulling a watch from his pocket, he said, 'I have invited Samuel to dine with us so that he can explain exactly what has happened. Fortunately, you have arrived just in time, my boy. I suggest that we foregather in the parlour in ten minutes. Now, I must see to my toilette if you will forgive me.' And he left the room.

Determined not to get involved in conversation until they had sat down to dine, John got to his feet. 'That gives me just enough time to change. I was out all night at Mr Fielding's and feel the worse for it. I'll ring for some sherry for you, Sam.' And he, too, withdrew, still barely concealing a smile.

Sitting beneath the gracious portrait of his mother some while later, waiting until the servants had served the first course, John felt fairly certain he could guess the cause of his friend's agitated fervour. Millie had obviously been told that she must now enter the ranks of the whores and was resisting, as many an innocent had done before her, and sure enough, as soon as the cover had been set, Samuel burst into agitated speech.

'I went to the house in Leicester Fields the other night, to continue investigations on behalf of John,' he added hastily, seeing Sir Gabriel's raised brows, 'and there Millie told me such a tale of woe. She has been asked to join the other girls as a... a...' His voice choked over the word and John looked at him in genuine surprise. It simply had not occurred to him that his friend did more than fancy the little maid, but now he was not so certain.

Sir Gabriel seemed to have come to the same conclusion, for he said smoothly, 'This is obviously of great concern to you, my boy.'

Samuel's neck went the colour of poppies. 'It concerns me that any girl should be forced into such a life against her will.'

Sir Gabriel made no comment, his fork toying with a morsel of fish, and it was left to John to say, 'There's rather more to it than that, I imagine. None of us likes to see a young woman enter a life of degradation but you have taken this particular case to heart, I believe.'

Samuel looked wildly confused. 'Well, I...'

'Oh out with it, man,' John went on, half irritated, half sorry for his oldest friend. 'You're infatuated with her, aren't you?'

Samuel braced his broad shoulders. 'More than that, I think. I feel that I have fallen in love.'

'How long have you known the young woman?' Sir Gabriel asked casually.

'Well, only a few weeks, to be honest. But I was drawn to Millie from the moment I saw her.'

'Is she the girl you mentioned the night we all met at Marybone?'

'Yes, Sir.'

'So you fell in love at first sight, presumably?'

'I am certain I did.'

'Hum,' said Sir Gabriel, and there was a fraught silence.

'What do you intend to do?' John asked, feeling some of his friend's wretchedness, his irritation and amusement gone by now.

'That's just the devil of it, I don't really know. I have no proper place of my own to take her to, and I most certainly couldn't afford to put Millie in lodgings.' Samuel turned to Sir Gabriel. 'I had wondered, Sir, if you might be looking for a servant.' He went an even brighter shade of red. 'I know it is most damnably forward of me to ask such a thing, but I really am rather desperate.'

Sir Gabriel put down his hovering fork and delicately sipped his wine. 'To be honest with you, Samuel, I am not. The household complement is full.'

'Oh I see,' said the younger man dejectedly.

'Furthermore,' John's father continued, 'it would put you in an awkward position, would it not, if I were to engage the girl in such a capacity?'

'I don't quite follow you, Sir.'

'You are my son's friend, your father is my friend, though somewhat distanced since he has moved out of London to Islington. If, as you say, Millie is the woman of your choice, then it would hardly be fitting for you as someone to whom our doors are never closed, to pay court to one of my servants.'

'I'm not sure that I approve entirely of these rigid structures in society,' said John.

'Whether one approves or whether one doesn't, the fact remains that they are there.'

Samuel put down his eating implements and stared glumly at his food. 'Then what shall I do?'

'It is obvious that you need to act quickly,' Sir Gabriel went on, 'so I suggest you get the girl out of her sordid surroundings as soon as you can. I can certainly put her up as a guest for a week or so, which should give you enough time to discuss the whole matter with your father.'

John smiled, thinking what a wily creature his parent was. No doubt, Master Swann would disapprove violently of his son's impetuous choice and try to persuade him otherwise. So at least by removing Millie from imminent harm, Sir Gabriel would allow time for the dust to settle before any further complications came about.

'That would be tremendously good of you, Sir,' Samuel was saying enthusiastically.

'Think nothing of it. My feeling is that the sooner your father is involved the better. The wisest course is for the three of you – you, he and Millie – to discuss the future sensibly.'

'He probably won't approve of her,' Samuel remarked pessimistically.

'That,' Sir Gabriel answered crisply, 'remains to be seen.'

It had grown unseasonably dark as they spoke and, glancing out of the window, John saw to his surprise that the street outside was grey with mist. 'Are you going to fetch Millie tonight?' he asked his friend.

'Yes, indeed. There is no time to lose.'

'Then I'll come with you. The weather looks threatening, not fit for a man to be out on his own in. Besides, I might be able to cause a diversion while you smuggle the girl away.'

'What a good plan,' Sir Gabriel said, nodding.

'Then shall we leave as soon as we can?'

'Yes,' John answered, 'let's put action to the words.'

As he spoke, a chill of excitement tempered by an inexplicable feeling of fear engulfed him and he shivered as he went to fetch his outdoor clothes.

By the time they left Nassau Street to walk in the direction of Leicester Fields, it seemed more like November than June. The mist had turned into a clammy swirling fog and John thought that, had it not been for the rescue of a harmless virgin, likely to be defiled at any moment, nothing would have induced him to have left the house. It was a night for footpads and blackguards to be abroad, and the Apothecary was never more glad than to see the glow of the linkman's torch as he walked steadily in front of them. And then all of a sudden the light was gone. He and Samuel had reached the open space of Leicester Fields and had walked into a rolling ocean of mist.

'I'm lost,' said his friend's voice, right beside him. 'Which way is it?'

'Over there,' answered John, striking out bravely, to become aware only a moment or two later that he was alone, that Samuel had disappeared into that grey sea and there was no-one to keep him company as he traversed the chilling stretch of land that lay before him.

'Samuel,' he called, but his voice bounced back at him, as if off a wall, and there was no reply.

Straining his ears, the Apothecary listened for any sign of life but could only hear the beating of his heart and the singing of his blood.

'Samuel,' he called again, more loudly. And then John was aware of a sound behind him and he swung round, a greeting on his lips. Thus, the hammer-blow to his guts. came without warning, harsh and terrible as it knocked the wind clean out of him.

'Oh God,' John gasped as he doubled over in pain. Then the clammy air stirred as another blow came out of the murk, this to the side of his head. Without a sound, the Apothecary dropped to his knees and the last thing he heard before he lost consciousness was the sound of a woman screaming in terror, quite close to where he lay.

Chapter Twenty-Two

He had not regained consciousness fully until he reached Nassau Street. Before that, John had been vaguely aware of being thrust into a hackney and put to lie on one of the seats, opposite the limp figure of a girl. He had also taken in the fact that Samuel was with them, large and capable, lifting him and the young woman to safety. Then finally had come a sea of willing hands, helping him through his own front door and up to his bedchamber, where John had summoned up sufficient energy to speak to Sir Gabriel, who hovered over him like an anxious elegant black moth.

'Father! What happened?' he had asked painfully, aware that there was a trickle of blood drying by his mouth.

'You were attacked in the fog. Samuel found you lying unconscious.'

'And the girl?'

'It's Millie. She heard a commotion and rushed out of the brothel to see what was happening. The next second she, too, was set upon.'

'By the same assailant?'

'So it would seem. And yet, my son, the motive is obscure. You see, you were not robbed. I have been through your pockets and nothing is missing at all.'

John sat up in bed, wincing as his head throbbed agonisingly. 'I fear that the murderer is growing alarmed.'

'What do you mean?' asked Sir Gabriel, blanching a little.

'I was warned by Mr Fielding to be on the alert. I feel that now the invitations are out for the reconstruction of the crime, it has grown imperative for the killer to make sure I am silenced.'

'My God,' said his father. 'We must arm ourselves. I shall see to it at once.'

John smiled weakly. 'Then I can rest assured. For at the moment I'm too feeble to fire a shot in my own defence.'

'Don't worry,' answered Sir Gabriel softly, 'for whoever it is who is coming after you will first have to deal with me.'

Then, having poured his son a draft of poppy juice, the Apothecary's father waited by his bedside until John fell into a deep dark sleep from which he did not wake until the evening of the following day.

The weather had changed again while he slept. Now it was unbearably hot and oppressive and every window of number two Nassau Street appeared to have been thrown open in order to get a current of air flowing through the house.

Trying to get out of bed, John found that he was weak as a baby and could do no more than crawl back beneath the covers and ring his bedside bell for attention. To which summons Sir Gabriel came so quickly that his son suspected he had been sitting in the servants' quarters for hours, awaiting that very signal.

'Ah, you are awake at last,' he said, looking down at John benignly.

'How long have I been asleep?'

'A night and a day. Even the girl Millie awoke before you did.'

'How is she after such a terrible experience?'

'Rather subdued, but then that is only to be expected. Samuel called earlier today, which raised her spirits somewhat.'

'Did she see who attacked her, by any chance?'

'She said it was a man, that is all.'

'Then she observed him more clearly than I did.'

'Obviously, and is therefore a vital witness. For that reason I have been trying to impress upon the foolish child that it is essential she come to the reconstruction, for she may notice something that you do not. However, she is not happy about doing so.'

'Why?'

'I think she is afraid, poor soul. Anyway, enough of that. I shall arrange for a table to be set up in here so that we may have supper together and meanwhile I shall go and change. I am in the mood for déshabillé.'

John smiled broadly. 'That sounds splendid.'

'May I ask Millie to step in and have a word with you?'

'By all means.'

He had thought her pretty when he had seen her in the brothel. But now, washed and dressed with care and without the terrible signs of fatigue about her, the girl had assumed the charm of a delicate piece of china. In fact, other than for a bruise on her forehead, she seemed quite perfect.

'Oh Master John,' she said, dropping a curtsey in the doorway, 'how glad I am to find you better.'

The Apothecary fingered his head carefully. 'It was a damnable hard knock. I get the feeling that whoever did it might well have wanted to lay me out for good.'

'You mean...?'

'Finish me off. Millie, how much did you notice of the attacker?'

'Not a lot really. It was very foggy. Anyway, it all happened so quickly after I heard you shouting.'

'I wasn't aware that I did.'

'Oh yes. You let out a great cry and I came running out of the door to see what was afoot – and then the person hit me.'

'I'll need you at Vaux Hall,' John said urgently, 'I really will.'

The forget-me-not eyes brimmed. 'But I don't want to go. I'm afeared for him to see me again.'

'I'm not exactly looking forward to it myself, but it's got to be done and that's all there is to it. Anyway, Samuel will be there. He'll look after you.'

Millie made a reluctant face. *'Must* I?'

'Yes,' John answered firmly, 'you must.'

Anything further the girl might have had to say about the matter was cut short by the arrival of Sir Gabriel, a sight to daunt a far mightier mortal than she. Clad in a black silk night-rail that swept the floor, a black turban woven about his head, a diamond brooch pinned casually within its folds, John's father loomed like some legendary figure from the Arabian Nights.

'Oh Sir,' she said, dropping a respectful salute.

'Supper has been laid for you in the small parlour, my child,' he said kindly, 'for I would be private with my son.'

'Yes, Sir.'

'So, good night to you my girl, and remember what I said about securing your window.'

'Oh I will, Sir Gabriel. You can depend on it.'

'What's this?' said John.

'A mere safety precaution. We want no trespassers during the dark hours, do we Millie?' His golden eyes flicked over her knowingly.

'Indeed we don't. Sir,' she answered, and turning on her heel went meekly about her business.

It seemed to John that his father had kept both the supper and the conversation deliberately light, for they supped on salad, sipped champagne and talked trivia. And yet he, who knew Sir Gabriel Kent so well, was aware of a tension in the magnificent being which, together with his dark clothes, made the Apothecary see the older man as a stalking panther, tensed for anything that might happen once night fell. None the less it was Sir Gabriel who drew the evening to a close, yawning and bidding John sleep well, yet securing the window personally before he left the room.

Still suffering from the effects of the blow and the large dose of poppy juice, the Apothecary did indeed fall asleep almost straight away, only to dream that he saw the Masked Lady walking through the most bewildering of mazes. 'Wait for me,' be called out in the dream, and woke to find that not only was he mouthing the words but also that he was listening intently.

There was absolute silence in the sleeping house, broken only by the distant tick of the great clock in the hall below, and yet John suddenly felt his spine tingle with fear. Somehow, even though he could hear nothing, a sixth sense told him that someone was creeping towards his room, someone who should not have been in the place at all. It would appear that Sir Gabriel's security arrangements had not succeeded. Sitting bolt upright in the darkness, John prepared to defend himself as best he could. And then, from deep in the heart of the house, a door flew open and he heard his father's voice call out, 'Who's there?'

Not a mouse drew breath, not a creature moved, and yet John was aware of an easing of tension and knew that the danger was past. His door opened to reveal Sir Gabriel, till clad in his night-rail and turban, a candle in his hand.

'Come with me, my son,' he whispered, 'you shall spend he rest of the night in my room.'

'Was there an intruder?' John whispered back.

'I fear that the net is beginning to tighten about you,' us father replied. 'The sooner tomorrow night's business over and done the better it will be for all of us.'

'Is Millie quite safe?'

His father nodded. 'Perfectly. Now come with me.' And he led John by the hand just as if he were still the child of long ago.

Despite the upset, the Apothecary spent the rest of the night comfortably, and the next morning, the day of the re-construction having finally come, set off, as had been previously arranged, to visit the Principal Magistrate in the Public Office. Walking briskly, John arrived at Bow Street just after the Court had risen but, thankfully, before John Fielding had sat down to dine.

The Blind Beak received his visitor in the spacious room above the Public Office, Elizabeth and Mary Ann buzzing in and out in a very companionable manner as the two men sat down to partake of sherry.

'So is all prepared, Sir?' John said, somewhat apprehensively.

'Yes, indeed. Mr Tyers has co-operated and a notice has gone up that the Gardens are closed to the public tonight. The Mesdames were not so helpful but the brothel, too, will not be opening.'

'Why?' asked John, surprised.

'I thought it a wise precaution to invite all the whores. There is just a chance that one of them killed Elizabeth Harper. I have tried to leave no stone unturned.'

'And what about the Comtesse and the Squire?'

'The former has declined on the grounds of her health. The latter has agreed to accompany his son.'

'And the rest?'

'They have all been ordered to come, Mr Rawlings, even the peers of the realm. It will be in their best interests to do so. If not, they can be apprehended and tried for contempt.'

'So you are confident that everyone, even the apprentice, will be present?'

'If he is hidden somewhere amongst their number, yes. If the lad was a stranger, no. We cannot cast our net that wide.'

'And how do you propose to arrange the evening, Sir?'

'I have requested that the company should dress in the clothes they wore on the night of the murder. Could you take note of that, by the way? When everyone has arrived I will ask them to foregather before the bandstand and from there I shall make an announcement asking people to take their seats in the boxes they inhabited earlier. Then the evening will proceed just as it did previously.'

'Until when?'

'Until the moment, Mr Rawlings, when you notice someone not in the place where they said they were. Or perhaps when somebody else sees something not quite right. Of those present not all will have been lying, and those who were telling the truth may yet prove valuable witnesses.' The blind eyes turned towards John. 'But be sure to look out for yourself, my young friend. I received a letter from your father this morning telling me about the attack upon your person and his suspicion that there was someone stalking the corridors of your very home. Because of this, it is my intention to put one of my best men to act as your shadow.'

'Thank you, Sir. It has been a little unnerving.'

'An understatement, that.' The Blind Beak deftly poured another sherry, his fingers acting as feelers. 'Now, tonight, you will arrive by water with Samuel Swann, together with your father and your house guest. I have specifically requested that they accompany you.'

'Thank you, Sir.'

The Magistrate nodded but before he could speak Mrs Fielding put her head round the door. 'Would you care to join us for dinner, Mr Rawlings?' she asked cheerfully.

'Thank you, no,' answered John, finishing his sherry and rising to his feet. 'I'd best be getting back.'

Yet despite his calm manner, he suffered a wave of fear so strong that he wondered if he would ever survive the rest of the day, let alone the dangers of the night. Intent on bracing himself up, the Apothecary turned his footsteps towards his shop, his plan to mix himself a potion. Thus, walking briskly down Great and Little Hart Streets, he made his way through the alleyways into St Martin's Lane.

A sudden overwhelming love of life swept him and he stood stock still for a moment, enjoying the fierce, terrible stink of London. Everywhere there was chaos and disorder, vigour and flurry. He saw eating houses offering meals for a shilling, hackney coaches and carriages crowding narrow streets. John read strange and mysterious signs in shop windows: 'Foreign liquors sold', 'Man for hire', 'Leave your Child for Education'. It was frightening, violent, and at the same time vastly reassuring, and in that moment John Rawlings, Apothecary of Shug Lane, despised the person who had deprived Elizabeth Harper of experiencing this tumultuous cacophony, however black-hearted the girl might once have been. So much so, that in the place of his former fear a steely resolve was born to find her murderer this very night and deliver him into the hands of justice.

Chapter Twenty-Three

It was like a dream. All together, John, Samuel, Sir Gabriel Kent and Millie made their way in Sir Gabriel's coach to the steps known as Hungerford Stairs. There, they hired a boatman to take them down stream to Vaux Hall Pleasure Gardens, drawing their cloaks about them as the Thames breeze rippled and whispered across the river, even on this finest of late June evenings.

John sat in silence, staring at the stars, hardly able to believe that only four weeks had passed since he and Samuel, free only for a few hours from the yoke of apprenticeship, had made this very same journey, laughing and carefree and unaware of the dramatic event that lay awaiting them, an event which would draw one of them into its web and change his life for ever.

In the same dreamlike manner, the boatman drew up at Vaux Hall Stairs and John saw that tonight, instead of the jostling throng of craft that usually heaved round their stony feet, there were only one or two other wherries at mooring, bobbing next to the Duke of Midhurst's private barge. Reinforcing the Vaux Hall beadles at the landing stage stood several other hefty fellows, and the Apothecary guessed that Mr Fielding's men must have arrived at the Gardens early in order to help keep order. This impression was further endorsed when, as Sir Gabriel Kent's party went ashore, one of them stepped forward and said, 'The Gardens are closed tonight, Sir. The Proprietor regrets any inconvenience caused.'

'I am here at the invitation of Mr Fielding,' John's father replied, and received the answer, 'Then please proceed.'

The feeling of illusion, of unreality, deepened as, once again, John and Samuel went through the swing doors in the mundane entrance and down the dark passageway that led to paradise. But tonight this particular piece of heaven had become sinister, a thousand lamps lighting a handful of fallen angels, its great avenues and walkways empty and deserted, a chilling sight somehow.

At the far end of the passage stood Joseph Jago, a spare quill behind his ear, another in his hand. With the aid of a portable ink well, held by an assistant, he was busy writing down the names of all who entered, then ticking them off a master list, also held by the junior clerk, who vas very young and very self-important and obviously quite overwhelmed by the circumstances in which he found himself.

'Ah, Mr Rawlings,' Joe said, on seeing John, 'may I have the names of your companions please?'

'This is my father, Sir Gabriel Kent, my friend Samuel Swann, who was with me that night, and his friend Miss Millie.'

'Then please pass inside and make your way to the bandstand,' Jago answered, and John suddenly found himself once more in the splendour of the Grand Walk, he statue of Aurora glinting as brightly as ever at the far end.

It was almost impossible to comprehend how still the place was. Normally, with the orchestra playing and the cheerful buzz of a thousand voices, the Gardens were full of sound, drowning the natural noises of brook and birdsong. But tonight, John thought, he could have reached out and touched the silence with his hand, so intense was the quiet. In this highly imaginative state, the Apothecary felt as if he were participating in a carnival for the dead, as he made his way to the bandstand through the great echoing hush of the abandoned Pleasure Gardens.

The Blind Beak was already in place, poised on the bandstand where Miss Burchell had stood when she had sung for the crowds below. Behind him, keeping herself to herself but clearly there to help her husband move through this unfamiliar territory, hovered Elizabeth Fielding. Glancing round, John saw that nearly all the principal players were gathered. Richmond was there with Henry Fox and Patty Rigby, who smiled and waved at the Apothecary. Terribly drawn and clearly ill at ease, the Duke of Midhurst stood close by.

'Where's the Masked Lady?' asked John, gazing all around him.

'She's making an entrance now,' his friend replied and quite involuntarily, despite the fact he was standing with Millie and should have known better, Samuel let out a whistle of admiration.

Dressed just as she had been on the night of the murder, the mysterious beauty was sweeping towards them down the Grand Walk, a vision in red and gold. The edges of the Lady's scarlet open robe were stitched with golden flowers, the centre of each one formed by a winking brilliant. The underskirt thus revealed was made of stiffened gold brocade, which shimmered and shone as she came nearer to the bandstand. A fan hung from her wrist on a golden chain, while on her head she wore the same red turban, the scarlet domino concealing her features as before. Despite the fact that her face was hidden, there was no doubt in anyone's mind that she was the most exciting woman present.

The Masked Lady drew level with John and he felt rather than saw her eyes turn towards him, then she flourished on, her heady perfume filling his nostrils, almost making him dizzy with its sensual impact.

''Zounds,' he muttered to Samuel, too low for either Sir Gabriel or Millie to hear. 'Can you imagine spending one precious night with her?'

But the time for small talk was over. From his place on the bandstand, Mr Fielding held up his hand for silence and the murmuring of the small crowd ceased.

'My lords, ladies and gentlemen,' said the Blind Beak in a resonant voice that seemed to echo throughout the Pleasure Garden's empty acres, 'the reason why I have asked you here tonight is to re-enact, as far as is possible, the series of events which culminated in the death of Elizabeth Harper. I hope that this will cause none of you any particular anguish or upset, but I believe we have now reached the point where no alternative course of action is open to us. In a few moments I am going to ask you all to return to the box which you occupied on the night of the killing. There, waiters will attend you and light refreshments will be served. The Duke of Midhurst will sit just where he did and will be accompanied by Miss Coralie Clive from Drury Lane Theatre, who will play the part of Elizabeth Harper.'

There was a cry of distress from someone and Mr Fielding managed to combine the expressions of sympathy and sternness as the black bandage turned in the direction of the sound.

'I realise that some of you may regard this as distasteful, but it is strictly necessary in order to remind all present of Miss Harper's movements. As to the rest of tonight's arrangements, after a while a bell will sound for the lighting of the Cascade. I would like everyone to proceed forward at that signal and take up your places exactly as before. After that, I ask you to await further instructions.'

'And what about those of us who weren't here?' called out Ralph Leagrave. 'What do you want us to do?'

'Mr Tyers has put several large boxes at my disposal. I would ask those who were not present on the night of the murder to take your seats there.'

'But surely, Sir,' shouted someone bolder than the rest, 'you should have invited everyone who was present to have been here. How do you know that the murderer is in the midst of this small gathering?'

'I don't,' the Blind Beak replied succinctly. 'I can only trust that with the help of you all we can establish, at least, those who are innocent of the crime.'

'Humph!' said Squire Leagrave.

'One last thing,' Mr Fielding went on, ignoring him. 'I would request you to do precisely what you did that night. Change nothing and hide nothing. Furthermore it is expected that each and every one of you must signal loudly if you see anything that differs at all from the original.'

His reproving blind stare swept the company and then the Principal Magistrate stepped aside to let Mr Tyers take his place.

'Honoured patrons,' declaimed the Proprietor in a beautifully modulated voice, 'though this occasion is a most unhappy one, my staff will be on hand to serve you. Please do not hesitate to ask them for anything you need.'

It was the most baleful soirée John had ever attended. Walking slowly, almost as if in a trance, the company broke up and went in the direction of the boxes, Sir Gabriel and Millie going off with the Fieldings, Samuel and John making for the same booth in which they had dined four weeks earlier. Next to them, ice-white and seeming on the verge of tears, sat the Duke of Midhurst with a delightful young woman of about twenty, who sparkled her gorgeous eyes in their direction before looking away.

'This is awful,' said Samuel miserably, 'I can't stop staring at her, just like poor dead Lizzie.'

'It's hateful,' answered John. He snapped his fingers. 'Waiter, a jug of the celebrated Vaux Hall punch. The Arrack,' he added, seeing it was exactly the same man who had served them on the other occasion.

Recognising them, the waiter smiled, despite the awful solemnity of the occasion, and came to a smart salute.

Out of the corner of his eye, John saw that Miss Coralie Clive was consulting a fob watch and suggesting to the Duke that they strolled forth, she taking his arm. At this sign, Patty Rigby waved at an empty box opposite and went to take her place in it, just as she must have done when she had joined friends on the night of the murder. Nobody else moved and the Duke and Miss Clive were clearly visible making their way down the deserted Grand Walk, looking uncannily like Lizzie and her escort but for the fact that the actress was not kissing him.

'I don't like this situation at all,' said Samuel, wiping his forehead and sinking a bumper of punch.

'I only hope some good comes out of it.'

The goldsmith lowered his voice to a whisper. 'Have you seen anyone remotely suspicious?'

John shook his head. 'No. Furthermore, if the apprentice is here, he's certainly concealed himself cleverly.'

'The only person present who's obviously disguised is the Masked Lady. You don't think...?'

John smiled. 'No, I don't.'

Samuel sighed. 'I wonder when the wretched bell will go. It seems an age, waiting like this.'

'I don't suppose Mr Fielding will hold it indefinitely.'

'I hope not. I swear to God one of the women will faint if this continues much longer.'

John burst out laughing. 'Women be damned! You don't look too light-hearted yourself.'

'I'm all right,' Samuel answered with dignity, and sank another bumper in one.

At that moment, with horrid clarity and sounding rather like the knell of doom, the bell rang. Startled, John and Samuel rose to their feet and joined the throng emerging from the boxes to make their way to the north side of the Gardens. Those who had not been present on the fatal night remained in their seats, with the exception of Mr Fielding who walked behind the crowd, led by his wife and Joe Jago. With a certain amount of pushing and shoving, people began to take their places before the curtained Cascade and John, very nervously, looked around.

It was just as if time had gone in on itself, had completed a full circle, for there was the scene he had memorised come back to life. He saw the Duke of Richmond in his stunning blue coat, talking to his brother-in-law Henry Fox. Next to them, with the crowd and yet not quite of it, just as she had been on the fatal night, hovered the Masked Lady. The Comte de Vignolles, standing not far from her, was giving her the same scrutiny he had then. Sulkily glaring, presumably because they were not making any money for once, the two old harpies in their silly identical dresses also looked her up and down. Right on the edge of the circle was a blob of green which John now identified as James Leagrave. He had seen someone there even then, though the face had not been distinct. It would appear in this instance, the Squire's son had been absolutely truthful about where he stood.

'Well, Mr Rawlings?' said John Fielding, close to the Apothecary's ear.

'The apprentice lad is missing, Sir.'

'Is he now?' the Blind Beak answered contemplatively. 'Are you sure?'

Into his mind's eye came the other picture and briefly, just before John lost it again, he was able to compare one with the other. Everyone was in place, just as they had been, with the exception of the owner of that small clear profile, a profile that somehow seemed suddenly familiar.

'Yes. He's not here, Sir.'

Mr Fielding clapped his hands for silence. 'Ladies and gentlemen, the Cascade will now be lit and afterwards I would ask you to make your way to the place you visited next. Miss Clive will continue to play the part of Miss Harper and therefore those who spoke to the murdered girl must re-enact exactly what they did. Monsieur le Comte and Lord Midhurst quarrelled with her, Lord Richmond smiled and winked. Please repeat those actions. To assist you with the impression of walking amongst a crowd I shall ask those in the boxes to join the throng.'

There was a general intake of breath, as if nobody wanted to participate in this next part, but for all that Samuel quietly left John's side and went off in dogged and admiring pursuit of Coralie Clive, who headed down the Grand Cross Walk towards the main part of the Gardens. Somewhat disobligingly, the Lords Midhurst and Richmond followed at a distance, while Lucy Pink and Giles Collings set off hand in hand towards the Dark Walk. Comte Louis de Vignolles proceeded last of all. Suddenly finding himself alone, John strode out in the direction of the Grand Walk, his ultimate destination, loath though he was even to have to think about it, the spot where the murder had taken place.

It was another night of quicksilver, of moon and stars, of sharp definitions and deepening shadows. And into this heightened atmosphere, this harsh time of solitary thought, ideas began to come, pell mell in the speed with which they presented themselves. What was it, John wondered, that still bothered him about the night he had been attacked? And where, oh where, had he seen the apprentice's profile before? Then the Apothecary stopped dead in his tracks as the pieces finally fell into place.

Way ahead of him, in the dim distance, John saw the Comte de Vignolles accost Miss Clive, then watched her spurn him and go off in the direction of the Dark Walk. Next he saw the Duke of Midhurst hurry in after her, the young rake Richmond leer and wink. Now, of course, John finally knew the answer and knew, too, that he was himself in danger. Still, the game must be played to the finish. Hurrying onwards, the Apothecary got into position to await the actress's scream. Yet when it came he felt himself to be totally unprepared. Gritting his teeth and more afraid than he had ever been in his life before, John rushed forward into the darkness.

Chapter Twenty-Four

The leaves on the tall trees must have grown even more dense in the four weeks since Elizabeth Harper had died. For now, or so it seemed to John, the luxuriant canopy above his head met and wove and joined so that not even a chink of moonshine slanted through to cast light upon the wooded walkways below. Not quite sure of where he was going, the Apothecary rushed hither and thither in his search for the place where poor Lizzie had died. Yet despite the darkness, or perhaps because of it, he was acutely aware of every sound. With a sudden stark recognition of what it must be like to be blind, John drew to a halt and stood still, listening.

Somewhere high above his head a nightingale was singing and all around him the grasses rustled with the movement of the wildlife that dwelt within this rural part of Vaux Hall Pleasure Gardens. Yet it was not these natural noises which caught his attention and made his scalp seethe with sudden fright. It was the sound of something else, the faint catch of panting breath, indicating that he was not alone, that another person had followed him into the Dark Walk and now stood close by, that had John's heart pounding with fright as he attempted to locate where his pursuer stood.

'Who's there?' he said, trying to control the quiver in his voice.

'I am,' came back an unrecognisable whisper.

'You will have to answer for your crime,' said John, praying that these words would bring the stalker out of hiding.

'But only you know who I am,' came the same terrifying murmur. 'Even the clever Mr Fielding hasn't guessed.'

'And what about Sir Gabriel?'

'He has an inkling but he isn't sure.'

'But if you kill me he will know, and what then?'

'I shall take a boat across the river and simply disappear.'

'Back to the darkness from whence you came,' John answered, and lashed out with his right hand, certain now that he knew where the voice was coming from.

Too late, his eyes, used to the gloom by now, caught sight of a flash of steel. Too late to do more than throw up his arm to ward off the lethal blow. Nauseated by pain, the Apothecary felt the sleeve of his coat slice apart and the skin beneath it suffer the same fate.

'Oh God!' he shouted aloud.

And then another voice spoke from the shadows, a young strong female voice. 'That will be enough of that,' it said. 'I'll have you know I'm carrying a pistol and will shoot to kill.' And a shot was fired, briefly lighting the scene. John had just enough time to see that his saviour was Coralie Clive, before a crash from the undergrowth told him that the Beak Runner who had been assigned to protect him was sprinting towards the site.

Yet it would seem that the actress had missed her target, for John heard the owner of the whispering voice spin on their heel and run.

'After her,' he yelled. 'She mustn't be allowed to escape.' And he took off, hardly feeling the pain of his injury in the excitement.

The Beak Runner must have harkened to him, for John was aware that the man's footsteps had turned and were heading towards the Grand Walk.

Behind him he heard Miss Clive call out, 'I can't go fast in these damnable high heels.'

'Leave it to me,' he called back over his shoulder. 'I'll thank you properly later for saving my life.' And then Samuel was there, come out of nowhere, running beside him just as if they were boys again, playing racing games.

'Who is it?' he panted. 'Who is the murderer?'

But John didn't answer, aware that the figure in front of him was gaining distance.

They had left the Dark Walk and were charging along the Grand Cross Walk, the light getting better with each step they took. By now, everyone else had become aware that a chase was on and had started a hue and cry. So it was accompanied by shouts of, 'Stop that woman!' and 'Get her!' that John and Samuel hurtled along the Grand Walk towards the entrance, followed by a pack of pursuing people who reminded the Apothecary horribly of a kennel of slavering hounds.

A Beak Runner had been posted at the swing doors to deal with just such an eventuality, but it seemed that the quarry had taken him by surprise and got through for he, too, was giving chase. Pushing their way past the portals, John and Samuel were aware that everyone behind them was following Mr Fielding's man and had gone heading down the path that led to Vaux Hall Stairs.

'No. This way,' said John, and pulling Samuel's arm, turned left, away from the Stairs in the direction of Marble Hall, a dancing establishment standing in its own small gardens, the Long Room of which overlooked the river and was considered one of the most beautiful spots for assemblies in London.

'Why there?' asked Samuel, very out of breath by now.

'Because the water runs deep just below Marble Hall.'

'What difference does that make?'

But John didn't answer, quite certain in his own mind that this was where the murderer would have gone.

The lights in the Long Room were lit and from within its gracious confines came the sound of music and laughter. The glow of the chandeliers was reflected in the river, for just below the assembly room lay an inlet with a small landing stage, nothing as imposing as Vaux Hall Stairs but sufficient to allow wherries to come in and out with passengers. There was something about the dark sheet of water that reminded John of Benbow's mill, and he was acutely aware that this was what had drawn him to the spot.

The moon was riding high, casting an argent pathway across the rippling river. Rushing to the very edge of the landing stage, John stared out across the reaches of the Thames, his eyes searching the waters, certain of what he was going to see.

'There!' cried Samuel, and pointed a craftsman's finger. John narrowed his eyes and peered, seeing a dark shape in the water, not struggling or fighting but calmly giving itself to the cold cleansing element that was claiming it. He stood silently for a moment, watching Eleanor Benbow die, knowing that this was what she wished – before he and Samuel stripped off their coats and shoes and dived into the river.

By the time they had struggled ashore with her, other people had arrived and a dozen pairs of hands were there to help them. Passing the girl's body up first, John and Samuel scrambled out of the water and on to the jetty. And it was only then that the Apothecary saw his friend stare at the face of the dead woman and reel with shock.

'Oh God's mercy, John,' Samuel exclaimed, bursting into grief-stricken tears. 'It's Millie. There's been some terrible mistake.'

Putting his arm round his friend's shoulders, the Apothecary drew him close. 'I'm afraid not, Sam,' he said gently. 'You see, it's not Millie at all. It grieves me to tell you, but tell you I must, that that is the missing Eleanor Benbow.'

Chapter Twenty-Five

Without being instructed or even invited, all those who had been involved in one way or another with the killing of Elizabeth Harper, made their way to the Public Office in Bow Street. Had he not been feeling so weak through loss of blood, John would have wondered about the invisible thread that led so many very different people to do the same thing without consulting one another. As it was, acting contrary to the order of the surgeon who had stitched him and very much against Sir Gabriel's wishes, John had also gone to see John Fielding in company with Samuel, who had sobbed brokenly for an hour before finally getting a grip on himself and deciding that he must learn the truth at all costs.

So it was that they were almost the last to arrive and the Apothecary was amazed to find the waiting room filled with those people from whom he had parted company only a short while earlier. Last to join the proceedings was the Blind Beak himself, the great man having waited until the remains of Eleanor Benbow had been removed to the mortuary before thanking Mr Tyers and leaving the Vaux Hall Pleasure Gardens to close quietly down for the night.

The very sound of his cane tapping on the front steps of the Bow Street house was enough to bring a hush to the assembled company. Yet despite the sudden stillness, the blind man obviously sensed their presence, for he turned towards all those who sat so silently and said, 'I think you had better come upstairs, ladies and gentlemen. I feel that every one of you has earned the courtesy of an explanation.' The sightless gaze circled the room. 'Are you amongst the number, Mr Rawlings?'

'Yes, I am, Sir,' John answered, hoping his voice did not betray how feeble he felt.

'And are you up to filling in those parts of the story that I do not know?'

'I think so.'

'I'm glad of that,' the Beak answered, and with that he started to climb the stairs, leaving the ubiquitous Joe Jago to point the way to the rest of the company.

They settled down in the large first floor room and John, staring round, saw that even the Duke of Midhurst had found the courage to attend, bolstered up, perhaps, by his fellow peer Richmond and the bubbling Miss Rigby, who sat on either side of him. Also amongst the gathering was the Comte de Vignolles, as darkly morose as John had ever seen him, Lucy Pink and Giles

Collings, sitting neatly together, and Sir Ralph and James Leagrave, who seemed to have drawn closer in friendship as a result of the terrible events they had just witnessed. John was not surprised to observe that both the Masked Lady and the two Madames were conspicuous by their absence.

Elizabeth Fielding, like the remarkable woman she was, had already alerted the servants that a number of unexpected guests had arrived, and it seemed only a matter of minutes before some claret, together with rhenish and sugar for the sweet toothed, to say nothing of a dish of ham and a custard, had appeared. Much to his astonishment, John found himself tucking in heartily.

'My lords, Monsieur le Comte, Sir Ralph, ladies and gentlemen,' Mr Fielding commenced, 'you have come here, I believe, for an explanation and you shall, indeed, have one.' He looked round from the high-backed chair in which he had taken his seat, just as if the assembled group was visible to him. 'My clerk has already told me who is present and so I am advised that all of you, to a greater or lesser degree, have been drawn into this tale of rural tragedy. So first let me start with the victim. She was known to some in this room as a mistress, others merely saw her at Vaux Hall Gardens. Mr Rawlings, who is by profession an apothecary, found her body and thus was enmeshed in the web.' Mr Fielding cleared his throat. 'I shall tell you her story as briefly and simply as I can but I beg you all, if I make any mistake in the telling, to correct me.'

There was a murmur of assent, during which the Blind Beak sipped his wine.

'Let me begin with her early life,' he continued. 'Elizabeth Harper was born an uneducated country girl who soon realised the extraordinary power she wielded over men. She was seduced at a tender age by her stepfather, a fact which I believe his daughter, Eleanor Benbow, discovered. Thus, probably, were sown the seeds of hatred which were to culminate in violent death. As a young woman, Lizzie went to work for Sir Ralph Leagrave, the Squire, where – forgive the plain speaking, gentlemen, but these are things that have to be said – she granted her favours to both father and son.'

James gave a great gulp at this, while Sir Ralph attempted to look nonchalant, an expression that ill became his ruddy features.

'Meanwhile,' Mr Fielding went on, disregarding them, 'she had allowed the local blacksmith, Jemmy Groves, to fall in love with her, another cause of her ultimate destruction as Eleanor Benbow nursed a passion for Jemmy herself. For reasons best known to the Squire and which need not concern us here, his sister, Miss Edith Leagrave, saw fit to terminate Elizabeth's employment and thus she, an ambitious creature I believe, came to London to seek her fortune.

'Like many an innocent before her, she was seen at the coaching inn by the procuresses, those women who call themselves the Mesdames de Blond and who run the house of ill-repute in Leicester Fields. With her extravagant beauty the girl at once became popular with the clientele and was soon taken into keeping by the Comte de Vignolles, am I not right, Monsieur?'

The Frenchman nodded glumly. 'But even that was not good enough for her. She looked around for someone both younger and richer and I lost Elizabeth Harper to the Duke of Midhurst.'

The nobleman hung his head but said nothing, and the Blind Beak turned to John. 'Mr Rawlings, pray continue he story. I believe that you are more au fait with the rest of it than I.'

The Apothecary gathered his strength together, determined to play his part to the last. 'It is my belief that during the time the girl worked at Leicester Fields she was seen by her former employer, Sir Ralph. Not only in Vigo Lane, as he freely admitted to me, but also in the brothel. Is that not correct, Sir?'

'It is, it is,' said the Squire, looking excessively glum. 'I did indeed run into her. Trouble was that I promised Lizzie not to tell Jacob Benbow. I hadn't realised there was anything rum between 'em and simply thought she had run away from home and didn't want the secret to come out. Usual old story. Anyway, I said nothing until one day that great booby Jemmy Groves comes a'sighing and a'weeping to me. I weakened then and, more fool me, told him her address in London. I suppose in a way I contributed to his suicide, for the poor bastard wrote – as best he could – and begged her to come home. Reckon she must have ignored him or written back telling him to go to hell, because the next thing I knew he'd ended up good and dead in the mill pond.'

'And the day afterwards Eleanor Benbow vanished without trace,' John went on. 'She had got Lizzie's address from Jemmy and had given it to Master Leagrave while she was at it. Full of hatred, both for her father and her adopted sister, I believe she came to London disguised as a boy in a coat she had purloined from her employer's son.'

'Did she deliberately set out to incriminate me?' asked James, looking bewildered and slightly upset.

'I don't believe so,' John said truthfully. 'In fact I'm quite sure she didn't. I think Eleanor merely wanted to disguise herself as a boy, and taking the coat that you believed you had lost seemed the best way of doing it.'

Diana, the only one of the whores to have come to Bow Street, spoke for the first time. 'Of course! The boy who came asking for Lizzie. It was Millie all the time. Why did I never guess?'

White-faced and stiff-lipped, Samuel asked an agonised question, each word obviously costing him dear. 'But why did she pretend to love me, John? Tell me the answer and spare nothing, I beg you.'

The Apothecary looked over at Mr Fielding, who must have guessed that his eyes were upon him, for he nodded.

'Let me tell you the rest of the story. Then maybe you can understand. Obviously, Eleanor went to Vigo Lane in the same guise, but too late to find Lizzie. She had abandoned the Comte in favour of Lord Midhurst and moved on.'

'I'm sorry,' said the Duke, staring de Vignolles in the eye for the first time. 'I had no wish to wound you. Truth to tell, as Mr Rawlings already knows, I took Elizabeth on to prove to the world that I was a man and not the weak-kneed quean that all believed me to be.'

The Frenchman returned his glance with grudging admiration. 'It must have cost you dear to say that. I appreciate your courage.

John Fielding cleared his throat once more, and everyone looked at him.

'It is my belief, based on the evidence to hand, that Eleanor went to Vaux Hall Pleasure Gardens purely by chance. Still dressed as a boy, she probably roamed the fashionable haunts of London in the hope of meeting her quarry and when she did acted both quickly and lethally, little guessing that Mr Rawlings, with his extraordinary pictorial memory, would take particular notice of an over-dressed apprentice lad and thus be her undoing. But, be that as it may, Eleanor Benbow saw her hated rival, followed her, perhaps even pretended to be attracted to her, then she took one of Lizzie's own stockings and strangled her with it.'

'But, that once done, why did she come to the brothel to work?' asked Diana. 'She must have known what happened to girls who took employment there.'

Mr Fielding shook his head. 'London is a terrible city, as you well know, young woman. I think the poor creature went to the only place she could think of to get a job. It was probably that or starve. Anyway, we know that she took the name of Millie, a reference, no doubt, to the fact that she was a miller's daughter. Yet I am positive that, for all her murderous intent, the girl was none the less a naive soul and had no idea she would be expected, one day, to join the whores, nor that she would encounter Squire Leagrave.'

'Gave me quite a shock, I can tell you,' Sir Ralph interjected. 'I'd believed her dead along with everybody else. But I promised not to give her away and I didn't let her down.'

Samuel spoke again, still in the same terrible voice. 'But none of this answers my question. Why did she pretend to love me? Just as a means to get out?'

'I suppose,' said Mr Fielding with enormous command, 'that it does not occur to you that she did love you? Just because she had committed herself to taking revenge on Elizabeth Harper, does not mean that Eleanor was incapable of other emotion.'

'But she tried to kill John. She must have been thoroughly evil.'

'On the contrary. Mr Rawlings was the one person who could have identified her as the murderer. It was an act of self-preservation to silence him.'

'There's one thing I've got to know,' said the Duke of Richmond, his voice laconic despite the tense atmosphere. 'When and how did our admirable friend guess who was behind it all?'

'Not until tonight,' answered John, and there was a crack in his voice which suddenly revealed how completely exhausted he was.

'Nuff said,' replied Richmond, holding up his hand. 'I'll hear the story another time. I'm for my bed. I think we've trespassed on Mr Fielding's hospitality long enough.' He looked round the assembled company. 'All to dine at my London house in a week, eh? Then we'll hear the rest of the tale.'

'All?' repeated Diana. 'Does that include me?'

'Yes,' Richmond replied, with a grin. 'That includes even you.'

They left in groups. Lucy and Giles with the air of those who have decided to wed; Richmond, Midhurst, James and Miss Rigby all in the same hackney, arranging to meet one another next day. Diana, already known to Squire Leagrave through the house in Leicester Fields, departing in fine fig, flirting with him for all she was worth. Only the Comte de Vignolles vanishing alone into the night, his unhappiness hanging round him like a pall.

'My young friends,' said Mr Fielding, as he bade Joe Jago see John and Samuel into Sir Gabriel's waiting coach, 'go home and rest and mend yourselves. I shall visit you both just as soon as you are restored. Send word when that time comes.'

Then he took John's hand and shook it before the two of them went their separate ways, the problem that had beset them both for so long, finally solved.

Chapter Twenty-Six

Strangely, John's stab wound, deep but not to the bone, mended more quickly than Samuel's broken heart. Aided by some ointment especially prepared by Master Purefoy, John's old teacher, his skin healed cleanly so that it was safe to remove the stitches that held it within a week. Samuel, however, with the delicate sensibilities of many a big man, languished like a lily until Sir Gabriel finally ordered him to go to his father in Islington in order to breathe in the sweet country air and recuperate.

'I truly hadn't realised in quite what high regard he had held Millie,' John said sadly, watching his friend depart in a hired hackney.

Sir Gabriel smiled his worldly smile. 'Neither did he until she was dead.'

'Do you mean that, had she lived, he might have tired of her?'

'There is no might about it, my son. Samuel would soon have grown bored with such a rural miss.'

'You married one such and did not grow weary of her.'

'Your mother was an exceptional woman and there will never be another like her, alas.'

'Do you miss her terribly?'

'Every day of my life. Yet she has come back to me in you, and thus the blow is softened.'

John looked at his father with affection and a certain shrewdness. 'Tell me something, Sir. Did you guess about Millie? I suspect that you did.'

'Oh yes, indeed. You suspect quite rightly.'

'What? And you didn't warn me of what you feared?'

'I was not certain enough to say anything. And, besides, I knew that you must be very near the solution yourself. For it was growing apparent, was it not?'

John looked thoughtful. 'It must have been the most terrible shock to the poor wretch when I walked into the brothel and announced myself as a friend of Samuel's. What an evil twist of fate.'

Sir Gabriel nodded. 'It gave her two reasons for wanting to kill you. For now you stood between her and her new love as well.'

'I must have come to represent her Nemesis. Yet Millie couldn't have been responsible for breaking into my shop. Or could she?'

'That we will never know. Perhaps she went there looking for evidence, perhaps it was the work of rowdies seeking potions.' Sir Gabriel sighed. 'Tell me when you first suspected that the girl was not all she seemed.'

'It was the attack in Leicester Fields that initially aroused my suspicions. You see, Millie said I let out a cry and she came running out of the brothel to see what was amiss. Yet I was so winded, so short of breath, that I could have sworn I did no more than groan as I fell.'

'It was the night when I heard someone prowl the landing near your bedroom that convinced me,' answered Sir Gabriel, leading his son into the library where a tray of coffee lay awaiting them. 'I knew full well that every window in the place was secure, yet still I heard a midnight walker.'

'Was that why you insisted she come to Vaux Hall? So that I would see her in the right place and connect her face with that of the apprentice?'

Sir Gabriel's fine profile was etched against the light of the window. 'My son, it was you who told her she must go, if you remember.'

'Yes, but it was not until I was there, in situ as it were, that the last pieces of the puzzle slid into place.'

'But slide they did, though too late to save you from her knife.'

'Poor Millie, poor Eleanor,' John said sadly. 'She could not have had much of a life when all's said and done.'

'No,' answered Sir Gabriel softly, 'yet perhaps in dying in the same way as her tragic Jemmy Groves, it ended just as she would have wished.'

Sitting in his study, Joe Jago at his side, the Blind Beak insisted that John should bare his arm that he might feel the extent of the wound and how well it had healed in the time since he had last seen him.

'Yes, I'm afraid that will scar, my friend,' Mr Fielding said, when he had finished his careful examination.

'It will give me character,' John answered cheerfully. 'One day I shall recount the story to my grandchildren.'

'Aye, and you might add that you joined, albeit temporarily, that band of Brave Fellows, known to the mob as the Beak Runners, who are the first proper squad of men whose full time employment is the keeping of the peace.'

'I'm proud of that,' said John. 'Yet not so proud that I stood still a moment and watched Millie die. For perhaps I could have saved her had my reactions been quicker.'

The Blind Beak shook his head. 'Put such thoughts from your mind, Mr Rawlings. Tell me, was there not a boat moored in the inlet beneath Marble Hall?'

'Yes, there was. Why?'

'Eleanor had ample time to get in it and row herself across to the fields below Mill Bank. From there she could have vanished quite successfully. I doubt that anyone would ever have seen her again.'

'Strangely, my father said that he thought she wanted to die.'

'And you know it too. Now, cast such foolish notions aside.'

John nodded. 'Yes. I will.'

The Principal Magistrate rumbled his melodious laugh. 'Good. So tell me, what are your future plans?'

'Soon I am going to apply to the Court of Assistants to be made free of the Society of Apothecaries.'

'Well done, well done.' The Blind Beak stood up and held out his hand. 'My heartfelt gratitude is yours but now, without a doubt, it is time for you to pursue your chosen career. I wish you well, my fine young friend.'

'Goodbye, Sir,' said John, bowing to the Magistrate even though he could not see him.

John Fielding smiled as he took the Apothecary's hand in his own. 'Goodbye is such a final word, don't you think? Shall we simply say *au revoir*?'

From the reign of Charles II onwards, coffee and chocolate house life had thrived in the metropolis, no meeting place being more fashionable than White's Chocolate House in St James's Street, where the *beau monde* assembled daily, and where young noblemen, according to the critics of the time, were fleeced and corrupted by gamesters and profligates. However, in 1736, White's had realised where its ultimate future lay and had been converted into an exclusive gambling club. The consequent increase in its popularity had made the search for new premises a pressing one, though so far with little success. Thus the place was always packed with players, winning and losing with equal *élan*. And never more so than on this hot summer's night when the heat from the company assembled within swept through the doors and out into the street beyond.

Stepping from his carriage, Sir Gabriel Kent delicately lifted a lace handkerchief to his nostrils and turned to his dinner guest, the Comte de Vignolles.

'Damnable hot, don't you think, my dear fellow?'

'Damnable,' replied the Frenchman, and smiled to himself at the eccentricities of the English who invited total strangers to dine on the strength of both having been involved in a murder enquiry.

'I'd suggest we don't go in were it not for the fact that I have arranged to meet my son here.'

'Oh,' said the Comte, his initial mistrust of John never having quite been dispelled.

'But if you'd rather...'

'No, no,' Louis answered, just a trifle impatiently. 'Let us enter.'

'I take it you're not a gambling man?'

'No, to be honest with you, Sir Gabriel, I never set foot in such places. Thus it will be a most interesting experience.'

'I'm sure it will,' the other replied quietly, and smiled behind his handkerchief.

'Mon Dieu!' exclaimed Louis, he and his host having deposited their cloaks before walking into the famous room. 'What a crowd!'

'Yes, indeed. Various games of chance are being played at different tables, d'you see. There, it is faro. There, whist. Dice at the large central table. And

there, my dear Comte, they are dealing quadrille. Shall we make up a set?'
Louis hesitated. 'Surely that would be a mistake. That woman wearing a mask is considered the most formidable gamester in London.'
'Really? But that is my son sitting with her! I must go to his rescue at once. Come.'

And refusing to be crossed and behaving in quite the most curious manner, Sir Gabriel seized his guest by the arm and led him to the table at which sat the Apothecary, looking decidedly anxious at being placed with so notorious a player.

John rose as the Comte approached. 'My dear Monsieur, a very good evening to you. I am glad you decided to come. It is my wish to make amends for any upset I caused in the past, albeit inadvertently. So, I cannot tell you how delighted I am that you accepted my father's invitation to dine.'

The Frenchman bowed with gallic courtesy. 'My dear young friend, let bygones be bygones. I hope that we can begin our friendship afresh.'

'Oh, so do I,' John answered enthusiastically, and his father shot him an unreadable glance.

'Now, won't you present me to the lady?' the Comte continued.

John gave a crooked smile. 'I would if I did but know her name. Nevertheless, Madam, may I introduce to you the Comte Louis de Vignolles. Monsieur le Comte, the Masked Lady.'

'Enchanted,' he said, and kissed her outstretched hand.

'How dee do?' she answered gruffly.

'And now,' said Sir Gabriel, 'to deal.' And he handed the pack to the Masked Lady, who cut the cards with her long white fingers.

There was silence while each player concentrated on their hand, then play began in earnest. Unfortunately, this seemed to be a signal for John to indulge in idle chatter, a fact which annoyed his companions considerably, all of whom were trying to concentrate on their game.

With a look of concern, the Apothecary turned to the Comte. 'Monsieur, pray tell me, how is your wife these days?'

Louis flicked up a black eyebrow. *'Comme çi, comme ça.* Some days she seems a little better, on others she just takes to her couch and stays there.'

John looked disappointed. 'What a pity. I thought my medicine had worked splendidly on her.'

'Like everything else she tries, it seems to wear off after a while.'

'Oh,' said John, and relapsed into silence.

The Masked Lady laid a winning card.

'Oh well done, Madam,' the Apothecary started once more. 'You really are a gamester to be reckoned with.' He let out a wild and most unseemly cry of triumph which succeeded in attracting the attention of the entire assembly. 'There you are, I told you it had done her good,' he said at the top of his voice.

The Comte de Vignolles frowned. 'What has done who good?'

'My physick.'

'Elucidate, dear boy,' ordered Sir Gabriel.

'I thought that my medicine would cure the Comtesse de Vignolles and, by God, it has. Hasn't it, Madam?'

There was an unbelievable silence, a silence which spread round the entire room. All play ceased and everyone present looked across to where the Masked Lady sat with her three card partners. Very deliberately, John turned to her. 'It has, hasn't it?'

She stood up, aware that every eye was upon her, then wheeled round to face the door. But she had not moved quite fast enough, for the Comte, too, had risen to his feet. The couple stood staring, like two cats confronting each other before the opening hiss.

'Well?' he said at last.

'Well, what?' answered that strange gruff voice.

'Are you who John Rawlings says you are?'

'Yes, *are* you?' called out a fresh young nobleman.

'I challenge you to remove your mask,' said Louis between gritted teeth.

'And if I do,' the Masked Lady answered, 'what is it worth?' She turned to face the assembled company. 'Well, gentlemen, let's hear your wagers. Am I the Comtesse de Vignolles or am I not? Lord Dorchester, I see you nod. Will you take my wager for five thousand pounds that I *am* the Comtesse de Vignolles?'

'Certainly,' the young gamester replied. 'You're too spirited, Madam, to be that wan creature. I'll take you.'

'Two thousand guineas that you're a wealthy widow,' called somebody else.

'Ten thousand pounds that you are my wife,' said Louis quietly.

The Masked Lady laughed her fascinating, husky laugh. 'Come, come, gentlemen, this is not like you. Surely you are not all done?'

Entering into the spirit of the occasion, there was a general chorus of 'No', and private bets began to be laid throughout the room until everyone, with the exception of Sir Gabriel and his son, had made a stake of some kind or another.

Then came the call of 'Show yourself', and the Masked Lady laughed yet again. Then slowly and with obvious enjoyment, she untied the strings of her domino and let it slip downwards about her neck. Beneath it, it could be seen, was revealed the face of a stunning beauty wearing a scarlet eye patch, the ultimate disguise.

There was a roar of approbation and Lord Dorchester shouted out a proposal of marriage, to which the Comte replied, 'I believe she is already spoken for.' Then, with shaking hands, he raised the patch to reveal his ailing wife, lovely and vivid and full of zest.

'By God's wounds,' called out old Lord Ilchester. 'I would never have believed it. If this is the result of your physick, Apothecary, I'll take a case.'

'Gladly, Sir,' John called back. 'You will find me in my shop in Shug Lane tomorrow. Or, better still, I'll compound for you this very night and deliver personally in the morning.'

There was a sudden rush of gentlemen to his table, demanding to know whether his medicine was truly strengthening.

'Oh very,' said the Comtesse, flashing her handsome eyes, 'just look at what it did for me.'

'I love you,' said Louis.

'I know, fool,' she replied, and kissed him as if it were something she had wanted to do for a very long time. 'Now, no more roving, d'ye hear?'

'My darling,' he answered quietly, 'I roved from a boring girl but now I find I am married to an exciting woman.'

'Enough said on that score, I think,' put in Sir Gabriel, laughing.

The Comtesse wheeled to face John. 'How did you know?' she asked.

Raising her fingers to his lips, the Apothecary kissed them. 'Your hands, Madam. Your beautiful strong, yet slender, hands. When you snapped your fingers beneath my nose it seemed to me that they were somehow familiar. That I had seen them before, so adeptly handling both cards and dice. Then there was Patty Rigby, who knew you personally. She thought she saw you at Vaux Hall on that fatal night, and when I mentioned it to you your face momentarily gave you away. And yet it seemed odd to me that nobody else had seen the sickly Comtesse de Vignolles out at night and remarked it. So I finally concluded that what Miss Rigby had observed was the back view of the Masked Lady, as she strolled alone as was her custom.'

The Comtesse nodded, smiling. 'I once told you that I thought you a clever creature and, my dear friend, I am still of that opinion.'

Her husband put his arm round her waist and turned to the assembled company. 'Gentlemen,' he said clearly, 'I would like to give you a toast. Let us raise our glasses to a young man who has worked a miracle. I give you the health of John Rawlings, Apothecary.'

'John Rawlings,' they chorused, and drank deep.

Historical Note

John Rawlings, Apothecary, was born circa 1731, though his actual parentage is somewhat shrouded in mystery. However, by 1754 he had emerged from obscurity when on 22 August he applied to be made Free of the Worshipful Society of Apothecaries. He became a Yeoman of the Society in March, 1755 – the reasons for the delay are interesting but not to be told here – giving his address as number two Nassau Street. Well over a hundred years later, this was the address of H.D. Rawlings Ltd, Soda Water Manufacturers, proving conclusively that John Rawlings was probably the first apothecary to manufacture carbonated waters in this country. His ebullient personality has haunted me for years and now, at last, I am bringing him out of the shadows and into the spotlight.

Breinigsville, PA USA
07 September 2009
223635BV00001B/25/A